LETTERS AND LAWSUITS

An Isle of Man Ghostly Cozy

DIANA XARISSA

✿ Created with Vellum

For Steve.

AUTHOR'S NOTE

I had to count twice to be sure, but this marks the twelfth book in the Ghostly Cozy series. I enjoyed telling a bit more of Mona's story in this title. I always suggest that you read my series books in order (alphabetically), but each book should be enjoyable on its own if you prefer not to start at the beginning.

I've tried to write this series in American English, except where characters who are British or Manx are speaking. They speak in British English, sometimes providing Fenella with an appropriate translation when needed. The longer I live in the US, the greater the chances of me getting things wrong, though. If you notice a glaring mistake, please let me know, and I will correct it.

I talk in every book about the wonderful and special place that is the Isle of Man. I encourage everyone to learn more about the island and its rich history. A UK crown dependency, the island has its own government, currency, and language.

This is a work of fiction. The characters are all products of the author's imagination. Any resemblance to actual persons, either living or dead, is entirely coincidental. The restaurants and businesses mentioned in the book are also fictional and if they resemble any real businesses on the island, that is also coincidental. The historical sites and landmarks mentioned within the book are all real, but the events that take place at these locations in the story are fictional.

Hearing from readers is one of my favorite parts of being a writer. Please feel free to get in touch, using any of the means of contact detailed in the back of the book. I have a monthly newsletter to keep you up to date on new releases. If you are interested, you can subscribe to the newsletter on my website.

Thank you for spending time with Fenella and Mona.

❈ I ❈

"We have two things to discuss today," Doncan Quayle said as Fenella Woods sat back in the comfortable chair in the advocate's expensively furnished office.

"Two?" she repeated. "I thought you wanted to talk about Mona's birthday celebration."

"I do, but something else has come up as well," he told her.

Fenella frowned. "I don't think I like the sound of that."

"Let's start with the birthday celebration," Doncan suggested.

Fenella took a sip of the tea she'd been given and then nodded. She wasn't about to argue with Doncan. He was the expert, after all. No doubt she was paying him a great deal of money for his help and advice, but as she had plenty to spare, she didn't mind. The thought of trying to find a new lawyer, or rather, advocate, as they were called in the Isle of Man, was out of the question. Doncan had been her aunt Mona Kelly's advocate, as had his father before him. If he was good enough for Mona, he was good enough for her.

"As we've discussed previously, Mona left you her entire estate, aside from one small provision. A lump sum was set aside to fund what I would consider a fairly lavish birthday celebration each year. Mona left me the guest list and complete instructions for the event. Obviously, as you're now living on the island, you will be invited to the party, but beyond that, the rest is in my hands."

"Can you share any of the details with me?"

Doncan shrugged. "Mona was very specific about what she wanted. One of the things that she requested was a level of secrecy about the evening. I'll tell you that each party is to have a theme, but Mona was adamant that no one find out the themes in advance. She didn't want other people copying her ideas."

"If there's a theme, shouldn't we be dressing in appropriate clothing?"

"When the invitations go out, there will be suggestions for appropriate dress on them."

"When will the invitations be going out?"

"On Friday. That's exactly a fortnight before the party. As I said, Mona was very specific about everything."

"So I'll be getting an invitation soon?"

"You will. It will be for you and a guest. One of the things we do need to discuss is whether or not you want to add anyone to the guest list."

"Can I do that?"

Doncan chuckled. "Mona wasn't certain if you were going to want to move to the island or not. She did her best to plan things for all contingencies. There is space on the guest list for a dozen or so of your friends, although I'm sure we could accommodate a few more if necessary."

"I don't think I know a dozen people on the island," Fenella replied, making a face. "Actually, now that I'm taking classes and doing some research, I'm starting to meet a lot more people."

"How is your class going?"

"I'm enjoying it a lot. When I started I wasn't sure why everyone else in the class had taken it multiple times, but now I want to take it again the next time it's offered."

Fenella was taking a class in reading old handwriting through a program at the Manx Museum. The museum was full of fascinating letters and documents dating back hundreds of years. Very little of what was in the collection had ever been transcribed, and some of it hadn't even been catalogued much beyond basic notes. Holding a doctorate in history and having spent her career teaching undergraduates at a large American university, Fenella was thrilled to be able to spend time studying some of the papers in the museum's collection.

"As I said, the invitations are going to be posted on Friday. I'll need your guest list by Thursday morning if I'm to have time to include your additions."

"I can probably give it to you now, although I suspect most of the people I'd like to invite are already on the list. I assume Shelly is there."

Doncan nodded. "She is," he confirmed.

Shelly Quirk was Fenella's next-door neighbor. Although she was over sixty and thus more than ten years older than Fenella, the pair had become close friends in the months since Fenella had arrived on the island. It had been Mona who had helped Shelly through the first difficult months after she'd been unexpectedly widowed, and Shelly had repaid the favor by helping Fenella settle into her new life on the island after she'd inherited Mona's estate.

"What about Peter Cannell?" Fenella asked.

Peter lived in the apartment on the other side of Fenella's. When she'd first arrived, he'd taken her out to dinner a few times, but the relationship had evolved into a comfortable friendship rather than anything romantic. While Fenella liked Peter a great deal, she was happy just being friends.

"He's also on the list."

"Is everyone allowed to bring a date? If they aren't, I'll invite Tim for Shelly."

Shelly had been seeing Tim Blake for a few months now. Fenella wasn't sure how serious the relationship was, but she was happy for Shelly, who seemed to be enjoying having a man in her life again. Tim was around sixty, and Shelly had first met him during another murder investigation. He played in a local band, The Islanders, for fun, but his real job was as an architect for ShopFast, the island's local grocery store chain.

"All of the invitations include a guest, aside from the handful of married couples who've been invited, such as myself and my wife."

Fenella nodded. "What about Donald Donaldson?"

Donald was a handsome and very wealthy man who'd seemed determined to win Fenella's heart when they'd first met. His work kept him off the island frequently, though, which had interfered with his pursuit. It had seemed as if he'd been ready to intensify his efforts when his daughter, Phoebe, had been badly injured in a car accident in the US. Donald had been gone for months now, staying with his daughter and coordinating her recovery efforts. He and Phoebe had recently relocated to London, which made it possible, although unlikely, that Donald might be able to attend Mona's party.

"He's also on the list. He was part of Mona's social circle. Everyone from that circle will be invited."

Fenella nodded. "I may not know many of the guests, then."

"You may not, although I'm sure you've met many of them at the various charity events you've attended since you've been here."

When Donald was on the island, he'd often dragged Fenella to one charity fundraiser or another. Fenella felt as if she'd met hundreds of people at the numerous events she'd attended, but she doubted she'd remember any of them if she saw them again. In the last month or so, she'd starting receiving invitations to events herself, but thus far she'd turned them all down, instructing Doncan to send a check along with her regrets. Perhaps one day she'd feel brave enough to start attending parties on her own, but for now she was giving the extravagant charity affairs a miss.

"I'm not sure who else to include," Fenella said, frowning.

"What about Daniel?" Doncan asked. "He wasn't on the island before Mona's death, so he's not on the list. Or were you going to bring him as your guest?"

Fenella's frown deepened. Daniel was a complication. The handsome police inspector had first come into her life when she'd stumbled over a dead body, and he'd been in and out of her life ever since. She'd been sure they were heading toward a relationship before he'd been sent to take some classes in Milton Keynes in the UK. When he'd returned, he told her that he'd met another woman taking the class, someone he'd considered getting involved with, but circumstances had prevented anything from happening. Since then the pair had been spending time together, but there was still some awkwardness between them. Daniel had asked for her help with a cold case in January, and she'd been instrumental in helping him solve it, but they hadn't really spoken since the case had been resolved.

"He's really busy with work right now," Fenella made an excuse for the man that may or may not have been true. "It might be easiest if you sent him his own invitation. Maybe he'll even bring a guest himself."

"Is that likely?"

Fenella shrugged. "I haven't spoken to him in a few weeks. I've no idea." She winced slightly when she heard how bitter she sounded.

Doncan glanced at her and then made a note. "I'll add him to the guest list, then. Is there anyone else?"

Fenella thought for a minute and then sighed. "I could include Marjorie Stevens from the museum. She's teaching the class I'm taking and working with me on the research I'm doing, but if I include her, I'll feel as if I should include the others in the class, too. I'm not sure I like all of them enough to include them."

Doncan laughed. "Why don't you think about it for a few days," he suggested. "It's only Monday. As I said, I don't need the list until Thursday. Give me a ring Thursday morning with any more additions."

"I can do that," Fenella promised. "I'll ask Shelly if she can think of anyone to add, too. She might have some ideas." I'll ask Mona, as well, she added to herself. Of course, Mona had written the original guest list, so it seemed unlikely she'd have anyone to add to it. While she was prepared to discuss the party with Mona, Fenella wasn't ready to tell Doncan about the ghost who was now haunting what had been Mona's luxury apartment.

"I think that's all there is to discuss on that matter, then," Doncan said, making a small neat tick on the pad in front of him. "Invitations will be posted on Friday, which means you should receive yours on Saturday. Do let me know if it doesn't arrive in a timely fashion."

"You can't tell me anything more about the party before I get my invitation?"

"I'm sworn to secrecy on all things," Doncan said seriously. "I've booked the venue under another name so even they don't know that they're hosting Mona's first posthumous birthday celebration."

"That seems a bit, well, over the top," Fenella suggested.

Doncan chuckled. "That was exactly how Mona liked things. Make no mistake, though, this party will be one of the highlights of the Manx social calendar. The guest list is full of everyone who is anyone on the island, as well as a number of very special guests from across and further afield. Mona's parties were legendary, and this one won't be any different. I consider myself fortunate to have made it onto the guest list, really."

"What else did we need to talk about, then?"

"Ah, yes," Doncan said. He cleared his throat and then sat back in his chair. "I've had a letter."

"A letter?" Fenella repeated when he fell silent.

"This feels awkward, although I'm not sure why," he told her. "I've had a letter from a woman who claims that she's Maxwell Martin's daughter."

"Maxwell Martin's daughter?" Fenella echoed.

She knew who Maxwell Martin was, of course. The man had been Mona's wealthy benefactor from the time Mona had been eighteen until his death. From all accounts, the pair had been passionately devoted to one another, unless they were fighting, which apparently had been a regular occurrence. Max had installed Mona in a room in one of the hotels he'd owned, and over the years he'd showered her with gifts including jewelry, cars, and property. When he'd turned the hotel into luxury apartments, he'd had the largest and most luxurious one designed for Mona. Fenella was now living in that apartment, sharing it with Mona's ghost.

"That's what she's claiming anyway, although she does mention having the support of Maxwell's sister, who's apparently accepted her into the family."

"Does that mean that Maxwell's sister is sharing Maxwell's estate with this woman?"

Doncan chuckled. "Knowing Maxwell's sister, I think that's highly unlikely. I should add that the woman in question, the possible missing daughter, is insistent in her letter that she isn't after anything. She simply wants to visit the island and meet you."

"Meet me? Why would she want to meet me?"

"Let me start at the beginning," Doncan said. "Her name is Rosemary Ballard. Her mother was Charlotte Sharp. According to Rosemary's letter, Charlotte met Max in London and they had a relationship for several months. Rosemary claims to have letters that Max sent to Charlotte that not only confirm that the relationship happened but also discuss Charlotte's pregnancy."

"What year are we talking about?" Fenella asked, sure that Mona would demand the same information.

"Rosemary was born in 1955."

"So she's in her early sixties?"

"She is. According to the letter, her mother raised her on her own, with some level of financial support from Max. She claims her mother told her Max's name and that he lived in the Isle of Man, but not much else about him. Apparently, Rosemary wasn't all that interested, either. Charlotte remarried when Rosemary was three, and from what she wrote, she's always considered her mother's husband as her father. Recently, however, one of Rosemary's children has been working on a family genealogy. That led to Rosemary reaching out to Max's sister. After an allegedly warm welcome there, she decided to get in touch with you as well."

"Again, why would she want to meet me?"

"As she tells it, Max's letters to Charlotte often refer to Mona." He stopped and cleared his throat. "From what I can ascertain, they aren't always terribly complimentary, either. According to Rosemary, Max claims in his letters that he would very much like to marry Charlotte, but can't for fear of upsetting Mona."

"That doesn't even make sense. Why would he care about upsetting Mona? If he had really been in love with Charlotte, he would have married her."

Doncan held up a hand. "I'm on your side," he reminded her. "You're right, of course. Rosemary seems to hint that Mona may have known something that she was holding over Max in order to get him to do what she wanted. Obviously, Rosemary wants to believe that there was some obstacle that kept Max from marrying her mother, other than Max simply not wanting to be with Charlotte."

"I still don't understand why she wants to meet me."

"She wants to visit the island, her father's homeland, as she puts it, and she wants to meet Mona's family and friends. I believe she's hoping to understand Mona and Max's relationship better, maybe find something to support her belief that Mona kept Max and her mother apart all those years ago."

"I don't want to meet her."

"Then you don't have to meet her. Obviously, I can't keep her from visiting the island, though. Once she's here, she won't have any difficulty in discovering where to find you. It might be easier for everyone concerned if you agreed to meet with her here, in my office, for a very brief conversation."

"I don't believe her story. From everything I've heard, Max and Mona were devoted to one another."

"They fought almost constantly, though. If Max had traveled to London while he and Mona were at odds with one another, it's entirely possible that he might have had a brief affair."

"Surely he would have told Mona if he'd had a child with another woman?"

"Perhaps he did, and she kept his secret for him."

Fenella shook her head. Mona wouldn't have stayed with Max if he'd betrayed her in that way, she was certain of that.

"Is Charlotte coming, too?"

"Charlotte passed away in the nineteen-eighties. Apparently, that's another reason why Rosemary never did anything to find Max. She said something in the letter about not wanting to betray her mother's memory."

"What is she really after?" Fenella demanded.

Doncan shrugged. "I don't think we'll be able to find that out until we meet her. I'm going to meet with her, whatever you choose. I may involve an advocate from the firm that Max used as well. I've seen Max's will. It doesn't mention any children."

"It also doesn't mention Mona, as I understand it," Fenella said, flushing as she realized that it was Mona who'd told her that piece of information.

"It does not," Doncan agreed. "Max made certain that she was well provided for before he passed away. He left his estate to be divided evenly between his sister and his business partner, Bryan Westerly. I believe Max was concerned that his sister would challenge anything bequeathed to Mona."

Fenella nodded. Mona had told her as much. "Surely if he had a child, he would have included that child in his will."

"Rosemary suggests in her letter that he provided for her before his death. Perhaps he kept her hidden to avoid upsetting Mona, even after his death."

Fenella thought about that for a moment. There was no doubt in her mind that Mona had loved Max deeply. She was going to be devastated to learn about Rosemary if the other woman was actually Max's daughter. "What about proof?" she asked.

"She claims to have letters from Max, as I said. Beyond that, if she were to try to make a claim on the estate, we could insist on a DNA test, but if she truly is just coming to try to learn more about her father and the island, then we'll simply have to take her at her word, I'm afraid."

"I don't believe her story."

"You don't have to believe her story. You also don't have to meet her. If you truly want to avoid her, though, I suggest you take a short holiday somewhere far away. I can let you know when she's arrived and when she's gone."

"Is she planning to visit soon?"

"Next week."

Fenella made a face. "Don't put her on the guest list for Mona's party."

Doncan laughed. "I definitely won't be inviting her," he assured her. "Think about it and let me know what you decide with regards to meeting Ms. Ballard. If you'd rather avoid her, let me know where you're going and when."

"I could hide in one of my other houses on the island," Fenella suggested.

"You could. Do you want me to check what's available?"

Along with her gorgeous seaside apartment, Fenella had inherited properties that were scattered around the island, everything from apartments and houses to farms and businesses. She'd recently stayed in a large four-bedroom house on the outskirts of Douglas while she'd been looking after a handful of cats. Once the animals had found good homes, however, she'd told Doncan that he could turn the house back over to the company that handled renting out her properties. The house's location, across the street from Daniel Robinson's house, had made staying there complicated.

"Is Poppy Drive rented out?" she asked about the house, even though she didn't really want to stay there again.

"It was rented out within an hour of you telling me we could list it. It's a large house in a very desirable area."

"I'm going to have to think," she said after a minute. "I don't believe this woman is who she claims to be, but there's a part of me that would like to meet her anyway. I'm curious what she's after. I'm pretty sure it's money."

Doncan nodded. "If she's going after money, though, she should be filing a lawsuit against Max's estate, not Mona's."

"You said Max's sister has acknowledged Rosemary's claim?"

"In the letter, Rosemary states that Max's sister has welcomed the chance to meet the niece she never knew she had."

"I'm surprised she isn't worried about Rosemary suing her."

"Max's sister is shrewd and tough, and she has her own team of solicitors to deal with her affairs. If she's acknowledged Rosemary as Max's daughter, she must have sound reasons for having done so. Whatever her reasons, I'm sure she's taking steps to make sure she's protecting every penny of her money, as well."

"What is Max's sister's name?" Fenella asked.

Doncan looked surprised and then laughed. "Mona hated the woman," he told her. "She made me promise that I'd never speak her name out loud. She said it was as dangerous as summoning the devil."

Fenella laughed. "That sounds like Mona," she said. "Don't tell me, then. We can just call her Max's sister."

Doncan nodded. "Max always referred to her as 'my sister,' never by name. Mona preferred to pretend that Max's sister didn't exist."

"What else do you know about Rosemary?"

"Quite a lot, all of it public record. As soon as I got the letter, I started doing some research. Her birth certificate lists her mother's name, but the father's name was left blank. She was Rosemary Sharp at birth. Although her mother remarried when she was three, Charlotte's husband never formally adopted Rosemary."

"I wonder why."

"According to Rosemary's letter, Max threatened to cut off his support if Charlotte allowed it. I don't know how much support Max was providing, but apparently it was enough to prevent Rosemary's adoption."

"I'm surprised Max didn't encourage the adoption. From all accounts, he didn't want anyone to know about Rosemary. Surely, if she was adopted by another man, the secret would have been even easier to keep."

Doncan shrugged. "I'm inclined to agree with you, but presumably Max had his reasons. Anyway, Charlotte and her husband went on to have three additional children. Two of them died young, and the third passed away last year after a long battle with cancer."

"How sad."

"Rosemary married at nineteen and had three children in fairly rapid succession. She and her husband were divorced when the youngest was three."

"How old are the children now, then?"

Doncan grinned. "I'm glad you asked. I felt a bit nosy, digging up all this information about the woman and her family, but I also felt it would be best to know as much as possible about the people with whom we're dealing."

"I think you're right about that. I don't believe she's who she claims to be and I'm suspicious of her intentions. Tell me everything you've discovered."

"Her oldest child is forty. She's April Malone now, after her third marriage. Her husband is Joe. He's a few years older than April. He has two children from two separate earlier relationships, but April doesn't have any children."

"Was she at least born in April?" Fenella asked.

Doncan flipped through the papers on his desk and then shook his head. "Date of birth, fifth of June," he told her.

Fenella shrugged. "That doesn't even make sense. June is also a girl's name."

"Maybe you could ask Rosemary about it when you meet her."

"When we run out of other things to talk about."

"Exactly that. Anyway, her son, Matthew Ballard, is thirty-eight. His wife is Viola. She's two years younger than Matthew. They are also childless."

Fenella suddenly felt as if she should be taking notes. She dug a pen and a small notebook out of her handbag and jotted down everything that Doncan had already told her. "And the third child?" she asked eventually.

"Another daughter, named Autumn. She's Autumn Tate now and she's thirty-six. Her husband, Randy, is forty. They have four children between them, although none together."

"So Rosemary is a grandmother," Fenella said thoughtfully.

"She is, although only one of the four children is Autumn's. Randy has three from former relationships."

"Tell me about Autumn's child."

"He's called Mason and he's twenty."

"Twenty? Then Autumn had him when she was only sixteen?"

"It would seem so."

"Tell me she was born in the autumn."

Doncan laughed. "Date of birth, tenth of January."

Fenella sighed. "I suppose Autumn is a better name than Winter would have been."

"Any more questions?"

"What else do you know about the family?"

"Not much, really. Everything I've told you is public record. Rosemary was only married the one time. She lives in a rented flat in a decent but not great part of London. Hers is the only name on the rental agreement, but that doesn't mean there isn't anyone else sharing the flat with her."

"Does she live anywhere near Max's sister?"

"I doubt Max's sister would be willing to go anywhere near where

Rosemary lives. As I said, it's a decent area, but not the sort of place that Max's sister would frequent."

"What about the children? Do any of them live near Max's sister or have any connection to her?"

"I couldn't find any connection to Max's sister, and I did look. April and her husband live a few streets away from Rosemary in a similar rented flat. Matthew and Viola own a small house on the other side of the city. Again, it isn't the best area, but not the worst, either. They bought during the height of the property boom and now owe the bank more than the house is worth, but if they hold onto it for a few more years, they should be okay. Houses in London just keep climbing, really."

"And the third child, Autumn? Where does she live?"

"Liverpool," Doncan told her. "She and Randy have a flat in a nicer area of Liverpool. Her son lives in the same building in a flat with his girlfriend."

"I wonder why they're in Liverpool."

"Randy was born and raised there. I'm not sure how he and Autumn met, but Randy's other three children all live in the same area with their respective mothers."

"How many mothers?"

"Two mothers," Doncan told her.

Fenella sighed. "All of this is fascinating, but I'm not sure what to do with the information. If I do meet Rosemary, I won't want her to know how much I know about her and her family."

"If you meet her."

"Which isn't likely. I really can't see any reason why I'd want to meet her."

"Aside from morbid curiosity?" Doncan suggested.

Fenella laughed. "I suppose I am curious. If she truly was Max's daughter, why did she wait until now to come forward? Max has been dead for years, hasn't he?"

"Another question for her, not me. I have a long list of questions about the entire situation. What I can't seem to work out is what she's hoping to gain by coming forward now and visiting the island."

"Unless she truly is just interested in learning more about her father."

Doncan nodded. "I can hope that's the case, but you said yourself that you don't trust her. As an advocate, I'd advise against trusting anyone, really. I simply can't see what she's hoping to accomplish."

"Can she sue Max's estate?"

"She could, if she can prove that she's telling the truth. She'd need DNA test results. Of course, if she starts making threats in that area, Max's sister might make her an offer to get her to go away. If I were her advocate, I might even suggest such a thing. Max's sister has plenty of her own money. She could probably afford to pay Rosemary off easily."

"Can she sue Mona's estate?"

"She can probably try, but I can't see that sort of suit being successful. Even if everything Mona owned had been given to her by Max, and that wasn't necessarily the case, everything was given to Mona legally and in Max's lifetime. I believe Rosemary would struggle to convince the courts that she was entitled to anything."

"But she could try."

"She could try, but it wouldn't be inexpensive and it would take time. You have much deeper pockets than she does, I'm sure. Again, I suspect she may make some threats, hoping for a quick out-of-court settlement."

"I have no intention of giving her a penny."

Doncan nodded. "Even if she is Max's daughter, you've no obligation to give her anything. If she does decide to sue, you know I'll do everything I can to protect you."

"If she is Max's daughter," Fenella echoed.

❧ 2 ❧

"Of course she isn't Max's daughter," Mona said angrily a short time later. "The very idea. It doesn't bear thinking about."

"You're positive?"

Mona narrowed her eyes at Fenella. "I can't believe you're questioning me. I knew Max better than anyone else in the world did. If you'd told me that he'd fathered a child before he'd met me, I might have given the matter some thought, but the idea that he'd cheated on me once we were together? Impossible."

"A lot of women feel that way and then get a nasty shock."

Mona shook her head. "I knew Max and all of his secrets. This woman was not one of them."

"She has letters."

"Good for her. I know who's behind all of this. Max's sister will have set the whole thing up for her own amusement. She'll have written the letters, copying Max's handwriting and his style. If pushed, I'd be willing to bet she'd even fake her own DNA to get a match with this Rosemary woman."

"Why would she want to do that? Surely it's her share of Max's fortune that's in danger?"

"She's trying to hurt me, or rather, you. She can't stand the idea that you're sitting here with all of the things that Max bought me over the years. She's just hoping to shake things up. Maybe she thinks you'll feel sorry for poor abandoned Rosemary and share some of your fortune with her. I'll bet Rosemary has agreed to share everything she can get from you with Max's sister."

"That's crazy."

"So is Max's sister. She hated me and she hated that Max cared more about me than he did about her. It's entirely possible that she's simply doing this to embarrass me. I'm sure she knows that my birthday is coming up. She may even know about the party I'm having. Maybe she's paid this Rosemary woman to come and make an appearance at the party. If Rosemary showed up and announced to everyone that she was Max's love child, the product of an affair that had gone on behind my back, well, Max's sister would love that."

"You're dead," Fenella pointed out. "Surely you're beyond being embarrassed or upset about such things, or at least you should be, as far as Max's sister is concerned. Why should she imagine that I'd care about Max's behavior?"

"She wants to ruin my reputation. The one thing everyone always says about me is that Max was devoted to me. If everyone finds out that Max had a child with another woman, then Max's sister will win."

"Are you sure she's behind this?"

"She must be. Doncan told you that Rosemary said she'd been accepted by the woman. There's no way Max's sister would have accepted her if she'd just turned up on the doorstep, not without DNA tests and goodness knows what else. The only way it makes sense is if Max's sister found Rosemary somewhere and set the whole thing up. No doubt she's been coaching her for weeks or even months, setting the stage for whatever she has planned."

"You think Rosemary is going to try to ruin your birthday celebration?"

"Or maybe just my reputation," Mona sighed dramatically. "She'll come over and meet with Doncan first and then with Max's advocates. No doubt she'll follow up those visits with a visit to the local paper. She'll claim she's just looking for interesting articles about her father, but in the end she'll let them talk her into giving them an interview, and within a day the entire island will be talking about how Max had betrayed me."

"I'm sure that will be very sad for you, but I really don't see why it matters otherwise."

"No, I suppose you don't," Mona said, wiping a tear from her eye. "Max and I had a very special relationship. It breaks my heart to think that people will be discounting its significance now."

"So we need to find a way to prove that Rosemary isn't who she's claiming she is."

"I'm not sure how we can do that. No doubt Max's sister will refuse to submit to a DNA test. I'm sure Rosemary will be vocal about her willingness to take one. She'll know she's safe because Max's sister will never agree."

"Does Max's sister have children?"

Mona laughed harshly. "No chance. You have be human to have children, I believe."

"She's married?"

'Oh, yes, she found herself a very wealthy and incredibly cold man to marry when she was in her early twenties. Aside from a single peck on the cheek at their wedding, I doubt they've even touched one another in fifty years."

"My goodness. How sad."

"They deserve each other. They both love money more than anything else, although Max's sister had a weird obsession with Max. That's why she hated me, of course. She always felt that I'd replaced her in Max's affections."

"Did you?"

Mona looked surprised and then laughed. "In some ways, maybe. Max had been close to his sister before he moved to the island, but once he'd moved, he and his sister started drifting apart, long before I came onto the scene. She wouldn't blame Max although it was his decision to move to the island, so she blamed me instead."

"And you think she's still so mad at you that she's engineered all of this just to make your memory look bad?" Fenella asked.

Mona sighed and then shook her head. "There must be more to it than that, mustn't there? She has to think she can get some money from you or from my estate. I just can't see how she thinks she'll be able to do it."

"If Rosemary truly is who she claims to be, surely she could sue for a share of Max's estate."

"She isn't who she claims to be, though. I wonder if Max's sister has been planning this for years. Maybe she needed to wait until I was gone in order to put things into motion. She had to know that I'd refute the woman's claims, of course."

"We need to work out what she's hoping to gain. How can she expect to get anything by suing your estate?" Fenella asked.

Mona sighed. "What did Doncan say? Could he think of any way she could sue you and win anything?"

"He didn't seem to think so. Everything Max gave you he gifted to you during his lifetime. If he'd wanted to give anything to his daughter, he had ample opportunity to do so."

"She wasn't his daughter," Mona said tightly. "Maybe she thinks that she'll be able to persuade you to give her some share of my estate out of misplaced guilt or something."

"If you weren't here, she may have been able to do just that," Fenella speculated. "I mean, I do feel rather sorry for her, not knowing her father and all."

"She may well have known her father. Rosemary's mother may have left the man's name off Rosemary's birth certificate for any number of reasons. That doesn't mean that Rosemary didn't know him, though."

"I suppose you're right. I wish I knew why she was coming to the island. What could she be hoping to accomplish?"

She and Mona talked for another half hour before Mona finally gave up and faded away. "I'm going to talk to Max," she told Fenella, "but I'm not going to say one word about this woman and her ridiculous claim."

Fenella would have argued if Mona hadn't disappeared immediately. "I don't see how you can be so sure," she muttered toward the now empty chair.

"How about a walk?" Shelly asked her the next morning when Fenella opened the door to her knock.

"A walk?" she echoed. "I suppose I could."

"You look as if you didn't sleep," Shelly said, sounding concerned.

Fenella looked down at her crumpled pajamas. "I didn't sleep well," she agreed. She vaguely remembered crawling into bed not long after Mona had left, but her sleep had been restless and filled with nightmares. Fenella's kitten, Katie, had given up after the first hour and gone to sleep in the spare bedroom rather than suffer through any more of Fenella's tossing and turning.

"Have you fed Katie?" Shelly asked.

Fenella thought for a minute. Katie nearly always woke her at exactly seven o'clock to demand her breakfast, but just occasionally the kitten would let her have an extra hour of sleep. "What time is it?" Fenella asked.

"Half nine."

It took Fenella a minute to work out that Shelly meant nine-thirty. After nearly a year on the island, she still thought in American English, in spite of her efforts to adapt. "I must have fed Katie, then. She never would have let me sleep this late."

A quick trip into the kitchen confirmed that Katie had indeed been fed. It looked as if Fenella had filled the animal's food and water bowls without opening her eyes. The empty packet from the cat food was sitting in the middle of the kitchen counter and there were bits of kibble scattered across the floor. Katie's bowls were empty, but she'd clearly left behind the food that hadn't been served to her properly.

"How about if I clean up in here while you shower?" Shelly suggested. "Then we can take that walk and you can tell me what's bothering you."

"What makes you think something is bothering me?" Fenella asked.

Shelly took her hands and then stared into her eyes. "You're still in your pajamas at half nine and your pajama shirt is on back to front."

Fenella looked down at herself and then frowned. "Okay, I'll go and take a shower. You don't have to clean up after me, but I'd be forever grateful if you'd start a pot of coffee."

Shelly nodded. "It will be ready when you are," she promised.

Fenella felt slightly better after her shower. She got dressed and then walked back into the kitchen, deeply inhaling the wonderful smell of coffee brewing as she went.

"Coffee," Shelly said, handing her a cup full of the black liquid.

Fenella took a sip and then sighed happily. After two more sips, she began to feel more like herself. "Thank you," she said, looking around her now spotless kitchen. "I don't deserve a friend like you."

Shelly laughed. "My goodness, I just wiped the counter and swept up a few kitten treats. It wasn't a big deal."

"You made coffee. That was a big deal."

"Your coffee maker made coffee. All I did was add water."

Fenella waved a hand. "Whatever, I'm hugely grateful, and I'm starting to feel better, too."

"That's good to hear. Are you ready for a walk?"

"I think a walk is just what I need."

The pair set out at a brisk pace, heading for the Sea Terminal building at one end of the promenade.

"I won't push you, but if you want to talk about it, I'm happy to listen," Shelly said after several minutes.

"It's something rather odd, really, that's bothering me," Fenella replied. "I feel as if I'm betraying Mona somehow by talking about it, though."

"Should we talk about the weather, then?"

Fenella shook her head. "I know you won't repeat anything I tell you. I met with Doncan yesterday, you see."

"You were going to talk about Mona's birthday celebration, weren't you?"

"I was, and we did talk about it. He's making all of the plans. I'm really just an invited guest, the same as everyone else. I'm allowed to add a few people to the guest list, though. Do you have an suggestions of people I should invite?"

Shelly shrugged. "It's up to you. It's going to be a huge social event, really. I'm sure everyone on the island is hoping for an invitation. If I were you, I'd invite just about everyone I know."

"I feel odd about inviting people, though," Fenella told her. "It's really Mona's party. Inviting my friends seems odd."

"Then don't invite anyone. Maybe you'll feel differently next year when the party comes around again. If anyone says anything, you can always say you didn't properly understand that you could invite extra guests. No doubt Doncan will back you up on that if it becomes an issue."

"He would, I'm sure. He's very good at what he does."

"Yes, he is. You really shouldn't let the party bother you, though. It's meant to be a fun evening, not a source of stress."

"It isn't the party that's bothering me," Fenella said. "Although if this other matter hadn't come up, it probably would be worrying me a lot."

"This other matter is where you feel as if you'd be betraying Mona if you talk about it?"

"Yes, exactly. The thing is, Doncan has had a letter from someone claiming to be Maxwell Martin's daughter."

Shelly stopped dead in her tracks. "Say that again, slowly."

Fenella repeated her words.

"I don't believe it. Max was devoted to Mona. Everyone knew that."

"You never met Max, did you?"

"Well, no. I didn't move in the same social circle as Mona when we were younger. I only met Mona when I moved in next door to her right after John died. Max had been dead for years by that point."

"So you only know what Mona told you about Max."

"Just because I'd never met Mona or Max doesn't mean I'd never heard of them. They were the talk of the island for many years. Everyone knew how devoted they were to one another. Everyone knew about their enormous fights, too. And while there were always rumors about Mona and other men, I never heard anyone suggest that Max ever so much as looked at another woman in his life. It's a small island. If he'd cheated on Mona, everyone would have known about it."

"Allegedly the affair took place in London."

Shelly frowned. "That makes it seem a little bit more possible, but I still don't believe it."

"If you're right, and this Rosemary Ballard is lying, why would she?" Fenella asked. "That's what kept me up all night."

"She's after Max's money, of course," Shelly said.

They'd reached the Sea Terminal and now turned to walk back the other way.

"How can she get to Max's money, though?"

"She can sue Max's estate, can't she? Max's sister got everything, didn't she? I'm sure I read that at the time. Everyone on the island wondered why Max didn't leave anything to Mona, not that she needed any more money, of course."

"Max's estate was divided between Max's sister and his business partner, Bryan," Fenella told her. "Apparently Max's sister has recognized Ms. Ballard's claim and welcomed her as the niece she never knew she had."

"Has she handed over some portion of Max's estate to Ms. Ballard, too?"

"I doubt that very much. From what Doncan said, though, it doesn't seem likely that she'll be suing Max's sister."

"And Bryan is dead, too, so she can't sue him."

"He left everything to his wife, and she left everything to charity, apparently."

Shelly's frown wrinkled her nose. "Surely this woman wouldn't sue charities, would she?"

"I can't imagine she'd sue charities, but I suppose you never know."

"She can't be planning to sue you, can she?"

"I wish I knew. Doncan doesn't seem to think that she could get anything from Mona's estate, even if she does sue, but I hate the idea of being tangled up in a lawsuit. The whole thing feels ugly."

"What sort of proof does she have for her claim?"

"Doncan said she has letters from Max to her mother that refer not only to their relationship, but also to the mother's pregnancy and to Rosemary herself."

"I'm surprised Max didn't marry her, then," Shelly said. "Everything I've ever heard about Max suggests that he was an honorable man who conducted all of his business and personal affairs with the utmost of integrity. Sixty years ago, if you weren't married and you got a girl pregnant, you married her."

"According to Doncan, Max told Rosemary's mother that he couldn't marry her because of Mona."

"What does that mean?"

"Apparently the letters suggest that Mona had some sort of hold over Max, something that made it essential that she not find out about the affair."

"That doesn't make sense. That wasn't how Mona described their relationship at all."

"Maybe Max just used Mona as an excuse to not marry the woman," Fenella suggested.

"It sounds as if you believe her story."

"I don't know what to think," Fenella admitted. "Men cheat. I should know. The man I loved got another woman pregnant while I was recovering from miscarrying his child."

Shelly pulled her into a hug. "I'm sorry. This must be very difficult for you."

"I need to talk to people who actually knew Max," Fenella said. "I need to find out if he would have cheated on Mona or not."

"You already know people who knew Max," Shelly pointed out. "Donald knew him and so did Peter. Ask them what they think."

Fenella frowned. "I'd rather not tell them about Rosemary, though."

"So make something up. Tell them that you're considering writing Max's biography. I'm sure there would be some interest among the island's historians for such a book. Max was a very important man, after all."

"That's an idea," Fenella said thoughtfully. "I could say I'm writing Mona's biography, instead. I could ask the same questions, really, and I'd much rather write about Mona than Max."

"You're missing the point," Shelly laughed. "I wasn't suggesting you actually write anything, just that you could ask a few questions as if you were."

"I know, but now that you've mentioned it, I might enjoy writing about Mona. She did lead a fascinating life."

"I can't argue with that."

Fenella didn't feel comfortable calling Donald. His phone calls seemed to have become less frequent, and that suited her. The last thing she wanted to do was make him think that she was chasing after him. Peter, however, she was happy to call.

After her long walk with Shelly, she rang his apartment. "Hi, it's

Fenella. I wanted to ask you something, but it isn't anything important. Maybe we could get a drink at the pub tonight? I'll invite Shelly, too," she told his answering machine.

"I'll come," Shelly said quickly from where she'd been standing behind Fenella. "Do you want to get dinner before we go to the pub?"

"We probably should. I don't have any food in the house and I'm not in the mood to go grocery shopping right now."

Shelly had some errands to run, so she left Fenella to read and pace and think too much while she did them. Mona was conspicuously absent, which didn't improve Fenella's mood. When Shelly came back, they went to a small Italian restaurant that was only a short walk from their building.

"That was delicious," Shelly said as they made their way back out of the restaurant an hour later.

"It was," Fenella agreed, even though she'd barely tasted her food. Her mind was racing in a million directions and she couldn't seem to stop it.

Their favorite pub was also nearby. Even in her distracted state, Fenella smiled brightly as she walked into the Tale and Tail. The addition of a large bar to the middle of the room was the only change that had been made to what had once been the private library of a large mansion on the promenade. The rest of the building had been turned into an expensive hotel, but the library was open to everyone, and Fenella thought it was the most wonderful place in the world. Bookshelves covered nearly every inch of every wall and all of the shelves were crammed full of books. Once you recovered from the shock of seeing so many books everywhere, you might notice the resident cats who lounged in beds scattered throughout the room.

"Peter called me back and said he'd meet us upstairs," Fenella told Shelly.

"Let's get drinks, and then go and find him."

The circular staircase to the upper level was another thing that Fenella loved about the pub. Going up was always fun, but nearly everyone used the building's elevators for going back down again.

Peter was sitting near the top of the stairs, sipping a glass of wine and reading a book.

"Hello," Fenella called as she and Shelly approached him.

"Hello," he replied, shutting the book and getting to his feet. "It's good to see you both. I must start making more of an effort to spend time with you two. Life has been far too busy of late." He gave them each a hug and then they all took seats around the small table.

"I don't think I've seen you since Christmas," Shelly said in surprise. "How have you been?"

The conversation covered a dozen subjects over the next twenty minutes. After Peter got a second round of drinks for everyone, he turned to Fenella. "You wanted to talk to me about something, or ask me something, didn't you?"

Fenella nodded. "I was going to make up some excuse for asking, but it seems easier to just tell you the truth. Doncan has had a letter from someone claiming to be Maxwell Martin's daughter."

Peter looked surprised. He sat back in his seat and took a sip of wine before he spoke. "How old is she?"

"I think Doncan said she's sixty-one," Fenella replied.

"Then I don't believe her," Peter told her. "Oh, her mother may have told her that Max was her father, but I don't believe that he was. To be that age, she would have had to have been conceived after Max had met Mona. I don't believe that Max ever cheated on Mona."

"Did Mona cheat on him?" Fenella asked.

Peter took another drink of wine before he replied. "I doubt it, in spite of her reputation. I think she found it amusing for people to think that she was wild and, well, free with her favors, but truly, I think Max was the only man for her in the same way as she was the only woman for him."

"According to this woman, her mother and Max had an affair in London," Fenella explained.

Peter shook his head. "I still don't believe it. Max traveled a lot, that's true, but Mona sometimes went with him. If Max had a woman in London, he wouldn't have included Mona in his trips."

"Apparently the other woman knew all about Mona, though," Fenella added.

"I liked Max, and I did a lot of business with him over the years. I trusted him, and he never gave me any reason to doubt his integrity. I can't believe that he'd cheat on Mona, and I also can't believe that he'd have a child with a woman and not do the right thing by her and marry her."

Shelly nodded. "I said the same thing. In those days, if you got a woman pregnant, you married her, unless you were married to someone else already, of course."

"From what Doncan told me, in Max's letters to the woman's mother, Max used Mona as the excuse for why he couldn't marry her. Allegedly, Mona had some sort of hold over Max that kept him tied to her."

"I can believe that part," Peter said. "They had an odd relationship, really. They were either madly in love or fighting like cats and dogs. Much of the time their fights seemed almost staged to me, as if they were both enjoying the drama more than anything else, but I do remember one particularly bad argument between them. Max said something almost nasty to Mona, which never happened. She went very still and then told Max to think very, very carefully before he spoke again. Max flushed and then began to apologize profusely. Mona just laughed at him and then walked away."

"Do you remember what they were arguing about?"

"Not at all, but I do remember thinking at the time that Mona must have known where the bodies were buried, as it were. It was odd, because Max was one of the most powerful men on the island, but Mona clearly had the upper hand in their relationship."

"Maybe just because he loved her so much?" Shelly asked.

"That may have been part of it," Peter agreed. "I was too much younger than she was to ever attract Mona's attention, but I can tell you that there was something incredible about her. She had this sort of magic about her, that's the only way I can describe it. When she was in a room, all eyes were drawn to her, even when she was simply standing quietly in a corner." Peter stopped and laughed. "Not that Mona ever stood quietly in a corner."

"If this woman's story isn't true, can you think of any reason why she'd be lying?" Fenella asked.

"As I said, perhaps it's the story her mother told her, so she believes it," he suggested. "It's difficult for me to imagine being an unwed mother in the nineteen-fifties, but I would think if I were, I might be tempted to tell my child that his or her father was someone rich and powerful, rather than admit that I'd had an affair with the local butcher or a window cleaner, or some other rather ordinary man."

"Whatever her mother told her, why is she coming to the island?" was Fenella's next question.

"If she truly believes that Max was her father, she probably wants to see the island for herself. No doubt she'll want to meet people who knew Max and find out everything she can about him."

Fenella nodded. "I can't help but worry that she's after more than just a chance to find out more about Max."

"She can't possibly think she has any claim to any of Mona's money," Peter told her. "I suppose she might have the basis for a lawsuit against Max's estate, assuming he truly had acknowledged her as his daughter but didn't mention her in his will."

"He didn't mention her in his will, that's for sure. I'm not sure about the other part. The woman claims that her mother and Max discussed the pregnancy in their letters, though."

"I would think she'd need a DNA test if she were going to try to claim anything from Max's estate. He's been dead for a long time, though. I'm not sure even a really good advocate could do much for her."

"According to the letter she sent Doncan, Max's sister has accepted her as a long-lost niece," Fenella said.

"But has she offered to give this woman a share of the estate? I've never met Max's sister, but I've heard enough about her to suspect that the answer is a definite no."

"I truly hope she is only coming to learn more about her father, if Max even was her father."

"I still don't believe it," Peter said firmly. "Max was devoted to Mona. Besides, if she truly did know some secret or secrets that he didn't want getting out, he never would have risked an affair."

Fenella finished her wine while she thought about what Peter had said. A third drink was tempting, but it was getting late and Katie needed her bedtime snack. The trio walked home in companionable silence.

"It was good to see you both again," Peter said as they got off the elevator on the sixth floor of their building. "We should do this again soon."

"You'll be getting an invitation to Mona's birthday celebration soon," Fenella told him. "If I don't see you between now and then, I hope you'll be there."

"I don't want to miss that," he assured her. "It's going to be the island's social event of the year. Maybe that's what this woman is after, an invitation to Mona's party."

"Considering the circumstances, she isn't going to get one," Fenella replied.

Shelly and Peter both laughed, and then they all let themselves into their own apartments. Fenella gave Katie a few small treats and then headed for the bedroom.

"I wish I knew what she was after," Fenella told Katie as she brushed her hair and took off her makeup. "I don't believe she just wants to learn more about her father."

"Max was not her father," Mona said emphatically.

Fenella jumped and then sighed. She'd spilled eye makeup remover everywhere. "I didn't hear you come in," she said to Mona as she reached for a roll of paper towels.

"I must remember to start making noise," Mona replied. "I wasn't planning on visiting, though. I was just passing through. Your comment made me stop."

"For what it's worth, Peter doesn't believe Rosemary's story, either, although he suggested that perhaps that it was Rosemary's mother who made up the story and that Rosemary believes it to be true."

"Max's sister is behind all of it, I'm sure of that. I'm still trying to work out what she's hoping to gain, though. If she simply wanted to embarrass me, she'd have done all of this while I was still alive."

Fenella tried to word her next question carefully. "The letters suggested that you knew something that let you control Max. Peter agreed that that was possible."

Mona laughed. "I knew all of Max's secrets, darling."

"And did that give you a hold over him?"

"Max had so many inconsequential secrets," Mona replied. "He dyed his hair, for example. I was the only one who knew that, but it wouldn't have been the end of the world if other people found out."

"Did you know any secrets that were more important?"

"Max only had one important secret," Mona told her. "Of course, I knew it. If others had found out, it could have been devastating for poor Max. He spent his entire life keeping that one secret at all costs, and he'd have done whatever needed doing to make sure that I didn't reveal it either."

"So you could have used it to control Max, to keep him from marrying the mother of his child?"

"I never used it to control Max, even though I could have, if I had been a different type of person. It's irrelevant anyway, as Max never fathered a child with this woman or anyone else."

Fenella had a dozen more questions to ask, but the look on Mona's face stopped her. "Are you okay?" she asked instead.

"Not really. The whole idea that Max may have cheated has upset my equilibrium. I know he didn't cheat, but I don't know what this woman wants or what Max's sister is planning. Those things worry me. I worry about you, mostly, although the idea that my reputation will suffer is also upsetting. That this woman is claiming that I kept her mother and Max apart through some sort of blackmail infuriates me. I knew Max's secret and I could have used it in a dozen different ways for my own gain. I suppose there are some people who would suggest that I did just that."

Mona faded away before Fenella could reply.

3

F enella spent much of the rest of the week making lists of people to invite to Mona's party and then crossing their names off her lists. Once she'd scribbled out every name, she'd start again with the same names, second-guessing herself repeatedly on whether to include anyone or everyone. On Thursday she called Doncan.

"I can't decide whether I should invite everyone I know or no one at all," she told him when she was connected.

"Will you have more fun at the party if everyone you know is there?" he asked.

"Maybe," she replied, feeling as if she should laugh or maybe cry. "The problem is, if I invite one person from my class, then I should invite them all. I only like one or two of them, though, not all of them."

"Mona never cared what people thought. If she were here, she'd tell you to invite the ones you like and ignore the others."

"But I'll still have to see them for the next several weeks in class. It will be awkward."

"You could simply pretend that you had nothing to do with the guest list," Doncan suggested. "If anyone asks, you can tell them that my office handled all of the details and you had nothing to do with it."

"Won't people wonder why Daniel Robinson is included, then?" Fenella asked. "He wasn't even living on the island before Mona died. His being invited doesn't make sense."

"It was Mona. It doesn't have to make sense," Doncan insisted. "I'm quite happy to tell people that Mona left clear instructions and I simply followed them. As ninety-nine percent of the guest list has nothing to do with you, you'd be mostly telling the truth, anyway."

Fenella laughed. "I suppose that's one way to look at it. I'm not comfortable with lying though, mostly because I'm not very good at it. Add the men and women from my class to the guest list, please." She gave Doncan their names and then added a few more names from among the other people she'd met in the months that she'd been on the island.

"Is that all?" he asked when she was finished.

"I think that's just about everyone I've met since I've been here," she replied. "It seemed safer to simply include them all. Hopefully, they won't all be able to attend."

"As I said, this is going to be a big event on the island's social calendar. I doubt you'll have many refusals."

"How many guests are we talking about, then?"

"I'd estimate about three hundred," Doncan said. "Maybe three-fifty if absolutely everyone comes and brings a guest of his or her own."

"Three hundred and fifty people?" Fenella gasped. "And I was worried about adding a dozen extras?"

"There's a good chance you won't be able to find your friends in the crowd," Doncan laughed. "Not unless you go looking for them, anyway."

Fenella put the phone down and then picked up Katie for a cuddle. "Harvey was already on the list," she told the kitten. "I wish he could bring Winston and Fiona. The party would be a good deal more fun with a few dogs and cats to liven things up a bit."

"Merrow," Katie agreed, before wiggling away.

Harvey Garus was an octogenarian who lived in the building next door to Fenella's. He had a huge dog called Winston that he walked daily up and down the promenade. Several months earlier, Fenella had looked after Winston for a short time while Harvey had been missing. By the time he'd returned, safe and sound, Fenella had also taken on responsibility for a small dog called Fiona. Both dogs now lived happily with Harvey, and Fenella enjoyed seeing them on their frequent walks. She'd even kept them for a week in the summer when Harvey had gone away.

Having never had pets before in her life, Fenella was still surprised when she thought about how much she enjoyed owning Katie and spending time with Harvey's dogs. Very occasionally she thought about getting a dog of her own, but for the moment she wasn't ready to take on any additional responsibilities. Perhaps spending a week taking care of a cat and four kittens had dimmed her enthusiasm for more animals.

"What should I wear?" she asked Katie as she wandered around the living room. "To Mona's party, I mean," she added when Katie gave her a blank look.

"You must wait to see what the theme is before you select an outfit," Mona told her.

"Or you could tell me the theme now and help me choose something," Fenella suggested.

"What fun would that be?" Mona asked. "You must be patient, like everyone else. The invitations should go into the post tomorrow, which means yours should be here on Saturday."

"I assume there will be something appropriate in the wardrobe."

"Of course," Mona nodded.

Along with everything else that Fenella had inherited, the apartment had come with a wardrobe packed full of Mona's clothes. Nearly everything Mona had worn had been custom designed and created for her by a local designer. The dresses and gowns were fabulous and they all seemed to fit Fenella perfectly, even though she seemed to have a very different body shape than Mona. Every outfit also had matching shoes, a matching handbag, and often matching hairclips. Sometimes Fenella wondered how much of Max's fortune had been spent on Mona's wardrobe.

With nothing else to do, she walked into the bedroom and began flipping through the clothes in the wardrobe. "I'm sure I've never seen half of these dresses before," she muttered as she made her way from one end of the rack to the other. Someone knocked on her door as she reached the last dress.

"Let's go for a walk," Shelly suggested. "I'm a bit of a mess, and I need to get away from the world for a few minutes."

"The promenade isn't very far away," Fenella replied.

Shelly laughed. "It's far enough away for me."

Fenella ran a comb through her hair and then grabbed her handbag and slid on her shoes. She waited until they were marching down the promenade before she spoke.

"What's wrong?" she asked.

"You know I've been working on writing a book," Shelly began. "It's been going pretty well, or so I thought. This morning, when I opened the file, I started reading it from the beginning and, well, it's horrible."

Fenella smiled and then patted her shoulder. "It's perfectly normal to feel that way," she told her. "My friend who is a very successful writer told me that she feels that way most of the time when she's writing."

"But now I feel as if don't want to finish the story."

"You have two options. Force yourself to finish the story anyway, or abandon it and start something new."

"You missed out the third option, which is abandon it and never try to write another word."

"That isn't an option," Fenella said firmly. "You enjoy writing, don't you?"

"Yes, I do, really."

"And you're comfortably retired, so you can write in your spare time without worrying about how you're going to pay your bills, right?"

"Yes, I know, but..."

"But nothing," Fenella cut her off. "Even if everything you write truly is horrible, if you are enjoying doing it, then it's worth continuing. Maybe you'll have to write three or four books before you start to feel as if you've written something wonderful, but you'll never get there if you give up now."

Shelly hesitated and then nodded. "I just feel as if I've worked awfully hard to get this far. I can't imagine writing another book after this one, let alone three or four."

"So finish this one and then ignore it for a week or a month or however long you like. When you go back to it, maybe you'll find it isn't as bad as you first feared."

Shelly sighed deeply. "I was all upset and you're spoiling it by being reasonable," she complained. "Now I feel as if I have to go back and finish the story. I left my heroine in a very uncomfortable position, actually."

"Physically or emotionally?" Fenella asked.

"Both," Shelly giggled. "She's just locked herself out of her flat wearing nothing but a bath towel. She knows the hero is home, because she can hear noises in his flat, but it sounds as if he's having a party and she wasn't invited. He's the only person she knows in the whole building, in the whole town, actually, and since her mobile is locked inside her flat, she's going to have to knock on his door sooner or later, whether she wants to or not."

Fenella laughed. "I want to read this book when you've finished it," she said. "If nothing else, I want to find out how that scene ends."

Shelly shrugged. "I've no idea how it's going to end. If I were writing about a younger woman, it might well end in a love scene, but my main character is in her sixties and isn't about to fall into bed with a man, not even after he helps her out of a difficult situation."

"What would Tim do?" Fenella asked.

"What do you mean?"

"What would Tim do if this happened to you and him? From what I know of him, he wouldn't expect you to fall into bed with him, anyway."

"No, I think he'd be almost as embarrassed as I would be," Shelly said thoughtfully. "He'd be respectful, but I think he'd probably tease me about it for months afterwards."

"That sounds about right," Fenella agreed.

"Thank you so much. I was well and truly stuck and fed up and now I can see exactly where everything is going. Thank you," Shelly said excitedly. She spun around and began to walk back in the opposite direction.

"Are we done walking now?" Fenella asked as she ran to keep up with her friend.

"Oh, I am sorry," Shelly gasped. "I was so excited about the story that I started for home without thinking."

"It's fine. We can go home now," Fenella assured her. "I think it's going to rain, anyway."

Fenella spent most of Friday in the Manx Museum's archives, transcribing some eighteenth-century letters between a mother and her son. Most of the letters had to do with the running of the family farm, and Fenella found herself fascinated by what she learned. After a brisk walk on Saturday morning, Fenella checked her mailbox. The large envelope inside the box had her name and address written across by an expert in calligraphy.

The paper was thick and difficult to tear. Fenella headed for the elevator with the invitation in her hand. There was a fancy silver letter opener in the desk, another thing that Mona had left behind. Fenella used it to cut open the envelope.

"The pleasure of your company..." she began, reading out the invitation that had her name written in an appropriate space. "How very posh," she told Katie.

"Meerow," Katie replied, tossing her head and walking out of the room.

"I'm sorry you weren't invited," Fenella called after her. "Mona didn't know you when she was writing her will."

The kitten had dashed into Fenella's apartment shortly after Fenella had arrived on the island. Although Fenella had done her best to find Katie's owner, eventually she'd given up and accepted that Katie was hers, or maybe that she was Katie's, for better or worse.

She read through the invitation again. "Wear something blue," she read the last line. "What does that mean?"

"It means you should wear the first dress on the left side of the wardrobe," Mona told her.

Fenella walked into the bedroom and opened the wardrobe. The dress in question was a gorgeous seafoam blue color that darkened just slightly from the plunging neckline to the multiple layers of the uneven hem.

"It's wonderful," Fenella exclaimed, certain that she'd never seen the dress before.

"Yes, it was a real favorite of mine," Mona said. "It reminds me of the sea, especially with that unusual bottom. Timothy tried to make it look like waves."

"It does look exactly like waves," Fenella exclaimed.

Mona nodded and then faded away, leaving Fenella to try on the dress alone. It fit perfectly, of course, which meant that Fenella had nothing else to do but formally accept the invitation. She rang the number that had been given on the card.

"Good morning," a perky voice said. "How can I help you today?"

"I'm calling about the invitation to Mona's birthday celebration," Fenella explained.

"Very good. To whom am I speaking?"

"Fenella Woods."

"Excellent. Ms. Woods, will you be bringing a guest to the party?"

Fenella hesitated. She'd had Doncan send Daniel his own invitation. She couldn't think of anyone else she might like to bring. "Put me down for a guest," she said eventually. It was just possible she might remember someone she'd forgotten to invite.

"Very good," the girl said. "I hope you enjoy the party."

"Thank you." Fenella put the phone down and then dropped the invitation onto her desk. The party was two weeks away. She could only hope that Rosemary Ballard would be nothing but a distant memory by the time the party arrived.

A few hours later, her phone rang.

"Fenella? It's Donald, Donald Donaldson. How are you?"

"I'm very well, thank you," she replied, feeling oddly nervous about speaking to the man.

"That's good. I was just ringing to let you know that I've received the invitation to Mona's party. Thank you for including me."

"To be fair, I didn't include you," Fenella told him. "Mona made the guest list and left it with Doncan. I'm simply another invited guest."

"Really? I'm not sure if I should be flattered or insulted by that information," Donald laughed.

"If you hadn't been on the list, I'm sure I would have included you," Fenella said quickly. "How are you, though? And how is Phoebe?"

"I'm very well, thank you, and Phoebe is doing as well as can be expected, or maybe a little bit better. If I'm honest, I'm incredibly frustrated by the whole process. I'm used to being able to throw money at problems to make them disappear and it's difficult knowing that no amount of money can make Phoebe well again. I can pay for her to have therapy every hour of every day, but she has to make the effort and her body has to be up to the challenge. Right now, she's fighting hard and doing her part, but her body isn't cooperating."

"I am sorry."

"As I said, I'm simply frustrated, but my feelings are nothing compared to Phoebe's. She's recovered enough to recognize her limitations, and in some ways that's harder than when she was less aware. I can't imagine how difficult this must be for her, so I really mustn't complain."

"I'm sure it's terribly hard for both of you, and for your son as well."

"Yes, well, he's mostly pretending that nothing has happened, which is his way of dealing with it all." Donald sighed. "But I didn't ring to complain about my life. How are you?"

"I'm fine. I've been taking a class in reading old handwriting and doing some research at the museum. It's keeping me busy and reminding me of why I love history so much."

"Excellent," Donald replied, "and now we get to the awkward part of the conversation."

"Awkward? Go on, then, what's wrong?"

"The invitation specifically said that I could bring a guest," Donald replied slowly. "I was wondering if you really meant that."

"As I said, I had nothing to do with the invitations, but of course you can bring a guest. Were you thinking of bringing Phoebe if she's well enough?"

"She isn't up to such things, not yet, anyway," Donald replied. He took a deep breath and then chuckled. Fenella thought he sounded nervous or embarrassed.

"You have a new woman in your life," she guessed. "Of course, you're welcome to bring her."

"It isn't like that," Donald said quickly. "I still care very much about you, but, well, things are complicated."

"For heaven's sake, just tell me," Fenella said sharply. "You know we were never more than friends. I'm not going to get upset or angry with you."

Donald cleared his throat. "Phoebe has to have round-the-clock nursing care. I've managed to find a number of wonderful women to come in and look after her, but one of them is, well, particularly special. A short trip to the island, with a fabulous party to attend, seems like a nice way to thank her for everything she's doing for Phoebe."

"If you're truly interested in her, be careful how you ask. You don't want her to think that you're just trying to get her into bed, unless that's what you are doing."

Donald chuckled. "We aren't anywhere near that stage yet, and you're right. I'm going to have to be very careful how I phrase the invitation. I also don't want anyone else on Phoebe's team to feel as if I'm giving Betty special treatment."

"Good luck with that."

"Yes, well, perhaps it would be easiest if I simply came on my own."

"It's up to you, of course. Betty would be more than welcome, though, especially as I get the feeling she's important to you."

"She's starting to become important to me," Donald admitted. "I'm not exactly sure how I feel about that, though."

"Let yourself fall in love with her. If she breaks your heart, at least you tried. Life is too short to pass up on wonderful opportunities."

"You're right, of course. That's why I care for you so much. If I truly thought I had a chance with you, I wouldn't have given Betty a second glance."

"I'm happy for you, if you've found someone special, and it sounds as if you have. I'm looking forward to meeting Betty."

"Yes, well, we'll see. First I have to work out how to ask her without offending her and then I have to work up the nerve to actually ask."

"I'm just a phone call away if you want any advice," Fenella told him. "Now, can I ask you a question?"

"Of course."

"Do you think it's possible that Max ever cheated on Mona?"

"No," Donald said immediately. "Max never so much as looked at another woman from the day he met Mona until the day he died."

"A woman has written to Doncan claiming to be Max's daughter."

"Then she must have been conceived before Max met Mona."

"She's sixty-one, so if she's telling the truth, Max cheated on Mona."

"I don't believe it. I've told you before how infatuated I was with Mona when I was younger. I spent a lot of time watching her, and that meant I spent a lot of time watching Max, too. They were crazy about one another."

"But they fought a lot, too."

"They did, but only because Mona thrived on drama. She loved fighting with Max, and, I imagine, making up with him as well. The fights never felt serious, they were just how Mona and Max communicated."

"The woman is alleging that the affair took place in London. Does that change your mind any?"

"It does make it slightly more believable. Max couldn't have cheated with anyone on the island. Someone would have found out about it, I'm certain. In London, however, well, Max would have been a good deal more anonymous. I suppose it's just remotely possible that he had an affair while he was in London at some point."

"That's a worrying thought."

"If Max did get a woman pregnant, I have to believe that he would have married her, though. That was what men did in those days, unmarried men, anyway."

"She implies in her letter to Doncan that Max used Mona as his excuse as to why he couldn't marry her."

Donald laughed. "She did have an incredible hold over him, but if it was truly that strong, it would have kept him from straying in the first place. If he did cheat, he would have done the right thing by the woman, I'm almost certain."

Fenella sighed. "She wants to meet me."

"Why?"

"She's told Doncan she wants to meet everyone who was connected in any way with her father."

"Did you ever meet Max?"

"No, never."

"I can't see why she wants to meet you, then, but I imagine the polite thing to do would be to agree."

"I can't help but feel as if she's after something."

"Yes, I can see why you'd feel that way, but surely she can't be planning to sue you? The things that you inherited from Mona were given to her by Max during his life. I can't imagine that there would be any way she could make a claim to anything."

"That's what Doncan said, too, but I'm still worried."

"Understandably, of course. I wonder if Max's sister is still alive. She's the one who should be worried, I would have thought."

"She is still alive, and apparently she's accepted the woman as her niece."

"Really? I hope she's ready for a lawsuit, then. If the woman is who she claims to be, she may well have some sort of legal claim to Max's estate."

"I'm not looking forward to meeting her," Fenella sighed.

"So refuse."

"Doncan suggested that she could probably track me down if she were truly determined to talk to me."

"Come and visit me in London while she's on the island, then," Donald suggested. "I'm leasing a four-bedroom flat with an amazing view of the London Eye. One of the bedrooms is spare at the moment, although I may be moving a physical therapist in if Phoebe's doctors think that might help. Anyway, you'd be more than welcome."

"Thank you for the kind offer, but I'm not running away from the situation. I may even agree to meet her. I haven't decided yet."

She got her chance to decide just a few hours later.

"Fenella? It's Doncan. I've just been speaking with Rosemary Ballard. She'll be arriving on the island tomorrow and she'd very much like to meet you at your earliest convenience. I told her that I wasn't sure you were available. Are you?"

Fenella sighed. "How long is she planning on staying?"

"A week."

"I suppose I can't hide from her for an entire week. We can meet in your office?"

"If that's what you'd prefer, or some other space that might be considered neutral territory."

Fenella chuckled. "Maybe that would be for the best. Neutral territory sounds safest."

"There's a large conference room in the building here where I have my office space. I can book that."

"That sounds good. Is she coming alone?"

"I didn't ask that specific question, but from a few of the things she said, I believe at least one of her children will be accompanying her, and possibly all three of them."

"Then a large conference room sounds even better."

"We'd be rather too crowded in my office," Doncan laughed. "Ten o'clock on Monday? Just come to my office and someone will be able to direct you to the conference room."

"I'll be there," Fenella said grimly.

"It's going to be fine," Doncan told her. "If she says anything out of line, I'll deal with it. I'll make a lunch booking for us at twelve in Port St. Mary. That means we'll have to finish with Ms. Ballard by eleven at the latest so that we can have a leisurely drive south."

"You don't have to do that."

"No, but I will anyway. Whatever happens, it's going to be an odd meeting. I think we'll both deserve a treat after it's finished. The place I'm thinking of in Port St. Mary does excellent food and even better puddings."

"I'm sold," Fenella chuckled.

"I'll see you on Monday, then," Doncan said before he disconnected.

Fenella put the phone down and then began to pace around her apartment.

"Oh, do stop," Mona complained as she settled onto one of the couches. "You'll wear out the carpets, and they were expensive."

"Everything in here was expensive. Max was hugely extravagant with his money, wasn't he?"

"Not at all," Mona said sharply. "He was actually quite frugal most of the time. You don't amass a large fortune by spending lavishly."

"If he did have a daughter, would he have provided for her?"

"He didn't have a daughter."

"I know, but I'm just wondering what he might have done if he had."

Mona sighed. "Max would have married the woman, no matter what. That was the right thing to do in those days, and Max always did the right thing. That was one of the things we fought about, actually. He saw rules and regulations in black and white, where I always appreciated the shades of grey."

"If he didn't marry the mother, he would have provided for the child, though, right?"

"Yes, and generously."

"In his lifetime as well as in his will?"

Mona frowned. "In his lifetime, certainly, which is another reason why I know this Rosemary woman is lying. Max didn't have secrets from me, including financial ones. I know how much money he made and how much he spent. The only time he hid money from me was when he was buying me another gift. There's no way he was supporting a child in the UK behind my back."

"And no child was mentioned in his will."

"No, and he would have included her if she existed. Even if he'd worked his whole life to keep her a secret, he'd have no reason to leave her out of his will."

"If she did exist, surely his advocate would have known."

"Maybe, although Max didn't always tell his advocate everything. There were only two people in the world to whom Max confided everything, myself and Bryan, his partner. He would have told me, even though he'd have known that I'd have been devastated. He couldn't keep secrets from me, not from the very first day we met."

The rest of the weekend passed mostly uneventfully. Daniel called Fenella on Sunday.

"I finally have a day off and I've been going through my post," he explained. "Thank you for the very fancy invitation."

"It's Mona's party, really, although Doncan did allow me to add a few names to the guest list."

"The invitation is for myself and a guest. I don't really have anyone to bring with me, though."

"All of the invitations are worded that way," Fenella told him. "You're welcome to bring a friend or whatever, but it's entirely up to you."

The long silence that followed made Fenella nervous. Was Daniel going to suddenly mention a new woman in his life the way Donald had? She hadn't minded hearing that Donald was seeing someone else, but she felt rather differently about Daniel.

"My sister may be visiting the island that week," Daniel said eventually. "She'll be coming with her husband and their sons, though."

"It's not going to be a party for children, but if you want to bring your sister and her husband, that's fine," Fenella assured him. "I'm not bringing a guest, so one of them can officially be my guest if anyone is worried about the numbers."

"Are you sure? I think Deborah would love it. She always complains that she doesn't get many occasions to get dressed up anymore. I'm not sure her husband will be as keen, but I'd rather include them both, if you're sure."

"It's fine. When you call to RSVP, just tell them that you'll be bringing one guest. I've already said I was bringing one, but I didn't have anyone in mind."

"Thank you so much. Now I just have to find someone to mind the boys that night for them."

"Good luck with that."

Daniel laughed. "I'm sure I can find a young constable with nothing better to do for an evening."

They chatted for a bit longer about nothing much before the conversation seemed to run out of steam.

"I've been thinking of you a lot," Daniel said in a low voice. "Things are really busy at work, though. We're short two inspectors at the moment, so I'm doing triple duty."

"Oh, dear, I am sorry. I hope you'll be able to find time to enjoy your sister's visit."

"I've booked a few days off during her stay. Fingers crossed I'll actually get to take them. Anyway, if I don't see you between now and then, I'll see you at the party for Mona. Thank you again for letting me bring my sister and brother-in-law."

"No problem. I'll see you in a few weeks."

Fenella put the phone down and frowned at it. Maybe Daniel truly was busy with work, but maybe he was busy with another woman. It was also possible that he was simply avoiding her. She sighed. With Rosemary's visit looming, she didn't have time to worry about Daniel Robinson right now.

4

"Ah, Fenella, come in," Doncan said on Monday morning as Fenella was escorted into his office. "Ms. Ballard isn't here yet, so we may as well wait here. I'll have her and anyone who comes with her shown to the conference room. We can join them after they've all arrived."

Fenella nodded and then sank into a chair. "How are the replies coming for the party?" she asked, trying not to think about the upcoming meeting.

"So far everyone who has replied is coming. I believe we've had responses from about half of the guest list thus far. I expect we'll have many more today."

"It's going to be a big party, then."

"It is indeed."

Fenella glanced down at her hands and realized she was twisting her fingers into knots. After a long deep breath, she tried to force herself to relax. Doncan chatted easily about the weather and a movie he'd recently seen, but Fenella wasn't really paying attention. Eventually Doncan's assistant, Breesha, knocked on the door.

"Ms. Ballard and her family are here," she said.

"Come in and shut the door," Doncan told her.

Breesha nodded and then complied.

"What did you think of them?" Doncan asked.

The older woman raised an eyebrow and then shrugged. "Ms. Ballard seems to think she's someone very special. She didn't take kindly to being asked to wait in the conference room. I offered coffee or tea and everyone accepted. One of the men commented to his wife that biscuits would be nice. When I put out a plate of digestives, they fell on them as if they hadn't eaten in weeks, the lot of them. They remind me of Mr. Nelson's family, if you remember them."

Doncan nodded and then chuckled. "Oh, dear. I was quite relieved when they finally found themselves a different advocate. At least I'm not working for Ms. Ballard or any of her family members. Ready?" he asked Fenella as he got to his feet.

"Not at all, but I suppose I don't have a choice," she said in reply. She stood up and let Doncan escort her out of the room.

"Let me do the talking," he suggested as they walked. "If Breesha is right about them, they're going to be difficult from the outset."

Fenella nodded and then took a deep breath as Doncan pulled open the conference room door. For a moment she could hear raised voices, but all conversation in the room stopped as she and Doncan entered it.

"I thought we'd agreed on ten o'clock," the woman sitting at the head of the table snapped. She had short bright red hair that was clearly artificial and deep frown lines etched into her face. Doncan had said that Rosemary Ballard was sixty-one, but this woman looked older. She was wearing a black jacket over a red blouse that clashed with the red of her hair. The matching black pants appeared to be covered in cookie crumbs.

Doncan glanced at the clock. Fenella followed his gaze. It was three minutes past ten.

"Good morning," he said. "I'm Doncan Quayle and this is Fenella Woods."

The redhead frowned at Fenella. "You aren't what I was expecting," she said gruffly.

Fenella bit her tongue and looked at Doncan. He smiled and then winked at her. "Let's sit, shall we?" he suggested, holding out a chair for her.

She slid into the seat and then sat back and told herself to relax. Doncan could handle whatever this woman could throw at them, she was confident of that.

"Perhaps you could introduce yourself and everyone else?" Doncan suggested to the woman, who was still frowning at Fenella.

She shifted her gaze to Doncan and then sighed. "I'm Rosemary Ballard, only daughter of Maxwell Martin. Maybe I should say that I'm the only daughter that I'm aware of, though. Mr. Martin was very good at keeping secrets, it seems. His sister was unaware of my existence, and from what I've heard since I've been here, no one on the island knew about me, either. Perhaps my father had a dozen other children scattered around the place."

"Would you like a cup of tea?" Doncan asked Fenella before she could say something she might regret to Rosemary.

"Yes, please," Fenella said gratefully.

Doncan pushed a button and Breesha appeared a moment later.

"Tea for myself and Fenella, please," he told her.

"We all need more, too," Rosemary announced, "and more biscuits, something nicer than digestives, if you could."

Breesha smiled tightly and then left the room.

"Ms. Ballard, welcome to the island," Doncan said.

"Oh, call me Rosemary, everyone does," she replied. "While we wait for our tea, I'll introduce you to my children. This is my oldest, April Malone." She nodded toward the woman sitting to her left.

April looked as if she'd had a difficult life. Her bleached blonde hair framed her face in a style that Fenella remembered as popular in the nineteen-eighties. Her frown lines were nearly as deep as her mother's, making her appear older than the forty that Doncan had given as her age. April nodded at Fenella and then waved a hand toward the man sitting next to her.

"This is my husband, Joe. We've been married for a few years now, and so far it hasn't been too bad."

Joe chuckled. "She really does love me dearly," he said in a mocking tone. He looked younger than his wife. His full head of hair was dark brown, almost black, and it contrasted handsomely with his blue eyes. Both he and his wife were dressed in jeans and sweatshirts. April's had the name of an athletic shoe manufacturer across it, while Joe's advertised what Fenella assumed was his favorite beer.

"Then there's Matthew, my only son," Rosemary said, nodding toward the man next to Joe.

Matthew shrugged. As he opened his mouth to speak, the door swung open and Breesha walked back in, pushing a large cart. She passed out cups of tea to everyone and then put three plates full of cookies onto the table.

"Is there anything else right now?" she asked Doncan.

"Thank you, no," he said. "I'll buzz you if I need you."

She nodded and then pushed the cart back out of the room. Fenella grabbed a custard cream and took a bite.

"Yeah, I'm Matthew," the balding man said, shoving an entire custard cream into his mouth after his introduction. He was wearing a grey suit jacket over a pair of jeans and what appeared to be a dirty T-shirt. "This is my wife, Viola," he added around a mouthful of food.

Viola smiled shyly and then took a sip of her tea. Fenella thought that, at least so far, Viola seemed the most likeable of the bunch. She had brown hair cut into a shoulder-length bob and thick glasses. She was wearing a dress with a pretty flowered pattern that would probably have been better suited to spring or summer on the island.

"And on my other side is my other daughter, Autumn Tate," Rosemary said.

Fenella looked at the other woman. Her first thought was that Autumn didn't look anything like her mother or her siblings. She was strikingly attractive, with light brown hair that she'd pulled into a loose ponytail low on the back of her neck. She was wearing a comfortable-looking sweater with a dark skirt, and she looked both younger and happier than anyone else around the table.

"Good morning," she said in a pleasant voice. "This is my husband, Randy. We're happy to meet you both and excited to be visiting your beautiful island."

Randy nodded. "You'd think, as I grew up in Liverpool, that I'd have been here before, but I haven't. It's lovely, though," he said, smiling across the table at Fenella. He had thinning dark hair and a pleasant smile. He was wearing a sweater with jeans, and Fenella found herself smiling back at him.

"Right, that's introductions out of the way," Rosemary said. "What can you tell me about my father?"

Fenella took a sip of tea and left Doncan to answer.

"As yet, I've seen no evidence that Mr. Martin was your father," Doncan began. "Further, as I was not Mr. Martin's advocate, I'm not the best person for you to speak with about the man. I believe I gave you contact information for the firm of advocates that he used on the island."

"Yes, you did," Rosemary agreed, waving a hand. "I've an appointment to see them later, but I want to know what you thought of my father as a person. You were Mona Kelly's advocate, so you must have had numerous dealings with my father over the years. Tell me about him."

Doncan took a sip of tea and then nodded. "I always liked Maxwell Martin and found him to be a man of integrity and honor."

"So you were surprised to hear about me?" Rosemary suggested.

"I was indeed," Doncan replied.

Rosemary laughed. "I suspect everyone on the island will be equally surprised," she said. "I'm going to talk to someone at the local paper, see if we can make the front page with my story."

Fenella forced herself to take a deep breath. She looked over at Doncan.

"Why would you want to do that?" he asked in a mild tone.

"You aren't what I expected," Rosemary said to Fenella.

"What did you expect?" Fenella asked.

"I don't know. If I'd inherited a fortune from a blackmailing whore, I think I'd be embarrassed about it," Rosemary told her.

Doncan cleared his throat loudly. "I don't think this conversation is going to go well," he said before Fenella could react.

Rosemary laughed. "I should have known she'd spend the entire meeting hiding behind you," she said. "That's why she insisted that we meet here, rather than somewhere without her solicitor."

"The Manx term is advocate," Doncan said, "and you contacted me to arrange the meeting. If you didn't want to meet in my offices, you simply had to tell me, and I would have happily arranged this meeting for somewhere else."

"She's probably right to hide behind you," Rosemary replied. "Anything she says now will just be more evidence for my lawsuit."

"Lawsuit?" Doncan echoed. "You're planning on suing someone?"

Rosemary laughed. "I'm planning on suing your client there," she said. "She inherited a fortune from a woman who blackmailed my father. She shouldn't be allowed to live off of the money that my father would have given to my mother if it wasn't for Mona Kelly and her evil treatment of my father."

Fenella grabbed a random cookie and bit into it to stop herself from speaking. Doncan glanced at her with concern in his eyes before he turned back to Rosemary.

"Those are some pretty serious accusations," he said. "If you're planning to sue, than I can't see that we have anything further to discuss." He pushed his chair back from the table and started to stand up.

"Perhaps we could discuss what you could do to stop me from suing," Rosemary said quickly. "I'm sure no one wants to have this whole thing drag through the courts for years and years. I'm not getting any younger, for one thing. The faster we can find a mutually agreeable solution, the better for everyone, wouldn't you agree?"

"If we're going to discuss possible resolutions, perhaps you'd prefer to have your own advocate or solicitor present," Doncan suggested.

Rosemary shook her head. "I'm not sharing what I get with anyone," she said fiercely before she laughed and looked around the table. "This lot might get a few pounds once I'm gone, if I haven't spent every penny by that time, but I'm not sharing with a solicitor, that's for sure."

Doncan nodded. "I haven't had a chance to discuss this with my client, obviously, but I think I can safely say that we aren't prepared to make any sort of offer simply to make the threat of a lawsuit go away."

"I have letters," Rosemary said. "My father wrote to my mother for years, detailing how Mona Kelly was ruining his life. I'm sure your client would hate for those letters to be published."

"Is that a threat?" Doncan asked.

"Not at all," Rosemary said hastily. "I'm not trying to blackmail anyone, even though the concept should be quite familiar to Mona Kelly's niece. I'm just making it clear exactly what I have to bargain with, as it were. You make me a decent settlement from Mona Kelly's estate and I'll hand over the letters."

"That sounds like blackmail to me," Fenella said in a low voice.

Doncan nodded. "It does, rather."

"You'd prefer that I sue for my fair share of my father's money?" Rosemary asked. "That's all I'm after, you know. My father sent small amounts now and again, but nothing like what he could have afforded to send if he hadn't been buying up houses and cars for Mona. All I want is what I should have been given over the years."

"I'm not your advocate, so don't take this as legal advice, but it seems to me that if you're interested in getting money from the man you claim was your father, you should be suing his estate, not Mona's. Whatever he gave Mona in his lifetime, he left a considerable fortune when he died."

Rosemary shrugged. "That money went to his sister and his business partner. I feel as if they deserved it. Mona Kelly, on the other hand, only got money from my father by forcing him to buy her things. She didn't deserve what she was given."

"As I've not seen the letters to which you are referring, I can't comment on what is in them, but what you're suggesting is very much at odds with everything I knew about the relationship between Maxwell Martin and Mona Kelly," Doncan said.

"Let's cut to the chase," Rosemary told him. "I think five million pounds would be a fair settlement. I know Mona was worth more than that when she died."

Fenella nearly choked on her tea. Rosemary was correct, Mona was worth more than five million pounds, considerably more, but there was no way she was going to simply hand that sort of money over to anyone, least of all Rosemary Ballard.

"Out of the question," Doncan said casually. "Again, you might consider suing Mr. Martin's estate if you can actually prove yourself to be who you claim."

"I knew you'd get to that eventually," Rosemary said mockingly. "My dear aunt, Maxwell's sister, has recognized me as his daughter and rightful heir. That should be proof enough, surely."

"If she's recognized you as his rightful heir, then she should be turning her share of his estate over to you, as well," Doncan replied. "Perhaps once she's done that, we'll be in a position to consider your request."

"As I said, I've not asked her for any money," Rosemary countered. "She did everything she could to support her brother, even while he was under Mona Kelly's spell. Mona wouldn't allow him to contact her, did you know that?"

"What you're saying does not correspond with what I knew of both Mona Kelly and Maxwell Martin," Doncan replied.

Rosemary shrugged. "If you absolutely insist on proof, I'm sure my aunt would be happy to agree to a DNA test. As I said, she supports my claim."

"A DNA test would be a start," Doncan told her.

"We're wasting our time here," Joe said loudly. "They aren't just going to write you a check, but you knew that."

Rosemary frowned at him. "I told you to keep quiet," she snapped. "You all wanted to come along, and I only agreed as long as you promised to keep your mouths shut. Maxwell Martin was my father and this is my money I'm after."

"He was my grandfather," April interjected. "Some of the money should be mine, too."

"And mine," Matthew added. "Autumn will probably want a share, too, but she'll wait and ask you privately and get you to agree to giving her extra."

Autumn flushed and sighed. "I'm not going to get involved," she told her brother. "You can fight it out with Mother and April. Count me out of all of it."

"Until the money comes in," Matthew sneered. "Then you'll be right in the middle of everything, demanding your share. Except you'll be subtler than that. You'll just point out that Mason is Mum's only grandchild and demand a share for him, won't you?"

"Mason is my only grandchild," Rosemary said. "When I get my fair share of my father's money, I will put something away for him, obviously. He wants to go back to school and make something of himself. He deserves a chance to do that."

"Viola and I have been trying for kids for three years," Matthew said angrily. "We could use some money to pay for some treatments, and then maybe you'd have more grandchildren to spoil."

Fenella looked at Viola, who blushed bright red and looked down at the table.

"Maybe you just aren't man enough to make a baby," Joe suggested with a harsh laugh.

Matthew jumped up from his seat. "Say that to me again outside," he challenged.

Joe slowly got to his feet and squared his shoulders. "I'd be happy to," he sneered.

Fenella held her breath, waiting for someone to intervene. From where she was sitting, it looked very much like Matthew was going to get badly beaten up by his brother-in-law.

"Enough," Rosemary said, sounding bored. "Joe, sit down. You know you can't hit Matthew, not if you want to stay in this family. Matthew, sit down. You know Joe would put you on the ground with a single punch."

The two men were staring at each other and neither moved. After a minute, Rosemary spoke again.

"I said sit," she barked.

Joe dropped back into his seat and laughed. "One of these days you're going to challenge me to a fight when your mummy isn't around to protect you," he told Matthew. "I hope Viola doesn't mind visiting you in hospital for a few weeks."

Matthew sat back down and took Viola's hand. "I'm sorry," he said softly to her.

She nodded and then looked back down at the table.

"I'm going to repeat myself, because I don't think you were all listening," Rosemary said loudly. "I'm here fighting for my money. I was the one who was all but abandoned by my father. I'm the one who is entitled to a share of Mona Kelly's fortune, and I'm the one who is going to get it, one way or another. I let you all come along, but don't think that means I'm going to share anything I get with all of you."

"You say that as if we weren't just as abandoned by our father," April said.

"We don't even know who Autumn's father was," Matthew laughed.

Rosemary narrowed her eyes at her son. "I've told you all a million times that you all three have the same father. Peter Ballard didn't stick around long after Autumn was born, but that wasn't because he wasn't her father. He just decided he didn't like the responsibilities of father-hood, that's all."

"The fact remains that he abandoned us," April said. "At least when you were left, your mother remarried and gave you a family to grow up in."

"And I was too busy trying to bring up three kids on my own to try to find you a stepfather. If I'd had my fair share from my father when I was younger, we'd have all had a better life," Rosemary replied.

"Did Mr. Martin provide you with any support?" Doncan asked.

Rosemary looked at him and then shook her head. "I'm not going to answer that. Whatever support he provided was minimal, especially when compared to the things he lavished on Mona."

"You seem to know a lot about Mona," Doncan remarked.

"Max's sister told me some things, but there was a lot in the letters, too. My father often replied to my mother's requests for more help by detailing what he'd given Mona in the past month," she told him. "I'll show you an example."

She dug into her handbag and pulled out a sheet of paper, which she passed to Doncan. "It's a photocopy, obviously. The original letters are locked in a safe-deposit box in London."

Doncan glanced at the sheet and then handed it to Fenella. She read it quickly.

My dear Charlotte,

Thank you for the update on our darling Rosemary. It sounds as if she is growing up into a fine young lady. I can't believe that she's two already. It doesn't seem possible that more than two years have passed since I held you in my arms.

Things are difficult here. I'm enclosing a small amount of cash, which is all that I can spare at the moment. Mona insisted on an emerald bracelet for her birthday and I couldn't refuse. She could ruin me, you understand, with the things that she knows. She's the only one who knows everything, even the things I haven't told you.

Some days I despair of ever breaking free from her demands. When I first held you in my arms, I dreamt of a day when we could be together forever, but that day seems impossibly out of reach now. As much as it breaks my heart to do so, I urge you to find someone else, someone who could make you happy and who could raise our little Rosemary with you.

I'll write again soon. Your letters are my most precious treasures, and I keep them where I'm certain they will never be found. Please send more photographs of Rosemary when you can. I long to see her and to hold you again.

Yours, M

"I hope you won't mind if I keep this," Doncan said as Fenella passed the letter back to him.

"As I said, that's just a copy. Only I know where the originals are being kept. You're welcome to them, of course, all of them, if you agree to my price."

"Five million pounds? I don't think so," Doncan told her.

"It's your choice, or rather, it's Fenella's choice. Speak up, dear. Wouldn't you like to make this all go away? I'm sure five million pounds isn't much compared to what you've inherited from Mona, is it?"

"I'm not interested in settling," Fenella said, struggling to keep her voice level.

"Things are going to get ugly, then," Rosemary sighed. "It's a shame Mona's good name is going to be ruined on the island."

Fenella laughed. "Mona had a reputation on the island for being wild and wicked. She didn't have a good name for you to ruin."

Rosemary raised an eyebrow. "Really? And you're quite content for everyone to know that she was a blackmailer?"

"I'm quite content for everyone to know that some stranger from across is accusing her of all manner of things," Fenella countered. "You've a long way to go before I'll believe anything you've said, and I think the rest of the island will be as skeptical as I am about your claims."

"Four million," Rosemary said. "You can even pay it in installments of a million a year for the next four years. I'll have the letters brought over this afternoon, after the first check is cut."

Fenella shook her head. "You'll have to take me to court if you want anything from me. As Doncan said, you'd probably be better off suing Maxwell Martin's estate, though. Mona was only a bit player on the edge of his life."

"He spent a fortune on her," Rosemary countered. "His sister is quite bitter, you know. Once my father fell under Mona's spell, he rarely visited her."

"But Max did leave his sister half of his estate. That doesn't sound like the action of a man being blackmailed or under anyone's spell," Fenella suggested.

"Once he was dead, Mona didn't have any hold over him any longer," Rosemary told her. "Mona knew she couldn't get anything further once he'd died."

"What sort of information was she supposed to have been holding over him?" Doncan asked.

"I'm not answering any more questions," Rosemary said firmly. "You've seen that letter. It's pretty clear from that letter than Max was being blackmailed."

"I don't agree," Doncan replied, "and you may struggle to get the Manx courts to see things that way, as well."

"Oh, I'm not worried about that. This is one of the milder letters," Rosemary shot back. "The evidence is clear. You'd be much smarter to settle now. Three point five million, but I won't go a penny lower."

"It's been very interesting talking with you," Doncan said, getting to his feet. "Unfortunately, Ms. Woods and I have a meeting to attend in the south of the island in a short while. Let me show you all out before I go."

Rosemary laughed. "Afraid I'll steal the teacups if you leave me behind?" she asked. "I'm not interested in teacups. I'm going to have a good deal more than a few cheap bits of crockery before I'm done, see if I don't."

She got to her feet and looked at the others. "Come on, then," she told them. "We're leaving." The others got up slowly. Fenella watched as Joe grabbed a handful of biscuits and Autumn quickly swallowed the last of her tea.

"You know where to find me if you have anything else you want to discuss," Doncan told Rosemary. "I'll ask you not to contact Fenella in any way."

Rosemary glanced at Fenella and then laughed. "I'm sure that's what you want. If we come to an agreement without your input, you won't get your overinflated fees, will you?"

Doncan didn't bother to reply. Instead, he pushed the buzzer on the desk. When Breesha appeared in the doorway, he smiled at her. "Please show Ms. Ballard and her family out," he said.

"I'll give your secretary my contact details," Rosemary said. "Make sure you pass them along to Fenella, won't you?" She looked at Fenella. "Ring me. I'm sure we can work something out between ourselves. There's no need to involve advocates and solicitors."

"Sorry, but I'll be including Doncan in every conversation we have," Fenella said steadily. "I trust him to look after my interests."

Rosemary laughed. "You're a fool, then. He's only looking after his own. You won't be feeling as trusting once he's burned through every penny Mona left you fighting me through the courts."

She turned and swept out of the room, with her children and their spouses right behind her. As the door shut behind them, Fenella blew out a long breath.

"That was deeply unpleasant," she said sadly.

"It was indeed," Doncan agreed. "She's an unpleasant person."

"Yes, with an awful family."

"I didn't believe her story when I first heard it. Now I believe it even less. The letter from Max is worrying, though."

"Do you really think Max wrote it?"

"The writing resembles his, but I'm no expert in handwriting. Obviously, I will be submitting it to one if Ms. Ballard persists with her claims."

"I'd like a copy of the letter," Fenella said. "I haven't been through all of Mona's papers. I may be able to find something from Max somewhere. I'm no expert either, but I'd like to see for myself how closely this resembles his writing." And I want to have Mona take a look at the letter, she added to herself. If anyone would recognize Max's hand-writing, it was Mona. Mona would also be able to speak to the style of the man's writing. Fenella just had to hope that her aunt wouldn't be too upset by everything that was in the document.

"I'll have Breesha make you a copy before you go. I truly did make lunch reservations for us in the south of the island. Would you like to have lunch with me?"

Fenella slowly shook her head. "I don't feel like socializing right now. What I really want to do is crawl into bed and scream into my pillow for an hour or so. I nearly bit through my tongue several times when that woman was speaking."

Doncan chuckled. "Are we to refer to her as 'that woman' from now on, then?"

"I'd rather just forget she exists. Could we do that?"

"I wish we could, but I'm afraid she's just getting started."

"Can she really sue me in the way she's threatened?"

"I think she'll be able to find a solicitor to take the case, which is bad enough. She'll make a lot of noise, get a lot of newspaper column inches, and just generally make Mona look bad. I can't imagine the courts actually giving her any money, though."

"So why do it?"

"That's a very good question. I'm sure Mona would suggest that Max's sister is behind the whole thing and that it's all just an exercise in making Mona look bad."

"I can see why Max's sister might want to make Mona look bad, but I can't see why Rosemary is going along. What's in it for her?"

"She might believe that she can truly get some money from you, either in an out-of-court settlement or through her lawsuit. Otherwise, Max's sister might be paying her to play the part."

"Does Max's sister truly hate Mona enough to pay someone to make her look bad now, after she's been dead for a year?"

"I'd hate to think so, but maybe," Doncan replied. "That makes as much sense as any of this, anyway."

Fenella sighed. "I'd better get ready for some nasty articles in the local paper, then. I hope there isn't any negative impact on the party."

"I think Rosemary will wait a day or two before she starts talking to the papers. I believe her next move will be to ring you and try to get you to agree to a private meeting. She has to believe she'll have better luck persuading you to pay her off if I'm not around."

"I won't agree, of course."

"I should hope not. She'll have a whole list of reasons why you should, of course. If she's too difficult, just agree and then ring me. I'll come with you at any time, day or night."

"That's well outside of your responsibilities as my advocate."

"But well within my role as one of Mona's dearest friends. I cared a lot about Mona, and I don't believe that she was blackmailing Max. This woman is threatening to destroy the reputation of a dear friend and I'm not going to let her do that unopposed."

"I'll call you if I hear from her," Fenella promised.

❦ 5 ❧

"**O**f course Max didn't write that," Mona said scornfully. "The writing is similar to his, but he didn't write it."

"Do you have letters from him?" Fenella asked. "Are they in a box in the storage room or somewhere? It would be helpful to have something with which to compare this letter."

"Max very rarely wrote to me. We were nearly always together, after all. He sent odd postcards or notes when he traveled, but I never kept them. I didn't need notes, not when I had Max."

"Is the style like his?"

"Style? I wouldn't suggest that that letter has any style. It's clearly been fabricated to support Ms. Ballard's narrative, and that's all it does. No doubt Max's sister wrote it. She has no imagination. I'm sure that's exactly her idea of a love letter."

"Did Max write to his sister?"

"Sometimes. Actually, when we first met, he used to write to her quite regularly, long letters all about the island, but his sister never seemed to care. Over time he wrote less and less frequently. In the last few years before he died, I don't believe he sent much more than a card at Christmas and one for the woman's birthday. They spoke on the telephone on those occasions as well, but never otherwise."

60

"Did she call him for his birthday?"

Mona laughed. "Not once. She did send a card at Christmas, but never for his birthday. He never complained, but I know he was hurt by it."

"She'd have plenty of examples of his handwriting, though, to use if she wanted to forge a letter from him," Fenella said thoughtfully.

"Yes, if she'd bothered to keep them. The idea that she may have done surprises me, really."

Before Fenella could reply, the phone rang.

"Hello?"

"Ms. Woods? Fenella? It's Rosemary Ballard. How are you?"

Fenella made a face and then switched the call to speakerphone. Mona might as well hear what Rosemary had to say. It would save her from having to repeat the conversation later.

"I'm fine, thank you," she said flatly.

"I thought we got off on the wrong foot today. I didn't mean to upset you in any way. This is very awkward for me, you see."

"Is it?"

"I had a difficult childhood. My mother always talked about my father as this sort of almost mythical being. She kept his letters in a locked box and never let me see them. She'd been madly in love with Max and her heart was completely broken when he wouldn't marry her."

Mona rolled her eyes. "Poppycock," she snapped.

"She did find another man when you were three, though," Fenella said after a moment.

"Yes, and my stepfather was a good man. My mother never truly loved him, but I believe he knew that and accepted it. They had three children together and he always tried hard to make sure that he treated all four of us the same, even though I had a different surname and didn't resemble my half-siblings in the slightest."

"It sounds as if he tried his best."

"He did, of course, and I'm grateful to him and my mother for everything they did for me. I told myself for years that my real father didn't matter, that I was happy with my life. Then Autumn started researching our family history and I started to wonder where I'd really come from. I'd never opened that locked box of my mother's, ever. I decided at sixty-one that it was time to read those secret letters."

"Your mother died in the eighties?"

"Yes, and I'm sure you find it hard to believe that I didn't read the letters years ago, but I was married with small children when my mother died. I was too busy with my own life to worry about her past. I put the box on the top shelf of one of my wardrobes and forgot all about it for nearly forty years."

"I don't believe that, either," Mona said.

"Anyway, when I finally rediscovered the box and began reading the letters, I was shocked to learn that my father had been a very wealthy and powerful man. My mother had always refused to answer any questions about him, so I'd always assumed he'd been a married man, really."

"He probably was," Mona muttered.

"So you reached out to Max's sister?" Fenella asked.

"Yes, the dear aunt I'd never known I had," Rosemary agreed. "She was immediately kind and welcoming. She told me that she'd always wondered whether her brother might have had a child or two in secret. She, well, she told me a lot about my father and about his very difficult relationship with Mona."

"Or her version of it, anyway," Fenella suggested.

Rosemary laughed. "Her account matched what I'd already read in my father's letters, but of course you'll have a different idea about it, I'm sure. What did Mona tell you about my father?"

"The last time I saw Mona, I was a teenager, and we didn't discuss the men in her life," Fenella said dryly.

Mona made a face at her and then laughed. "I suppose that's true if you limit yourself to when I was alive."

"I didn't realize that," Rosemary exclaimed.

"I was born on the island, but we moved to the US when I was two and I grew up there," Fenella explained. "I only moved back to the island when I inherited Mona's estate."

"I'm sure I heard something about that, but I simply assumed that you'd known Mona better than that. You won't be able to answer any of my questions about her, then."

"No, I won't."

Rosemary sighed. "I really don't want to sue you, but I do feel as if I'm owed something. My mother kept note of every penny my father sent and how she spent it. It wasn't much, not considering how much Maxwell Martin was worth."

"Then you should sue his estate," Fenella suggested.

"I can't do that, not after my aunt was so kind to me."

"But you're prepared to sue me, without even giving me a chance to be kind?"

Mona snorted. "You can't possibly be kind to that woman."

"That isn't it at all. Mona wasn't entitled to my father's money. She got it illegally. It seems as if I should be entitled to some of her ill-gotten gains."

"We'll have to agree to disagree there."

Rosemary laughed. "Neither one of us wants this to drag through the courts for the next five years. The solicitors and advocates are the only people who will benefit from that. Your Doncan Quayle seems to be doing quite well for himself, even without the millions that defending Mona's estate will bring him."

"I'm happy to go to court if that's what it takes to challenge your claims," Fenella said firmly.

"And you're happy for everyone on the island to learn about how Mona blackmailed Max into keeping her in grand style?"

Mona got to her feet and began to pace angrily across the room. "She can't talk about me in that way," she said tightly.

"You'd better have plenty of proof to back up those sorts of accusations," Fenella told Rosemary.

"I have letters, lots and lots of letters. Some of them are considerably more sensational than the one I gave you today, too. If I were you, I'd want to take a look at a few of them before I refused to consider a quick settlement."

"I'm not interested."

"If the police get involved, you could lose everything, you know," Rosemary said. "Money gained through criminal activity can be confiscated. If I were you, I'd be very worried."

"I'm not the least bit worried," Fenella lied.

"We should meet. I really think you need to see a few more letters. As I said, some of them are even more specific about things. Let's have lunch tomorrow."

"We can meet in Doncan's office, if you really want to meet again," Fenella told her.

"You really don't want him reading these letters. Once he discovers what Mona was doing, you may well find yourself without an advocate. Meet me privately. I'll show you copies of the letters and we can talk, woman to woman. Then, if you do want to keep things between just us, you can ring Doncan and ask him to arrange a settlement. I promise not to insist on more than the five million we already discussed."

Mona gasped. "She can't be serious. I would never give her five million pounds."

"I'd prefer to meet in Doncan's office," Fenella countered.

"Really, Fenella, come on," Rosemary said. "You may not have known Mona yourself, but you must be familiar with her reputation. Everyone thinks she and Max were devoted to one another. You don't want the ugly truth spreading all over the island, do you? Spend an hour with me tomorrow. Read the letters. If, after that, you still want to fight it out in court, we can. I truly am doing this for your own good, though. I want to spare you a tremendous ordeal."

"That's awfully kind of you," Fenella said sarcastically.

The sarcasm was lost on the other woman, though. "I truly don't want to hurt anyone," she said. "I just want a portion of what I should have had from my father. I want to be able to enjoy life and then leave my children comfortable after my death. You can understand that, can't you?"

"Trying to lie and cheat your way into a fortune shouldn't be a lesson you want to teach your children," Mona said.

Fenella shook her head at her aunt. "Lunch tomorrow?" she asked.

"Meet me here, in my hotel room. I think that will be best. We won't be disturbed here."

"What about your family?"

"They're all going out to see the sights tomorrow," Rosemary told her. "I've booked some sort of bus tour for the lot of them. They'll be gone from early morning until after five. I love them all, of course, but I can only put up with them for a few hours at a time."

"Where are you staying?" Fenella asked.

Rosemary told her the name of the hotel and then added her room number. "Just come up around midday," she said. "I'll be here."

"Great, I'll see you then," Fenella told her.

She ended the call and then sighed deeply. "I have to call Doncan," she told Mona.

"Why?"

"I promised him I wouldn't meet with Rosemary without him present."

"But if you take Doncan, she'll never show you the letters. I want to see what horrible things Max's sister has dreamt up."

"I'm not going over there without Doncan."

"I've half a mind to go over there myself," Mona said thoughtfully. "Maybe I could catch her writing the letters herself. She probably isn't clever enough to manage that, though. I'm sure Max's sister has been creating the letters. I wonder if the paper could be tested. Surely Max's sister doesn't have paper from sixty years ago just lying around."

"It probably isn't impossible to get, though," Fenella told her. "You can get anything online these days."

Mona sighed. "Don't take Doncan. Go alone. You'll be able to learn more."

"What if it's all some sort of trap?" Fenella asked. "She could have it all set up to record everything I say, for example, and then she could try to trick me into saying something I shouldn't."

"Recordings like that wouldn't be admissible in court."

"I'm calling Doncan," Fenella told her. The call only took a few minutes.

"Come to my office around eleven," he told her. "We'll talk strategy before we walk over to Rosemary's hotel."

That left Fenella with the rest of the day to fill. She paced around her apartment until she'd annoyed both Katie and Mona and then took herself off for a long walk on the promenade.

"Woof," a loud voice barked from behind her.

"Winston, just what I needed," she said as she embraced the huge dog. He barked excitedly and then let her pet him and scratch his head.

"Hello, hello," Harvey Garus said as he caught up to the dog. "How are you today?"

"I'm fine, thanks," Fenella replied politely, if not entirely truthfully.

Harvey nodded. "Good, good."

"But where's Fiona?" Fenella asked, looked around for the smaller dog.

"She's staying with Mr. Stone for a few days," he replied, referring to the veterinarian who looked after both dogs as well as Fenella's Katie. "She caught a nasty virus from somewhere and she's been under the weather for about a week. He decided it would be best if he kept her so that he can make sure she's getting her medications exactly when she needs them. She's a bit sneaky when she doesn't want to take them, you see."

"Well, I hope she feels better soon."

"Mr. Stone assured me this morning that she's on the mend. She should be back with me by the weekend, if not sooner."

"Excellent."

"Thank you for the kind invitation to the party for Mona," he added.

"You'll have to thank Mona for that," Fenella laughed. "She wrote the guest list before she died." As soon as the words were out of her mouth, Fenella wondered if they were true. Perhaps Mona wrote the guest list more recently and then sneaked it into Doncan's files somehow. Or maybe she popped up in Doncan's dreams, instructing him as to whom to invite. Either idea seemed weirdly possible, really.

"I've already rung to confirm that I'll be there," Harvey continued. "I don't often go places without Winston, but for this party I'll make an exception."

Fenella nodded. "I did ask Doncan about including the dogs, but he didn't think it would be appropriate."

"Oh, no," Harvey laughed. "Mona's parties are far too fancy for Winston. He'd just knock over the champagne fountain or eat an entire table full of canapés and ruin everything."

"You would, too, wouldn't you?" Fenella asked Winston.

"Woof," he agreed.

Fenella laughed. "Well, I'm glad you're going to come, anyway. I don't know how many people I'll actually know there."

"I'm sure it's going to be an interesting evening," he told her. "Mona always had the very best parties."

Fenella gave Winston a few more minutes of attention before she headed back to her apartment, feeling better about the world. After a light dinner, she sat down in the front of the television with Katie on her lap.

"We should talk," Mona said when she appeared a short while later.

"What's on your mind?" Fenella asked, muting the television.

"This woman. What does she really want?"

"It seems as if she really wants money. If she just wanted to smear your memory, she could give those letters to the papers and then sit back and watch them run with them."

"But Max's sister doesn't need money," Mona said thoughtfully. "Certainly she doesn't need five million pounds. If Rosemary had asked for fifty or sixty million, I might have believed it was Max's sister behind the demand, but five million doesn't seem nearly enough to satisfy that woman."

"So maybe Rosemary is trying to make a deal behind Max's sister's back," Fenella suggested.

Mona stared at her for a minute and then began to laugh. "You could be right," she said eventually. "What a delightful thought. I can just about see it, too. Max's sister found Rosemary somewhere and set this all up, with the fake letters and whatever else as evidence. I'm sure she's paying Rosemary to destroy my reputation. No doubt Rosemary decided that she could get more from you than whatever Max's sister is paying. Knowing that woman, it isn't anything close to five million pounds, anyway."

"I can't see why Max's sister would pay someone just to damage your memory, not now that you're dead, anyway."

"She's a horrible, vindictive woman with nothing else to do with her money," Mona explained. "This time, though, I think she's failed to think things all the way through. She's sent Rosemary here with her toxic letters, and now Rosemary has gone rogue. No doubt Max's sister agreed to fake the results of a DNA test if Doncan demanded one. That's all Rosemary needs, of course, to successfully sue Max's estate. Max's sister truly hasn't thought this through, not at all."

"I'd love to see her turn around and sue Max's estate," Fenella grinned. "As you said, if Max's sister does fake DNA test results for the woman, she's opening the door for just such a thing to happen."

"Maybe you should have Doncan ring Max's sister," Mona said thoughtfully. "I'm tempted to warn her, just to make the whole thing go away."

"Rosemary said that she has other letters that are even more damaging. What could they possibly say?"

Mona shrugged. "I've no idea what horrible things Max's sister might have dreamed up. Maybe they'll accuse me of murder. Maybe I killed anyone who threatened to get between Max and me. That would explain why he had to keep Charlotte such a deep secret, right?"

"Tomorrow is going to be a long day," Fenella sighed, feeling as if today had been incredibly long already, and it was only eight o'clock.

"I'm going to go and talk to Max. I don't want to ask him anything directly, but I'm going to try dropping Charlotte's name into a conversation and see if he remembers ever meeting anyone by that name. They may have known one another, even though they never had an affair," Mona told her. She faded from view.

Fenella put the sound back on the television and did her best to get lost in a few comedy shows that she didn't fully understand. It was only nine-thirty when she gave up and went to get ready for bed. Katie was already asleep in the exact center of Fenella's king-sized bed when Fenella finished washing her face and brushing her teeth. She crawled in carefully and then pulled the covers up to her chin. Sleep was elusive, but she finally dozed off with thoughts of blackmail and murder in her mind.

"It can't be seven already," she complained as Katie began to pat her on the nose.

"Merrrooww," the kitten answered as she jumped off the bed.

Fenella sat up and looked at the clock. It was exactly seven. She sighed and pushed the covers down. Going back to bed was an option, of course, once Katie was fed. It was an option she thought quite hard about as she filled the animal's food and water bowls. When she found herself filling the coffee maker, she realized that she'd decided to stay up. Sighing, she went back into the bedroom and made the bed. A hot shower helped wake her up and the first cup of coffee did a lot more.

"It's going to be a long morning," she told Katie.

Katie shrugged and then headed into the living room. She found a sunny spot and then curled up for a nap.

"Maybe Shelly wants to do something," Fenella said. She grabbed her phone and called the apartment next door.

"Hello?" Shelly sounded as if she'd been sleeping.

"Did I wake you? Sorry. It's Fenella. I was just wondering if you wanted to go for a walk or something."

"Tim and I had a late night," Shelly said apologetically. "I need another hour or two of sleep before I'm going to be able to function."

"I'm sorry I woke you."

"No problem," Shelly assured her before she put the phone down.

"Where's Mona when I'm bored?" Fenella demanded.

Although Mona had insisted that she hadn't kept any letters or notes from Max, Fenella decided to hunt for some. She started by going through the large desk in the master bedroom, but she didn't find any correspondence at all in any of the drawers. A smaller desk in the spare bedroom was equally lacking in anything interesting.

"I'm going down to the storage room," she said to Katie, who didn't move.

Fenella grabbed her keycard that would open the door to the storage room and then headed for the elevators. Each apartment had its own small room on the ground floor of the building. For some reason, Mona's felt much larger inside than it actually was. Fenella opened the door and then stood just inside it waiting for the huge chandelier to fully illuminate the space.

The chandelier had once been one of many that had graced the ballroom when the building had been a hotel. Now it illuminated what looked like hundreds of boxes, all of them neatly labeled with their contents. Fenella started in one corner where there were dozens of boxes full of Christmas decorations. She'd already had most of those boxes open, as she used a selection from them to decorate the apartment for her first Christmas on the island.

Boxes full of plates, kitchenware, glasses, and the like were next. Fenella had emptied one of them to replace several items that her former boyfriend, Jack Dawson, had broken while he'd been staying at her house on Poppy Drive. She couldn't help but wonder why Mona had had so many extras of everything.

The next set of boxes held things like vases and picture frames. Some of them had obviously been expensive, but Fenella knew that she had things at least as nice in the apartment upstairs. By the time she'd finished opening and then resealing the boxes in that section, it was nearly time to meet Doncan.

She sighed as she headed for the door. She'd looked through a lot of boxes, but she hadn't found a single scrap of paper. As she rode the elevator back to the sixth floor, she wondered if her aunt had ever kept a diary. Now that she was thinking about it, the apartment had been lacking in personal papers when she'd moved in. Doncan must have been dealing with all of the bills and whatnot, but Fenella wasn't sure she'd ever seen anything with her aunt's handwriting on it, let alone Maxwell Martin's.

Back in her apartment, she changed into nicer clothes and then brushed her hair and touched up her makeup. While she wasn't looking forward to seeing Rosemary again, she wasn't going to turn up in jeans and a sweatshirt, either.

"Whatever the letters say, don't give her a penny," Mona told her as she headed for the door. "The letters are fakes; they have to be."

"I doubt she'll show me the letters when I turn up with Doncan, but I also won't be giving her any money."

"Good."

Fenella found that she was dragging her feet as she made her way to Doncan's office. Maybe she should simply have him call Rosemary and cancel the meeting, she thought.

"I can do that, if you'd prefer," he told her when Breesha showed her into his office.

"I don't know what I want," Fenella said with a shrug.

"In that case, it might be useful to talk to Ms. Ballard again. She may refuse to speak to you because you've brought me along, of course, but that in itself could be telling."

"Let's go and get this over with, then," Fenella sighed.

Doncan chuckled and got to his feet. "It won't be that bad," he said. "I suspect she'll open the door, take one look at me, and shut the door in our faces."

"That sounds good to me."

"Then I'll take you somewhere for lunch, since we didn't get to go yesterday," he offered.

"I may take you up on that, especially if it's someplace that has wine."

"That won't be a problem."

They walked out of the building and turned to stroll along the promenade.

"Do you know anything about the hotel where she's staying?" Fenella asked.

"It's a decent place, not the most expensive or luxurious, but it has a good reputation. She'll have had fewer choices at this time of year, of course. Several of the midsized hotels shut during the winter months."

"I assume the entire family is staying there?"

"I believe so. Ms. Ballard made all of her own travel arrangements. I didn't even know where she was staying until you told me."

"She said she was sending her children and their partners out on a bus tour of the island all day."

"I'm surprised she found one operating. Most of them don't bother in the winter months."

They'd reached the hotel building. Fenella looked up at the Victorian façade and sighed. "I really don't want to do this."

"We don't have to go inside. We can go and get lunch somewhere and you can ring Ms. Ballard from the restaurant."

Fenella was tempted, but part of her wanted to read the letters that Rosemary kept threatening her with, as well. "Let's just hope it won't take long," Fenella said as she started up the steps to the building's front door.

"Good morning," the woman behind the reception desk said

brightly as they walked into the hotel's foyer. "How can I help you today?"

"I'm meeting someone in her room," Fenella told her.

"I don't believe any of our guests are in at the moment," the desk clerk frowned. "We've only a small number of people staying here right now, and I believe they all went out this morning."

"I'm meant to be meeting Ms. Ballard," Fenella replied. "She told me she was sending her children and their spouses out for the day but that she'd be available."

She shrugged. "I saw a large group leaving this morning, but I didn't specifically see Ms. Ballard with them. She may be in her room, I suppose."

"Perhaps you could ring up to her room and check?" Doncan suggested.

"I can," the desk clerk said, picking up the phone on the desk in front of her. She checked something on the sheet of paper in front of her and then punched in a four-digit number. Fenella could hear the busy signal from the other side of the desk.

"It's engaged," the woman said, putting the phone down. "That must mean she's in the room."

"We'll just head up, then," Doncan told her. "Thank you."

She nodded and then turned her attention back to the magazine on the desk in front of her. She flipped the page as Doncan pushed the button to call the elevator. After what felt like a long wait, the elevator doors slowly slid open.

Fenella glanced at Doncan. "Are you sure it's safe?" she whispered.

"Probably," he replied, glancing back at the desk clerk in the foyer. "It may be slow, but it should get us there."

They boarded the elevator car and Fenella tried to ignore the slight drop she felt as she stepped inside. Doncan pushed the button for the fourth floor and they both waited for the doors to slide shut again.

"Maybe we should take the stairs," Fenella said in a low voice after a full minute passed.

Doncan pushed the button again. The doors slid together and then the elevator began its slow climb. Fenella was feeling quite claustrophobic by the time the doors opened again on the fourth floor.

"I'm going to take the stairs back down," she told Doncan.

He chuckled. "I'm not going to argue."

The carpet in the corridor was clean but worn. It didn't take them long to find the right room in the short hallway. Fenella knocked on the door.

"Maybe I should stay out of sight for a minute or two," Doncan suggested.

Fenella shook her head. "I just want to get this over with," she told him as she knocked again.

"The woman in reception said she was on the phone," Doncan reminded her.

"She knew I was coming, though. I expected her to be standing at the door, really." She knocked again and then counted slowly to one hundred. "I think that's long enough," she told Doncan. "Let's go."

"Are you sure? Maybe we should have reception try ringing her room again. Maybe she's taking a nap and isn't hearing us."

Fenella sighed. "We can try, but if she took the phone off the hook so it wouldn't disturb her nap, calling won't do us any good."

Doncan nodded. "At least we can say we tried."

Fenella looked around. "Where are the stairs?" she asked.

"They have to be at one end of the corridor or the other," Doncan suggested.

There was only a single door in the hallway that wasn't identified with a room number. The sign on it read "Staff Only."

"This looks more like storage than stairs," Fenella said.

"If it is storage, the stairs must be there somewhere, too," Doncan told her. "Maybe we should just take the lift, though."

Fenella shook her head. "If the door isn't locked, I'm going to peek. If there are stairs in there, I'm going to take them."

She grabbed the doorknob and was relieved when it turned in her grasp. There was a light switch right inside the door. Fenella turned it on and then frowned at the large laundry and cleaning carts that nearly filled the entire space. "No stairs," she said. "Unless they're behind door number two," she added as she noticed a second door along one side of the room.

The carts were packed fairly tightly into the space, but Fenella managed to maneuver her way past them to the second door. "Aha," she laughed when she opened it and found a steep and narrow flight of stairs behind it.

"Those will have been the stairs for the servants," Doncan told her. "At one time there would have been another flight for the family. Maybe they were removed when the house was converted into a hotel. It may have been where the lift is now, actually."

"These will do," Fenella said. "Anything is better than getting back onto that elevator."

He nodded. "I don't usually mind such things, but that one was too small and too slow for comfort." He took a step into the room and then frowned. "Don't move," he said in a serious voice.

"Don't move? Please don't tell me there's a spider. I'm terrified of spiders," Fenella said, trying to stand very still while looking in every direction at once.

"No spiders," Doncan told her. "But you've stepped in something and you've left footprints behind."

Fenella looked down at the white linoleum floor and gasped. "It looks like blood," she said in a strangled voice.

Doncan nodded. "Maybe someone spilled some red paint." He took another step into the room and then stopped next to the first laundry cart. After a deep breath, he carefully pulled back the sheet on the top of the cart.

Fenella watched as the color drained from his face. "What is it?" she whispered.

"I've found Rosemary Ballard," he replied before dropping the sheet and rushing out of the room.

6

Fenella stood still, listening to Doncan as he coughed and cleared his throat in the corridor. After a minute of silence, she shouted to him. "Are you okay?"

"I thought I might, um, contaminate the crime scene," he called back. "I'm going to ring 999 now. I think it might be best if you simply stay right where you are. You've already walked through the scene once. I don't think you should walk through it again."

"I could just go down the stairs."

"And possibly destroy or contaminate evidence. Just stay where you are and we'll let the police work out what happens next."

She shut her eyes and counted slowly to ten and then to twenty as she listened to Doncan's call to the police. He reported the body and their location in clipped tones.

"Someone is on the way," he said loudly a minute later. "I'm guarding the door here. You need to guard that door."

Fenella laughed. "I can't see anyone suddenly coming up these stairs. If they're as difficult to find on every floor as they were here, we're probably the only people who know about them."

"I was thinking more of staff. They probably use the stairs regularly."

Time dragged on endlessly as Fenella stood, shifting her weight back and forth, waiting for the police to arrive.

Constable Howard Corlett was the first on the scene. "Good afternoon," Fenella heard him greeting Doncan. "The dispatcher said something about a body?"

"In the first laundry cart," Doncan told him.

The constable appeared in the doorway. For a moment he looked startled when he saw Fenella, then he shrugged. "I shouldn't be surprised to find you here, should I?" he asked.

"I didn't find the body," she told him "I walked right past it, actually."

He raised an eyebrow and then looked down at the floor around the cart. "There's quite a lot of blood," he said softly.

"I didn't notice when I walked through the room. I was looking for stairs."

"Stairs?"

"The elevator was small and slow and it made me uncomfortable. I wanted to go back down via the stairs."

The constable nodded and then looked down into the cart. When he lifted the sheet, his eyes grew wide. He dropped the sheet immediately and then backed out of the room.

Fenella could hear him on his phone a moment later. Only parts of the conversation reached her on the far side of the room. She heard 'crime scene team,' 'definitely murder,' and her own name before the constable reappeared in the doorway.

"I'm going to ask you to stay right where you are," he told Fenella. "You're rather unfortunately right in the center of the crime scene."

Unable to think of any way to reply to that, she simply shrugged and then looked at her watch. It was only twenty past twelve, although it felt much later. Another familiar face appeared in the doorway a short while later.

"Ms. Woods, I thought we agreed to stop meeting like this," Mark Hammersmith said, giving her a wry grin.

"No offense, but I could have gone the rest of life without seeing you again," she shot back, frowning at how bitter her voice sounded.

He shrugged. "Inspector Robinson is on his way, but with you involved, it's probably best if we're partners on this investigation. Unless you simply want to confess?"

Fenella gasped and then sighed. "Very funny," she muttered, rubbing a hand over her face.

Mark Hammersmith was another CID inspector in Douglas. He didn't typically deal with murder investigations, but while Daniel had been away in Milton Keynes, Mark had handled the ones in which Fenella had been involved. Now it seemed as if he was going to be a part of every investigation that concerned Fenella in any way. Fenella was aware that the chief constable knew that she and Daniel were friends, but that didn't mean that Daniel couldn't manage this investigation on his own.

Daniel glanced into the room a short while later. "Hi," he said softly.

"Hi," she replied.

"I know you'd really like to get out of that corner, but we're still waiting on the crime scene team. Getting you processed will be their first priority when they arrive."

"Splendid."

"Did you know the victim?" he asked in a casual voice.

"She was threatening to sue me," Fenella replied, having decided to get the worst information out as quickly as possible.

Daniel looked surprised. "Sue you? For what?"

"For a share of Mona's money. She claimed she was Maxwell Martin's child and that Mona got money from Max through blackmail. She claimed she should have been entitled to some of the money that Mona received over the years."

Daniel sighed deeply. "I should have known it wasn't going to be something easy," he muttered before he turned around and said something to someone behind him.

"I'm going to talk to the police now," Doncan told her from the doorway a minute later. "If you want me with you when you speak to them, just tell them and they'll find me for you."

"I have nothing to hide."

"I know, but this is complicated."

"I'm sure Daniel and Mark will be able to work out what happened. They're both experts at what they do."

Doncan nodded. "I share your faith in them, but, well, just be careful when you speak to them, or ask for me to be present."

"It will be fine," Fenella insisted.

An hour later she wasn't so sure. The crime scene team had done a preliminary sweep of the room and the stairwell and then escorted Fenella, minus her shoes, down the stairs and into one of the guest rooms on the ground floor. "Someone will be in to take your statement shortly," she'd been told before the door had been shut and locked.

After standing for what had felt like hours waiting for the crime scene team to let her go, she'd sunk gratefully onto the bed. Two minutes later she was up and pacing the room in her sock-covered feet. Now that she had time to think, one thing became clear almost immediately. She had an undeniable motive for murdering Rosemary Ballard.

"Fenella? Ms. Woods," Mark said as he walked into the room a short while later. "I'm sorry to have kept you waiting so long."

"It doesn't matter," Fenella told him.

He glanced around the room and then shrugged. "I'd rather not interview you sitting on the bed, but we don't have much choice in here. Is this okay with you, or would you prefer to move to the station and a proper interview room?"

"I'd rather stay here," Fenella said quickly.

Mark nodded. "Let me get a constable to take notes." He left the room and then returned a moment later with a young woman in a constable's uniform.

"This is Constable Harkins," he said, nodding toward the woman.

"Nice to meet you," Fenella said automatically.

The constable nodded and then took a seat on the edge of the bed. Mark sat next to her and waved for Fenella to join them.

"This is weird," he acknowledged, "but as this is just a preliminary statement, it shouldn't take long. I've no doubt either Daniel or myself will want to talk to you further as the investigation continues."

Fenella nodded and then sat down and stared at her feet. Being without shoes left her feeling oddly vulnerable, almost naked, next to the two police officers.

"Let's start with why you were here," Mark began. "What brought you to the hotel today?"

"I was supposed to be meeting Ms. Ballard. She wanted to discuss a few things with me."

Mark nodded. "Doncan Quayle gave us a brief outline of the situation. Maybe we need to start further back, then. Tell me about your first meeting with Ms. Ballard."

Fenella did her best to remember everything she could about that first meeting. After she was finished, Mark had her repeat the telephone conversation that she'd had with Rosemary.

"You agreed to meet with her on your own, then?" he checked.

"I never agreed that I wouldn't bring Doncan," she replied. "I believe Ms. Ballard thought I was coming alone, though."

"So why did you bring Doncan with you?"

"Because I didn't trust her. She was clearly trying to extort money from me, one way or another. I didn't feel safe meeting with her on my own."

"Perhaps you should have rung the police, rather than your advocate. If the woman was genuinely trying to blackmail you, you could have had her arrested."

"I didn't want to get anyone arrested. I just wanted her to go away, really."

"And now she has."

Fenella flushed. "I didn't want her dead, of course. I just thought she should be suing Maxwell Martin's estate, rather than Mona's."

Mark raised an eyebrow and then typed some notes into his phone. The constable had been writing continuously since Fenella had first begun to speak.

"Right, tell me everything that you did today, starting with the time you woke up," he told her.

Her day sounded incredibly dull as she recounted it to the two police officers.

"Did anyone see you when you went into the storage area in your building?" he asked when she'd finished.

"Not that I noticed. I believe the building has security cameras, though. They should have recorded when I went into the room and when I came back out again."

Mark made another note. "Tell me again why you went through a door that was clearly marked 'Staff Only,' please."

"The elevator was horrible," Fenella explained. "I get claustrophobic. I don't take elevators unless I absolutely have to, really."

"Do you take the stairs in your building?"

Fenella flushed and shook her head. "The elevators in my building are large and brightly lit. They don't really bother me."

"And you didn't notice the large pool of blood on the floor when you walked through the storage room to the stairs?"

"I was looking for stairs. I didn't look down at the floor at all. When I spotted the other door, I headed for it, working my way between the carts and the wall. I never looked down, not once."

"Mr. Quayle noticed the blood almost immediately."

"As I recall, he noticed that I'd left footprints before he noticed the pool of blood," she countered. "I believe he was trying to work out the best way to get through the room when he noticed the footprints I'd left behind."

"Could you have afforded to write Ms. Ballard a check for five million pounds?"

Fenella thought about refusing to answer the question, as it seemed rather personal, but she didn't want to be accused of hiding anything from the police. "Yes," she said, frowning when she thought of Daniel reading her statement. Her money seemed to be an obstacle between them already. This could only make things worse.

"Then why didn't you just do that?"

"Because I didn't believe that she was who she claimed to be, for a start. Even if she was Maxwell Martin's illegitimate daughter, I still don't think she had any claim to anything that was Mona's anyway. I could understand her wanting to sue Maxwell Martin's estate, but not Mona's."

"You and Doncan both mentioned letters that she claimed were from Maxwell Martin to her mother. If Mona truly was blackmailing Maxwell into funding her extravagant lifestyle, wouldn't you think Ms. Ballard had a right to make some sort of claim to some of that money?"

"As I already said, I didn't believe her story. Even if she was telling the truth about her parentage, I don't believe that Mona was black-mailing anyone. Nothing I've ever heard about her suggests that she would do something like that."

"She was undeniably wealthy, and from what I know, her lifestyle was funded by Maxwell Martin."

"Because they were devoted to one another, not because she knew his secrets and demanded presents in exchange for her silence," Fenella said tightly.

"Obviously, we're very interested in finding the letters that Ms. Ballard claims to have had. Do you have any suggestions on where we might look for them?"

"I assume they were in her room, or rather, I assume she had copies of them in her room. She told us yesterday that the originals were in a safe-deposit box in London. As I said earlier, she'd offered to show me copies of some of the more incriminating letters today."

Mark took her back through her day a second time, seemingly trying to pin down the exact times she did different things. She did her best, well aware that without any witnesses to her activities, she was also lacking an alibi for the murder.

"I know you've been involved in murder investigations before," he said eventually. "You're familiar with the concept of motive. Can you suggest any motive for anyone in this case?"

"Other than myself?" Fenella asked dryly. "I mean, I realize that I had a motive, although I don't personally think it was a very strong one."

"No? Why not?"

"As I said, I could have simply written her a check for the amount that she'd demanded. I suspect she would have taken less, too, if I'd made her an offer."

"Perhaps when she rang you, she asked for a good deal more."

Fenella shook her head. "I've told you what she said. She promised she wouldn't ask for more than five million."

"Of course, we only have your version of events from which to work."

"Yes, of course," Fenella sighed, "but she'd originally made the offer in front of a number of witnesses, including Doncan."

"If she'd asked for more, how much could you have given her before it would have impacted your lifestyle?"

Fenella shrugged. "I've no idea, really. Quite a bit more than the five million, though, I think. Doncan has a clearer understanding of my money than I do, but I know I have a lot of properties around the island. While I do get rental income from them, I could probably sell a few and not really notice their loss."

Mark shook his head. "How does it feel, being super rich?"

"I don't know how to answer that, except to say that I don't really feel any different from how I've always felt. I still keep careful track of my spending and look for sales before I buy anything, just the same as when I was working and barely even aware of Mona's existence."

"Are you worried about Mona's reputation on the island?"

"I'm not sure anything anyone could say about her would make her reputation any worse, really. I've been told since I arrived that she was an amoral gold digger who slept with married men and never worked a day in her life."

"But accusations of blackmail are rather more serious," Mark suggested. "It's even possible that some or all of her assets could have been seized as criminal acquisitions."

"If I wanted to shut Ms. Ballard up, all I had to do was write her a check. Her murder is going to get a lot more press and publicity than anything I could have done. I would be much better off than I am now if she were alive and willing to be paid to go away."

"But maybe you didn't think that through before things got out of hand."

"Maybe I didn't, but as I said before, I didn't believe she was who she said she was and I didn't believe that the letters she claimed to have are genuine. If she'd passed a DNA test and had the letters examined and verified by an expert, I might have started to worry."

Mark nodded. "I'm sure I'll have additional questions for you, but maybe not today. Thank you for your time. I'll just have someone take your fingerprints and then you'll be free to go."

"My fingerprints?"

"You opened the door to the room where the body was found. We need to be able to identify which prints are yours."

Fenella nodded. "I don't mind. I was just surprised."

"I'll send someone in shortly," he said as he stood up. The constable jumped off the bed and rushed to the door. She had it open before Mark had taken his first steps away from the bed. "Thank you for your cooperation," he added before he walked out of the room.

The young man who took her prints said much the same thing a few minutes later. Fenella nodded and then headed for the hotel's foyer, eager to put as much distance as possible between herself and the crime scene. She was halfway across the foyer when she remembered her shoes. There was no way she could walk back to her own building without shoes.

"I don't suppose you have a gift shop that sells shoes," she said to the young woman behind the reception desk. The woman stared at her for a minute and then slowly shook her head.

"I didn't think so," Fenella sighed.

She walked out of the building while she tried to think. She'd left her handbag at home, bringing only her phone and her apartment keycard with her to the hotel. There were more than a dozen shoe stores along the shopping street that ran behind the promenade between the hotel and her apartment, but without any money or credit cards, they were useless to her. It was possible that one of the stores might extend her credit, if they knew who she was, but under the circumstances, Fenella didn't feel as if she could ask for any favors.

Three of her first four steps along the sidewalk in front of the hotel seemed to include small pointy rocks. She sank onto a nearby bench and pulled her phone out of her pocket.

"Shelly? It's Fenella. I have a strange request for you. Can you meet me in front of the Beachside Hotel with any pair of shoes from my wardrobe?"

"Shoes?" Shelly repeated, sounding confused.

"Yes, something comfortable would be best. If you do me that favor, then I'll tell you the whole horrible story while I eat some lunch."

"I'm looking forward to hearing it," Shelly replied. "I'll be there in a few minutes."

Fenella put the phone back in her pocket and sighed as a light rain began to fall. She stared out at the Tower of Refuge. The tide was in and the tower didn't look all that far from shore. It was difficult for her to imagine sailing in a storm so near to land but unable to reach it.

The tower had been built to provide emergency shelter to sailors whose boats were lost in storms. Shelly had told her that very occasionally the tide would go out far enough that it was possible to walk to the tower, but Fenella also knew that when the tide was in and the weather was bad, the tower could be someone's only chance for survival. Wishing she had some sort of refuge from the storm that was growing around her, Fenella blinked back tears and waited for her friend. Shelly arrived ten minutes later with the promised shoes and a large umbrella.

"This is going to be a good story, isn't it?" Shelly demanded as they began the walk back to their building.

"It's not good at all," Fenella sighed. "In fact, it's pretty terrible."

"Oh, dear," Shelly exclaimed. "I hope no one is dead."

Fenella's deep sigh shattered that hope.

"What's going on?" Mona demanded as Fenella and Shelly walked into Fenella's apartment a short while later. "You've been gone for hours, and there were police cars everywhere."

"I need food," Fenella said. "I never got any lunch. Let's talk in the kitchen."

Shelly and Mona followed her into the kitchen. Mona waited until Shelly had settled into a seat before selecting her own. Katie rushed into the room, loudly demanding her own lunch.

Shelly picked up the cat and snuggled her close. "Now, now, I know you're hungry, but Fenella has had a bad morning. You can wait a minute or two."

Fenella had to quickly hide a smile as Shelly put Katie down on the chair that Mona was occupying. Mona jumped up, frowning as Katie curled up on the seat and gave Fenella a smug smile.

"She did that on purpose," Mona said.

Fenella very nearly replied, only just stopping herself in time. "I'll feed her first," she told Shelly, "even though I did give her a snack before I left."

Mona and Shelly both looked impatient as Fenella filled Katie's bowls and then fixed herself a sandwich. After she'd eaten a few bites, she took a long drink from her soda and then sighed.

"Rosemary Ballard is dead. She was murdered, and Doncan and I found the body," she said in a flat voice.

Shelly gasped while Mona nodded. "I'm not surprised," Mona said. "Max's sister must have realized that Rosemary was double-crossing her and sent someone over to kill her."

Again Fenella nearly replied. She bit into her sandwich to stop herself.

"But what happened?" Shelly demanded.

"I've no idea, really," Fenella replied. She told the two women about the tiny dark elevator and her determination to find stairs, and then explained about finding the body. Shelly grabbed her hand when she was done.

"How awful for you," she said.

"It was deeply unpleasant," Fenella agreed.

"I wonder if Max's sister paid one of the woman's children to kill her," Mona said conversationally. "Perhaps one of the spouses would be more likely."

"Why were you meeting with her, anyway?" Shelly asked.

"I forgot, I never told you about the meeting yesterday, did I?" Fenella asked. She quickly brought Shelly up to date on everything that had happened since their last conversation. When she was done, Shelly patted her arm.

"Her children and their partners sound horrible," she said. "I'm sure one of them must have killed her."

"I don't know about that," Fenella replied. "Whoever she was, she'd done her homework and set things up very cleverly. Perhaps she's spent her entire life conning people out of money. She may well have made herself a great many enemies over the years."

"Tell Daniel to take a good look at Max's sister," Mona told her. "She won't have done it herself, of course, but she'll have paid for the murder. Daniel just needs to trace the hit back to her."

Fenella nearly choked on her drink. The hit? Mona sounded like a bad Hollywood movie.

"If she truly was a career criminal, she must have a police record, mustn't she?" Shelly asked.

"Unless she was good enough to not get caught," Fenella replied.

"Doncan thought the handwriting looked plausible, didn't you say?" Shelly asked. "Where would she have found samples of Maxwell Martin's handwriting?"

"Perhaps his sister supplied them," Fenella said. "Perhaps she had a hand in this."

"Max's sister? I mean, I don't know anything about her, except that she and Mona hated one another, but what could she possibly be after?"

"Mona's money?" Fenella suggested. "Everyone tells me that she and Mona hated each other. Maybe she just wants to do what she can to damage Mona's reputation."

"Mona's been dead for a year. Surely it's far too late for that."

"Not hardly," Mona said.

"If she really hated Mona, maybe she's still bitter, even a year after Mona's death. She could certainly have been one source for letters, anyway, and I find it suspicious that she recognized Rosemary's claim, too."

"If she truly did," Shelly replied. "Maybe Rosemary just told you that she had, hoping that you wouldn't contact her."

"That seems a huge risk to take, although the way Rosemary was pushing for a quick, out-of-court settlement suggests that she was trying to keep me from investigating her claims in any way."

"Of course, Doncan was never going to simply hand over money to the woman," Shelly said thoughtfully. "What are his thoughts on her murder?"

"I've no idea. I haven't talked to him since the body was found. I should call him, actually. There are probably things we need to discuss, not least the fact that I'm a suspect in the investigation."

"Daniel must know that you didn't kill anyone," Shelly told her.

"I'd like to think that he knows that, but I did have a pretty solid motive, and I'm not sure what motive anyone else had, really."

"Max's sister killed her," Mona said emphatically. "Rosemary wasn't behaving properly. I've no doubt Max's sister put a lot of time and effort into preparing everything. No doubt she was furious when she found out Rosemary was trying to get a quick settlement behind her back."

"How did she even know that, though?" Fenella asked.

"How did who know what?" Shelly wondered, looking confused.

"Sorry, I was thinking out loud," Fenella replied, flushing.

Mona laughed. "Maybe we should wait to talk until after Shelly has gone home."

"I was wondering if Max's sister had set everything up, and then Rosemary had gone behind her back to ask for a quick settlement. That might have made Max's sister angry."

"Angry enough to kill Rosemary?"

"I've no idea," Fenella sighed. "If she'd put a lot of time and effort into arranging everything, maybe."

"She must be quite old. Surely you aren't suggesting that she came over to the island and murdered Rosemary herself."

"No, of course not. She must have hired someone to do it, if she's behind the murder."

Shelly shook her head. "I still think it was one of her children or their partners. They're here and they sound horrible. Maybe the murder didn't have anything to do with Mona and Max. Maybe April finally snapped and killed Rosemary because Autumn was always Rosemary's favorite."

Fenella chuckled. "Matthew certainly seemed to think that Autumn was Rosemary's favorite, anyway, but that doesn't seem much of a motive for murder."

"People get murdered for all sorts of stupid or strange reasons," Shelly replied. "Maybe it was completely random. Maybe Rosemary went out for a drink last night and met a serial killer in a pub. There are so many possibilities."

"Maybe you should save your imagination for your books," Fenella suggested. "Let's talk about something else. I don't even want to think about murder or Rosemary Ballard for the rest of the day."

After Shelly left, Fenella curled up with a book about Henry VIII and lost herself in court politics and intrigues. His first divorce was getting increasingly messy when the phone rang.

"Fenella? It's Daniel. I need to ask you some more questions about the case. Are you free tomorrow afternoon?"

"I can be. Do you want to come here or would you rather grab lunch somewhere or something?"

"Actually, I'd rather you came down to the station, if you don't mind."

"The station?"

"We need to be absolutely certain that we do everything by the book this time around," he told her.

"By the book," she repeated and then shook her head. "You're treating me as if I were a real suspect."

"Could you be here around two?" he asked, ignoring her remark.

"Sure, why not," she said, only just resisting the urge to slam the phone down in his ear.

"Ask for me at the front desk," he told her. "I'll see you tomorrow."

She didn't bother to reply before she returned the phone to its cradle. "He's going to interview me at the station," she told Katie, who made a face at her and then jumped into her lap. When the phone rang again a short while later, Fenella thought about ignoring it. Curiosity got the better of her.

"Ah, Fenella, it's Doncan. I wanted to see how you were after this morning's ordeal."

"I'm fine, mostly. Daniel just rang and he wants to interview me tomorrow at the police station, though. I'm not very excited about that."

"He's right to be careful in this case. You did have a motive, after all. I hope you also have an alibi?"

"That depends on when she died, I suppose. I saw Harvey Garus on the promenade around nine, maybe. Then I was in Mona's storage room for a while, looking for letters from Max. I'm hoping there are video cameras in the lobby area that show me going into and coming out of the storage area, but I don't know for sure about that."

"I suppose we'll have to wait until the time of death is determined to be certain," Doncan sighed. "I think it might be helpful if we had a chat tomorrow morning. At this point, I'm not sure what Ms. Ballard's family is planning, but it seems likely that they'll continue to press you for a monetary settlement. We need to be ready to respond."

"They'll get the same answer I gave Rosemary. I'm not signing over any of Mona's fortune to anyone."

"Of course not, but this murder is going to generate even more negative publicity than Ms. Ballard's original claims would have done. Let's meet at ten tomorrow to discuss matters, assuming that doesn't interfere with your meeting with Inspector Robinson."

"No, I'm meeting Daniel at two. I'll be at your office at ten."

"We'll talk about a few strategies for dealing with the police, then, as well. I may have a colleague who specialized in criminal law sit in on that part of the meeting."

"I didn't have anything to do with Rosemary's death."

"I know that, but now you have to convince the police as well, and not just Inspector Robinson, but everyone up to and including the chief constable. That might not be easy."

Fenella felt like screaming, crying, or laughing. It all seemed horrible and absurd, really. Instead of doing any of those things, she dove back into medieval Britain, immersing herself in Henry's matrimonial concerns and refusing to let herself think about Rosemary Ballard's murder.

$$\text{\ding{96}} \quad 7 \quad \text{\ding{96}}$$

"It was kind of you to kill Rosemary," Mona said, "but I don't think you've done enough. In order to protect my reputation and my memory, you're going to have to kill the rest of the family as well."

"I didn't kill anyone," Fenella told her firmly.

"Save that for the police. I hope they'll believe you, as I've grown quite used to having you around. If you go to prison, what would become of my flat?"

"I'm not going to go to prison. I didn't kill anyone."

"Yes, yes, of course," Mona said patronizingly. "Now how can we get rid of Rosemary's children? You'll need to track down that grandson as well, of course, at some point. Once he's gone, there won't be anyone left from Max's little indiscretion."

"You knew about it?"

Mona chuckled. "I've told you many times before that Max didn't have any secrets from me. There's no way he could have hidden an affair and a child from me. He used to talk about her endlessly, Rosemary, I mean. Charlotte was just a passing fancy, someone who caught his eye at a party or some such thing. He was quite taken with Rosemary, though, his only child. I had a very difficult time keeping him from giving her his fortune."

"I can't believe you knew about her."

"He very nearly offered to marry Charlotte, you know," Mona told her. "When he found out she was pregnant, he told me he was going to marry her. I had to get quite cross with him to change his mind. As I said, she was simply a mild diversion. They never would have made one another happy."

"He wanted to marry Charlotte?"

"When I made it clear that wasn't going to happen, he suggested that we should adopt the baby when it arrived," Mona laughed. "Imagine, me looking after a baby. What a horrifying thought. Honestly, Max was quite beside himself about the whole situation."

"I'm sure."

"In the end, I offered to help him send funds to Charlotte so that no one could trace the money back to Max. He used to give me large amounts of cash and I would send some of it on to Charlotte for Rosemary. Although, thinking back, I didn't often send very much of it to Charlotte. It was usually just easier to keep all of the money for myself."

"You can't be serious," Fenella said.

"Can't I? I'm afraid I simply don't know whether I am or not. This is your dream, after all. I must say, if you're going to dream about me, you really should make more of an effort with my clothes." Mona glanced down at the plain white dress she was wearing and shook her head. "Ghastly," she muttered.

"This is a dream?" Fenella asked. "You didn't know about Charlotte, then?"

Mona laughed. "I did in this dream, clearly, but in the real world, there was no Charlotte for me to know about. Max didn't have other women, not ever. I'd stake my life on that if I were still alive."

Fenella shook her head. "I don't understand any of this," she complained. "Am I awake or not?"

Mona reached across and pinched her arm. Fenella didn't feel anything.

"You're asleep," Mona told her. "I do think now would be a good time to wake up, though."

Fenella quickly opened her eyes. Katie was standing next to her pillow with a surprised look on her face.

"It must be nearly seven," Fenella said, glancing at the clock. The numbers changed to seven as she blinked at it.

"Merroowww," Katie said as she jumped off the bed and raced away toward the kitchen.

"I was having the strangest dream," Fenella told the kitten as she prepared her breakfast. "Mona knew all about Charlotte and had done everything she could to keep her and Max apart. It was terrible."

"And it was just a bad dream," Mona said firmly. "I meant what I said, though. Max didn't have other women."

"And you'd stake your life on that?"

Mona chuckled. "I would have when I was alive, anyway. I suppose I could stake my afterlife on it, if that would make you feel better."

"Did you ask him about Charlotte?"

"I mentioned her name in a conversation, yes. He thought it sounded vaguely familiar. His best guess was that she worked for someone he did business with at some point in the fifties. That would tie in with Rosemary's story, of course, but that still doesn't mean that she and Max had an affair."

After a shower and breakfast, Fenella went out to get a copy of the local paper. The headline made her flush.

"'Max Martin's love child brutally murdered,'" Mona read when Fenella showed her the paper. "You should sue them for that headline. That woman was not Max's child."

"A woman claiming to be the illegitimate daughter of one of the island's most famous former residents was stabbed to death in her hotel room overnight," Fenella read out the opening sentence.

"I'm sure I get a mention somewhere in the article," Mona sighed. "Probably a quite disparaging one, suggesting that perhaps I didn't truly mean anything to Max after all."

Fenella glanced through the rest of the article. It was short on facts and long on speculation. She read the last few sentences to Mona. "This reporter finds himself wondering about the fortune that Max bestowed on Mona Kelly. Perhaps some of that money might have been better spent supporting the child that he'd fathered and then seemingly forgotten."

The phone rang before Mona could reply. Fenella glanced at it and then shook her head. "I'm not answering my phone today. I don't want to talk to anyone."

She was glad she'd made that decision when the answering machine picked up.

"Ms. Woods, this is Dan Ross at the *Isle of Man Times*. I'd like to get a statement from you regarding the unfortunate death of Ms. Rosemary Ballard. I understand you and your advocate found the body. I believe the pubic have a right to know why you were looking for Ms. Ballard. What business did you have with her? Were you, perhaps, trying to reach some sort of settlement out of the money that you inherited from Mona Kelly? Surely you must agree that, as Max's child, she deserved some portion of the man's fortune. Please ring me back so that I can make sure that your side of the story is fairly represented in my next article."

As soon as the line went dead, Fenella erased the message. "That's one call I don't have to return, anyway," she muttered.

She'd left Henry with his fourth wife, Anne of Cleves. Knowing that he was miserable there, she grabbed the book and read through to his next wedding. Okay, in the end he wasn't going to be any happier with wife number five, but at least he'd have a few good months before that all went wrong, she thought as she shut the book and got ready for her visit to Doncan's office.

"Whatever he thinks, don't give anyone a penny," Mona told her.

"I'm sure Doncan will agree with that."

"He's an advocate," Mona countered. "He may well argue that there are sound reasons why it would make sense to simply write a check to make the whole Ballard family go away. I'd rather you spent every penny I ever had fighting them."

"I don't know that I'm prepared to spend every penny, but I'm ready to spend quite a lot to fight them. I am just taking your word for it that Max never cheated, though. If it ends up that you were wrong, I could be in a lot of trouble."

"I'm not wrong. Trust me."

Fenella let herself out of her apartment with Mona's words ringing in her ears. Maybe if Doncan suggested a reasonable settlement, she should give the idea some consideration. Trusting the word of a ghost seemed oddly foolhardy at this point.

"You look tired," Breesha said sympathetically when Fenella arrived at Doncan's office.

"I didn't sleep well," she replied.

"I'm sure everything you went through yesterday was difficult. I can't imagine finding a dead body."

"That was more Doncan than me, at least this time."

Breesha nodded. "He wasn't himself when he came back to the office yesterday. The whole experience was quite upsetting for him."

"I'm sure."

"I'll let him know you're here." She used the phone on her desk to ring Doncan's office. He came out to collect her a minute later.

Fenella knew she looked tired, but she thought Doncan looked a good deal worse. "Are you okay?" she exclaimed when she saw him.

"I didn't sleep well," he replied. "I'd never found a dead body before. It's not an experience I'd like to repeat."

"I don't recommend it," Fenella said dryly.

"Of course, you've found quite a few bodies in the last year. I'm afraid I haven't been anywhere near as supportive of you as I should have been. The whole experience has been shocking and eye-opening, to say the least."

"We should have just taken the stupid elevator again," Fenella sighed.

Doncan chuckled. "You're right about that. Let's go to my office, then." He led her down the corridor and into his office.

She sank into a chair and sat back with her eyes closed. So much had happened since the last time she'd sat there that she felt a bit overwhelmed.

Doncan slid into his own seat and cleared this throat. "My colleague, the expert in criminal law, couldn't be here this morning. He's in court, actually. He did give me some pointers, though, for dealing with the police."

"I've dealt with them dozens of times before. This isn't any different."

"Except this time you have arguably the best motive for the murder."

"I don't see it that way at all. Killing Rosemary hasn't solved anything, really. Her family will probably end up suing me now, instead of her doing so. The entire thing has blown up all over the local paper, meaning I've no chance of keeping things quiet or protecting Mona's memory. Rosemary was pushing for a quick settlement. Things will probably drag through the courts for years now that she's dead."

"All good points, of course, but your motive also includes those letters, the ones that Rosemary claimed would prove that Mona was blackmailing Max. No doubt the police are considering the idea that you killed her to get your hands on those letters."

"Except she told us that they're in a bank in London."

"That's what she told us, but maybe she was lying. Maybe you met with her early yesterday morning and found the letters in Rosemary's hotel room somehow. You could have grabbed them and disposed of them in the hours before we found the body."

"Surely, if I killed Rosemary, the last thing I would have suggested was going back down the stairs, rather than using the elevator."

"Unless you didn't realize that the body was in that storage room. What if you killed her and dumped the body into a nearby laundry cart, maybe one that was in the corridor. When housekeeping arrived, they moved the carts into the storage room without realizing there was a body inside one of them."

"Wouldn't the cart have been a lot heavier than it should have been? And what about the blood? Someone said there was a pool of it under the cart. Surely, if there was blood dripping from the cart, someone would have noticed."

"If the cart was in the corridor, maybe not. Remember that the carpeting there was dark brown and badly stained. It's possible any blood may have gone unnoticed."

Fenella sighed. "You're starting to make me doubt my own innocence," she told Doncan.

He laughed. "You can see why the police are being so careful with you, therefore. We know you didn't do it, but they have to prove who did and you're still very much a possibility."

"Who do you think killed her?" Fenella asked.

"I'm hoping her death was the result of some sort of family argument that had nothing to do with Mona and Max," he told her. "I didn't like her children or their spouses. I'd happily cast any one of them in the role of murderer."

The phone on Doncan's desk buzzed. "Yes?" he said into the receiver. Fenella watched as he frowned and then sighed. "Send him in."

"Send who in?" Fenella asked.

"Joe Malone is here and has requested an urgent appointment," Doncan replied as he got to his feet. There was a knock on the door a moment later.

"Mr. Malone?" Doncan said as he opened the door. "I wasn't expecting to see you here today."

"I just finished talking to the police again," Joe replied. He glanced over at Fenella and then dropped into the empty chair in front of Doncan's desk. "I'm glad you're here," he told Fenella. "Maybe we can make this quick and easy."

Doncan returned to his seat and looked inquisitively at Joe. "I'm not sure what you mean," he said.

"Someone killed my mother-in-law. At the moment, I'm assuming it was something random. Maybe someone broke into her hotel room and tried to steal her jewelry or something. Whatever happened, she's dead now and the whole thing is generating a lot of negative publicity for Ms. Woods."

"I'm not sure I'd agree with that," Doncan countered. "So far the paper has mostly been filled with pointless speculation."

Joe shrugged. "You can call it what you want. I'm prepared to make it all go away."

"How do you expect to do that?" Doncan demanded.

"The family will withdraw any claims made about Rosemary's parentage, will drop any and all lawsuits, and will hand over all of the letters that were in Rosemary's possession that she claimed were written by her father."

"In exchange for what?" Doncan asked.

"Ten million pounds. Five today and a further five once the letters are delivered to Ms. Woods."

Fenella laughed. "You considerably overestimate what those letters are worth to me," she said. "As I see it, Mona's reputation has already been dragged through the mud. Your letters can't do much more damage."

"You haven't seen the letters yet," Joe said warningly.

"Rosemary was going to show me copies of them yesterday. If you have those copies, I'll take a look now," she suggested.

"I don't have the copies with me," he told her. "They're far too valuable to carry around in my pocket."

"Copies don't have any real value," Fenella scoffed. "If they're as incriminating as you claim, I might be prepared to pay something for them, but first I'll need to see them and have the handwriting verified."

"We can arrange that," Joe said.

"And I want to see the results of a DNA test between Rosemary and Max's sister," Fenella added.

"That might be more difficult," Joe frowned. "Rosemary's aunt accepted Rosemary into the family. That should be proof enough for you."

"Rosemary didn't demand any money from Max's sister," Fenella said. "If she had done so, Max's sister may well have insisted on a DNA test."

"Rosemary might not have demanded any money from Maxwell Martin's estate, but her family is considering taking action there as well. That's one of the reasons why we're eager for a quick settlement with you. We have other avenues we want to explore, you see."

"You're going to sue Max's sister?"

"I haven't said that. It's just something we're considering. Because the woman was willing to recognize Rosemary for who she truly was, we're hoping we might reach a quick settlement there as well. We aren't asking for much, just for what Rosemary should have been enti-tled to as the daughter of a very wealthy man."

"You may struggle to persuade Max's sister to part with anything,"

Doncan said. "I only had a few dealings with her over the years, and I always found her difficult."

"As I said, she was happy to recognize Rosemary as her niece. That suggests to me that she'll at least be willing to discuss some sort of settlement."

Doncan shrugged. "As Ms. Woods has indicated, we aren't prepared to discuss any settlement without first seeing copies of the letters you claim to possess and also the results of a DNA test. I'm sure you can understand our position."

Joe shrugged. "I thought maybe you'd want to get things sorted as quickly as possible. The stories in the paper are just going to get worse as time goes on, and there's always the possibility that your client might get arrested for murder, too."

Fenella felt her cheeks turn bright red. "I had nothing to do with Rosemary's death," she said in a low voice.

Joe stared at her for a minute and then nodded. "You'll want to keep saying that for as long as possible, of course. As I see it, you were the only one with a motive, unless it really was completely random."

"Perhaps Matthew simply grew tired of Autumn being the favorite," Fenella suggested, repeating some part of Mona's suggestion from earlier.

Joe laughed. "Good try, but all six of us were at the Manx Museum all morning. We had breakfast with Rosemary and then got on a tour bus. We went around the museum and even had lunch there. That was where we were when the police found us to tell us about Rosemary."

Fenella frowned. If the entire family had alibis, it was no wonder Daniel was being so careful with her.

"Perhaps you could ring my assistant when you have the letters and the DNA test results," Doncan suggested, getting to his feet. "She'll be able to make an appointment for you to meet with myself and Fenella at that time. Of course, we'll need to understand what's in Ms. Ballard's will, as well."

"What do you mean?" Joe asked.

"Any settlement that we make may depend on the provisions of Ms. Ballard's will. If she left everything to charity, for example, any settlement that we reach would have to take that into consideration."

"She didn't leave everything to charity," Joe replied. "I'm sure she left it to her children in equal shares."

"Nothing to her grandson?" Doncan wondered.

Joe shrugged. "Maybe, but I can't see why it matters. We can reach a settlement, just between us, on behalf of the entire family."

"I hope they all know that you're here, then," Doncan told him. "They'll all need to agree in writing to anything that we decide."

"I could get them to agree to something today, if you're willing to just settle," Joe tried again.

"I'm afraid we aren't," Doncan told him firmly. "We've no reason to believe that Rosemary was who she claimed to be, after all. Until you can provide proof, I don't think we have anything further to discuss."

Joe looked as if he wanted to argue, but after a moment he got to his feet. "I'll be in touch soon," he said before he turned and left the room.

"That was awkward," Fenella sighed as the door shut behind Joe.

"It was interesting," Doncan told her. "I'd be willing to wager a small sum that at least some of the family members had no idea that Joe was coming here. I think he was hoping that we'd be flustered and upset by the murder and willing to write him a check to try to make it all go away."

"He's an idiot."

Doncan laughed. "He may not be the only one in the family to start having those kinds of ideas, though. If anyone gets in touch with you directly, let me know."

"I will," Fenella promised.

Doncan spent an hour with her, discussing the finer points of answering police questions. When he was done, she sighed and sat back in her chair.

"I still don't believe that Daniel thinks I killed anyone."

"As I said, it isn't Daniel you have to convince. If Joe was correct, and everyone in the family was together all morning, then the police are going to struggle just to find other suspects."

"Could Max's sister be behind it all?" Fenella asked tentatively.

"Mona's been dead for over a year. I can't see why she'd bother with something this elaborate after all this time. I'm sure she was delighted when Rosemary showed up on her doorstep claiming to be Max's daughter, just because it would have upset Mona, but I can't see her orchestrating the entire con, if it is a con, of course."

"You think Rosemary was telling the truth?"

"I don't know what to think anymore. The murder has complicated things tremendously."

"What if Max's sister helped set up the con, but then when Rosemary got here, she went rogue and started trying to get us to agree to a quick settlement? What if Rosemary was trying to cut her out of her share of whatever she could get from me?"

"I wonder how Max's sister would know what was happening?"

"Maybe one of Rosemary's children or their partners is a spy for Max's sister," Fenella suggested.

Doncan reached across the desk and patted her hand. "I suppose all of that is possible, but it seems like a quite convoluted solution. In my experience, most murders have a more simple resolution. Perhaps Mr. Malone was correct. Perhaps Rosemary's murder was completely random."

"In my experience, murder is rarely random," Fenella said grimly.

Doncan nodded. "Of course, you have more experience with the subject than I do. If we rule out Rosemary's family and Max's sister, do you have any other possible explanations for the murder?"

"What if she was a professional con artist? Maybe she ran into someone on the island that she'd conned in the past."

"That's an interesting idea. I did some digging into her past before we met with her the first time. Maybe it's time for me to dig a little deeper."

"I suggest you look at her children and their spouses, too. Something about all of this is off somewhere. We just have to work out where."

"Actually, that's a job for the police, but that doesn't mean I'm simply going to sit idly by while they investigate. I don't expect to solve the case, but maybe we can learn more about what we're up against in terms of possible lawsuits."

Fenella stood up and stretched. "I just want to go home and go back to bed," she said. "I wish I didn't have to meet with Daniel this afternoon."

"Would you like me to accompany you to the meeting? You are entitled to legal representation when you talk to the police."

"I can't help but feel as if that would make me look even more guilty," Fenella said, forcing herself to smile at the thought. "No, I'll go on my own. I know how to reach you if I find that I need you."

He walked her back to the foyer. "Ring me after your conversation with Inspector Robinson. I want to know what he wanted to discuss with you."

Fenella nodded. "If I were you, I'd go home and take a nap now," she told him.

He laughed. "I may just do that, if I don't have anything on my schedule for an hour or two."

"Interestingly enough," Breesha said, "your next two meetings have both been canceled. You've no reason to be here for the rest of the day."

Doncan stared at her for a moment and then sighed. "You canceled my afternoon meetings?"

"I didn't say that," she replied, shuffling papers on her desk.

Doncan sighed. "I'm too tired to be cross with you," he admitted. "I'm going home to bed. Fenella, ring me after you're done with Inspector Robinson. I'll have to be back up by that time or I'll never sleep tonight."

Fenella nodded and then made her way outside. Home suddenly seemed a very long way away. There was a small convenience store right next door to Doncan's office. She went in planning to buy herself a cup of coffee and emerged a few minutes later unwrapping an ice cream treat.

The cold ice cream woke her up at least as successfully as the coffee would have, and it tasted much better. By the time she'd reached Promenade View Apartments she was feeling almost normal. It was nearly noon, so it was time for some lunch, but the ice cream had filled her stomach nicely.

"Yes, yes, I know," she told a loudly complaining Katie as she opened her door. "You need some lunch, even if I don't."

After filling Katie's bowls, Fenella checked her answering machine. The little light was flashing frantically. She listened to and deleted half a dozen messages from Dan Ross and two from a reporter from a newspaper in London who'd picked up the story. That left a single message.

"Ms. Woods, this is Autumn Tate. I'm Rosemary Ballard's youngest daughter. I hope you remember. Anyway, I wanted to talk with you about, well, things. I was hoping we could meet tonight. We've moved to a different hotel. We're at the Portsmouth now. Why anyone would name a hotel on the Isle of Man the Portsmouth is beyond me, but it seems nice enough. Anyway, they have a little guest lounge on the ground floor. Maybe you could meet me there for a drink around seven? I'd rather you didn't bring your advocate, but if you'd like, you could bring a friend. I just want to talk to you about, well, things. If you don't come, I'll understand. Maybe I'll try again another time. Thank you."

Fenella frowned at the answering machine. Part of her was desperate to talk to Autumn, if only to find out just how ironclad everyone's alibis were, but talking to anyone involved in the case was probably a very bad idea. She needed to see what Doncan thought of the idea, but he was probably at home, fast asleep at the moment. She would have to wait to discuss it with him after her meeting with Daniel.

In the kitchen she fixed herself a sandwich she didn't really want and ate it without thinking. After she'd cleaned up after herself she freshened up in the bedroom.

"I don't want to look as if I'm trying too hard," she told Katie, "but I do want to look nice."

"The bags under your eyes aren't particularly appealing," Mona told her.

Fenella nearly stabbed herself in the eye with her mascara wand. "Thanks. Auntie Mona. You really know how to make a girl feel good about herself," she said sarcastically.

Mona shrugged. "Put some concealer on them," she suggested. "Add some highlights to draw attention away from them, as well."

Sighing, Fenella did her best. When she studied herself in the mirror, though, the dark circles were all that she could see.

"Put your hair up in a shiny clip," Mona suggested. "Maybe that will be distracting."

Fenella twisted her hair into a messy bun and then clipped it into place with a large clip. The clip was on the back of her head, so it didn't do much to draw attention away from her tired eyes, but overall she felt as if she looked a little bit better, anyway.

"Wish me luck," she told Mona.

"You don't need luck. Daniel knows you didn't kill anyone."

"I wish I had your confidence," Fenella muttered as she headed for the door.

The local station was only a short distance away, but they had a large parking lot, so Fenella drove Mona's racy red sports car, counting on the experience to give her a confidence boost. She parked it in a distant corner of the lot and then walked toward the building trying not to think about the threatened lawsuit. Was it possible that she might lose everything Mona had left her? Did she even want to keep it if Max had been blackmailed into giving it to Mona in the first place? She shook her head. Mona was many things, but she wasn't a blackmailer, no matter what Rosemary had said. Fenella just had to have faith in her aunt.

❧ 8 ❧

"I'm here to see Daniel Robinson," she told the constable behind the reception desk.

"Do you have any identification?" the woman asked.

Fenella looked at her in surprise. "Identification? I have my driver's license." She dug around in her handbag and pulled out her wallet. "It's here somewhere," she said apologetically as she unzipped the wallet and began to sort through store loyalty cards, credit cards, and miscellaneous notes and receipts. One of these days she really needed to organize her wallet, she thought as she searched.

"Ah, here it is," she exclaimed eventually. She handed the card to the constable, who studied it carefully.

After a minute, she glanced up at Fenella and then picked up the phone on the desk in front of her. "Ms. Woods is here to see Inspector Robinson," she told someone. She put the phone down and gestured toward a few chairs near the door. "Have a seat. Someone will be right with you."

Fenella took her license back and settled into one of the hard chairs. While she was waiting, she separated receipts and notes from credit cards and loyalty cards. When Constable Clague appeared, she dumped everything together back inside her wallet and jumped to her feet.

"Ms. Woods, if you could come with me, please," he said.

She followed him through the lobby and into a small elevator. A wave of claustrophobia washed over her as the doors shut behind them. She took a few deep breaths and watched as the car rose slowly to the third floor. When the doors opened, Daniel greeted her with a tight smile.

"This way, please," he said, without a proper greeting.

Fenella followed him down a short corridor and through a door marked "Interview One." A cheap wooden table filled most of the space in the room. There were two chairs on one side of the table and one on the other. They were all the same type of cheap folding chair that Fenella had suffered through in the building's lobby.

"Have a seat," Daniel told her, gesturing toward the single chair. "Would you like coffee or a cold drink?"

"Something cold sounds good," she told him.

He turned and said something to Constable Clague, who was standing in the doorway. The constable nodded and walked away. Fenella sat down and tried to get comfortable. Daniel sat opposite her, seemingly unbothered by the rock-hard chair. Constable Clague walked in a moment later with three cans of soda in his hands. He handed one to Fenella and set another in front of Daniel before settling into the third chair with the last drink. Fenella opened hers and took a sip while Daniel took out a notebook and a pen. The constable did the same.

"We'll both be taking notes," Daniel told her. "I'd also like to record the session if that's okay with you."

"Of course it is," she replied. "I don't have anything to hide."

Daniel nodded and then looked at the constable. "Ready to begin?"

"Yes, sir," he replied.

"I'd like to start by having you go back through yesterday," Daniel told her. "Start with the time you woke up and keep going until you went to bed."

Fenella sat back and took a long drink from her can. "Katie woke me at seven, the same as always," she began.

"Katie is your cat?" the constable asked.

"Yes, Katie is my cat," Fenella sighed. She continued on with her recitation. Before long she began to feel as if the constable was interrupting just about everything she said with questions. They were all questions that she was sure he knew the answers to, as well. She understood the need for them to be thorough, but she felt he was taking things too far.

It felt like many hours later when she finally reached the end of her day. "And then I finally went to bed," she concluded.

"Alone?" the constable asked.

Fenella felt herself blushing. "Katie sleeps with me," she replied.

The constable raised an eyebrow and then made a note. Daniel hadn't said a single word the entire time. Now he cleared his throat. "Tell me about today," he said.

"Today?"

"What did you do today? I know you well enough to suspect that you spent at least part of the day with someone involved in the case," he replied.

"I went to see Doncan, and Joe Malone turned up to make some more vague threats and try to extort money from me, if that's what you mean."

Daniel sighed. "Maybe you'd better start with when you woke up again."

Fenella drank more soda to keep herself from sighing or screaming, both of which felt like suitable replies to Daniel's request. She swallowed and then began.

"I woke up one minute before seven, startling Katie, who was just about to wake me," she told the men, shooting the constable a look that dared him to question her.

He made a note but stayed silent.

Fenella told the two men about her meeting with Doncan, including everything that she could remember them discussing. Daniel looked slightly uncomfortable when she mentioned her motive and lack of alibi for the murder, but he didn't say anything. Both men seemed to take more notes when she began to talk about Joe Malone's visit.

"So he's still planning to take you to court," Daniel said thoughtfully when Fenella concluded her retelling of her meeting with Doncan.

"Thus proving that I didn't actually have any motive for killing Rosemary," Fenella suggested. "Things have exploded all over the papers now, too. I was better off with the woman alive."

"Except you couldn't have predicted the future," Constable Clague said.

"I'd met Rosemary's family. It was obvious that they were all supporting her claims. I'd have to have been pretty stupid to think that killing Rosemary was going to solve anything."

"What did you do after your meeting with Doncan?" Daniel asked.

"I walked home," she said, not bothering to mention the ice cream. "I had lunch and listened to my answering machine messages."

"Oh?" Daniel said. "Why do I feel as if that's significant?"

"I had a message from Autumn Tate. She wants me to meet her at her hotel tonight."

"Does she really? That's very interesting. I wonder if she knows that you've already spoken to Mr. Malone," Daniel said, scribbling notes rapidly.

"I doubt it. I got the impression that Joe was acting on his own this morning, even though he claimed to be acting on behalf of the whole family. His wife probably knew where he was and what he was doing, but I doubt anyone else did."

"I wonder if Autumn told anyone she was ringing you," Daniel mused.

"From what she said, I sort of doubt that, too. I think they're all a bit lost without Rosemary. I feel as if they're reaching out to me to see if they can get anything from me before the courts get involved."

"Are you planning to meet with Mrs. Tate, then?" Daniel asked.

"I need to discuss that with Doncan," Fenella told him. "I'd like to talk to her, obviously, but I don't want to do anything that might jeopardize my position in any future court cases."

"If you do talk to her, don't discuss the murder," Daniel said sternly. "This is one investigation I don't want you involved with in any way."

"I'm already rather involved," Fenella pointed out.

"You're a suspect," he snapped. "The further you stay away from the victim's family, the better."

"They're all suspects, too, I hope," Fenella said. "Someone in that group must have had a motive for killing Rosemary. I certainly didn't."

"We aren't going to discuss the case," he told her. "I appreciate your cooperation, but this is strictly a one-way street as regards information."

Fenella nodded. She'd expected nothing less under the circumstances, but his words still stung.

"Do you have anything else to tell me about anything to do with the case?" he asked.

Fenella thought for a minute and then sighed. "Max's sister hated Mona. Someone suggested that she might have been behind Rosemary's claims. It's just possible that she helped Rosemary forge the letters she threatened me with, for example."

Daniel raised an eyebrow. "If Mona were still alive, I might give the idea some consideration, but I can't see what she has to gain by harassing you."

"Maybe Rosemary was going to give Max's sister a share of anything she managed to get from me. Rosemary said something about using the letters to get Mona's entire estate confiscated. If that happened, Rosemary might have sued herself into a fortune."

"I'll take a discreet look at Max's sister," Daniel told her, "but I think her involvement is unlikely."

"She'd supposedly recognized Rosemary as her niece. I can't imagine why she'd do that. She had to realize that doing so opened her up to a lawsuit against Max's estate," Fenella argued.

Daniel made another note. "Perhaps she was just pleased to learn that her brother had left behind a child, a part of himself, as it were. Maybe she was willing to share some of her fortune with Rosemary in exchange for a relationship of some sort."

"If she were going to share Max's fortune with Rosemary, Rosemary didn't need to sue me," Fenella said.

"If the letters you told me about truly do exist, I can see why Rosemary might be angry with Mona and why she'd want to sue for some portion of her estate. Imagine discovering that your father was rich and had never provided for you properly because he was busy spending all of his money on another woman, one who may or may not have been blackmailing him."

"Mona wasn't blackmailing anyone," Fenella said firmly.

Daniel shrugged. "I'm not saying she was, I'm just trying to suggest what Rosemary may have thought, reading through the letters."

"But the letters are fakes," Fenella insisted. "Rosemary had to know that. If they were real, she would have read them when her mother died in the eighties, and she'd have turned up on the island to confront Max then, not wait until now to launch a lawsuit."

"As I said, I'm not in a position to discuss the case with you," Daniel said. "What I am going to do is send a constable to the Portsmouth Hotel bar tonight. It probably won't be anyone you know, but you may recognize him or her. It would probably be best if you pretended that you didn't."

Fenella nodded. "I'm still not sure I'm going to go."

Daniel chuckled. "That's odd, because I'm quite certain you're going to go."

Fenella opened her mouth to protest, but Daniel was right. She was going to meet Autumn for a drink, whatever Doncan said.

"Was there anything else?" she asked him after a pause.

He flipped back through his notebook and then looked the constable. "Do you have any additional questions?"

Constable Clague looked through his own notes and then flushed. "I don't think I do," he said.

Daniel nodded. "We're done, then," he said, getting to his feet. "I'll walk you out," he told Fenella.

She nodded and stood up. The constable stayed in his seat, adding to his notes, as Daniel took her arm and led her out of the room. They walked in silence to the elevators.

"Are there stairs?" she asked.

He glanced at her and then nodded. "Sure, we can take the stairs."

"I don't really like elevators," she explained as they walked a bit further down the corridor.

"I didn't know that about you," he replied.

"The ones in my building aren't bad. They don't really bother me."

"What about the ones in the Tale and Tail?" he asked.

Fenella tried to laugh, but the sound fell flat. "I only use those when I've had a drink or two," she said.

He nodded and then walked her down the stairs and through the lobby. "Did you walk here?" he asked in the doorway.

"No, I drove," she replied, gesturing toward Mona's car.

He walked her to the car and gave it an appreciative look. "It's a gorgeous car."

"It's fun to drive, too. I thought it might lift my spirits."

Daniel nodded. "I'm sorry. This case is making everything difficult. If we don't have it solved before the party, I'm not going to be able to attend. I can't be seen to be socializing with witnesses."

"You mean suspects," Fenella sighed. "I understand that I'm a suspect, even though I don't agree that I had a motive."

"Ms. Ballard was threatening to sue you. She claimed to have letters that would prove that Mona was blackmailing Max. You could have lost everything."

"And I still could. Killing her didn't help in any way. The letters, if they exist, are still out there somewhere. Her family will know where they are and they've already indicated that they're going to make use of them."

"Unless Rosemary had the letters in her hotel room and you took them when you killed her," Daniel said quietly.

"If I had the letters, I could have simply laughed in Joe Malone's face this morning."

"But you don't want him to realize that you have the letters."

"Rosemary told us all that the letters were in a safe-deposit box in London. I had no reason to believe anything else."

"She rang you and arranged to meet you. Maybe she told you during that conversation that she had the letters with her."

"Except she didn't," Fenella said, letting her frustration seep into her tone. "Look, I appreciate that you have to consider every possibility. By all means, consider me a suspect, investigate me as much as you need to, but don't stop investigating everyone else, because someone killed Rosemary Ballard and you and I both know it wasn't me."

Daniel stared at her for a minute and then nodded. "I do know it wasn't you," he agreed. "If nothing else, you'd have done a better job of it, and there's no way you would have stumbled over the body an hour later, either."

"We found the body an hour after she'd been killed?"

"I didn't say that, at least not exactly," he replied, shaking his head. "The coroner hasn't determined an exact time of death, but an hour is as good a guess as any at this point. It could have been more than that, though, so you aren't in the clear because you were with Doncan from eleven."

Fenella sighed. "And her family was all together at the museum?"

"I can't answer questions," he told her. "I've already said too much. Look, I know you and I know that you're going to be right at the center of this investigation no matter what I say. Please be very careful. Ring me before you meet with anyone involved in the case, even if you're going to meet them in a public place. If any of them show up on your doorstep, don't let them into your flat, and ring me immediately. This is an ugly and complicated case."

"It is, and I'm right in the middle of it whether I want to be or not."

Daniel glanced over his shoulder at the police station and then sighed. "I can't risk giving you a hug, not here, not right now. Know that I would if I could."

She smiled at him. "I appreciate that. You can owe me one until the case is over."

He chuckled. "I'll do that," he agreed. "I'm just hoping for a quick solution."

"As I said earlier, check into Max's sister."

"I was listening, and I take everything you tell me seriously. I'll see what I can find out about the woman, but if she's behind the letters and the lawsuit, surely she wanted Rosemary alive and well?"

"Unless she found out that Rosemary was going behind her back to try to get a quick cash settlement. That probably wasn't in her plans."

"I'll see what I can find out. For now, I'd better get back to work. I have other cases to deal with besides this murder, you know. Crime is up and we're short on staff at the moment."

"Good luck," Fenella said. "Call me if you solve the case."

He laughed. "I will do, but I have a feeling you'll be there when we wrap everything up. You usually are."

Fenella swallowed a sigh and then unlocked her car. She slid behind the wheel and slowly turned the key. As the engine roared to life, she decided to go home the long way, via Peel or maybe Laxey or Ramsey. After putting the top down in spite of the cold February air, she exited the parking lot, turned left, and simply drove. When she reached the coast, she made another left and kept going. The car handled well as she sped along various roads on her way around the island. After an hour, she realized she was feeling better. The letters were fake and Rosemary wasn't Max's daughter. Mona might tease her regularly about the afterlife, but she wouldn't lie to her outright, not about such important things.

After she'd parked the car in the garage next to her other, much more sensible vehicle, she gave it an affectionate pat. "We'll do that again soon," she promised. The beep that followed her words must have come from another car in the garage, she told herself as she headed for the elevators.

Mona was pacing anxiously when she walked into her apartment.

"That was a very long interview," she said. "I was afraid Daniel had arrested you."

"I went for a drive after the interview," Fenella said sheepishly. "Your car is such fun to drive."

Mona sighed dramatically and then dropped onto the nearest couch. "I can't disagree," she said after a moment. "You did worry me, though."

"I'm sorry. I needed to relax and unwind a little bit after my talk with Daniel."

"Tell me everything," Mona demanded.

"Let me ring Doncan. Then I can tell you both at the same time." She didn't give Mona time to argue before she dialed Doncan's office number.

"He's home, having that nap, I hope," Breesha told her. "I'm sure you have his home number."

"I do, but I hate to bother him there."

"He wanted you to ring after your session with the police," Breesha reminded her.

Fenella put the phone down and opened the desk drawer.

"What now?" Mona asked.

"I have to find Doncan's home number."

Mona rattled off the number before Fenella could drag out her address book. "Are you sure?" Fenella asked.

Mona sighed. "Yes."

"Ah, Fenella, thank you for ringing. I had a short nap and I'm feeling much better. How did your conversation with Inspector Robison go, then?"

Fenella gave him a shortened version of everything that had passed between her and the inspector. When she mentioned Autumn's phone call, he made a noise.

"What?" she asked.

"We'll talk about that at the end," he replied. "Continue for now."

When she was done, Fenella felt exhausted. All she'd done all day was talk to people. What she needed now was a few hours of solitude with her book.

"I should come with you if you're planning to meet Autumn later," Doncan said.

"She won't talk to me in front of you," Fenella argued. "I can take a friend, if that will make you feel better."

"You're thinking of Shelly Quirk, aren't you?"

"I am."

"Would you be willing to take Breesha instead?"

"Your assistant? Surely Autumn will remember her from your office."

"She might, but I doubt she paid Breesha much attention. Anyway, I know Breesha can do wonders with her hair and makeup. I can promise you that she'll be barely recognizable if you agree."

Fenella hesitated and then nodded. "I suppose that makes sense," she said when she realized that Doncan couldn't see her nodding. "Have her meet me here, just in case she truly isn't recognizable."

"Unless I ring you, she'll be at your flat by half six," Doncan promised. "She's not an advocate, but she's worked for advocates since she was eighteen. She probably knows the law better than I do."

"He's probably right," Mona said as Fenella put the phone down. "Breesha should have been an advocate. She's much smarter than Doncan."

Fenella didn't argue. It was already past five, so she didn't have long before she'd have to get ready to go back out. She made herself a frozen meal for dinner and quickly read through the final days of poor Catherine Howard. At least Henry would finally find some happiness with Catherine Parr, she thought to herself as she headed into the bedroom to change. If Henry was truly capable of happiness by that point, of course.

She found a pretty sweater dress in Mona's wardrobe and put it on with a pair of long boots. After washing her face, she redid her makeup and then brushed out her hair and put it back in the clip. The mirror told her that she still looked tired, but she'd done the best she could under the circumstances. After giving Katie her dinner, she paced around her apartment for a few minutes, waiting for Breesha.

When she opened the door a short while later, she was surprised to see just how different Breesha looked. "Wow, I'm not sure I would have recognized you if I hadn't been expecting you," she said honestly.

"I don't wear a lot of makeup at the office," Breesha told her. "I try to look warm and welcoming, maybe comforting, even. Most people who need the services of an advocate also need comfort."

There was nothing comforting about Breesha's look tonight. She looked at least ten years younger than Fenella thought she was, in a figure-flattering dress and expertly applied makeup. "You look wonderful."

"Thanks. It's fun to dress up and go out once in a while, but I don't make a habit of it. Tonight should be interesting, anyway. Doncan suggested that you call me something other than Breesha though, just in case Autumn was paying attention in his office."

"What should I call you, then?"

"How about Brenda? That should be close enough to my real name that I won't forget to answer to it."

Fenella laughed. "Let's hope I don't forget."

"As long as we both limit ourselves to one drink, we should be fine," Breesha said confidently.

"Is it raining? I looked as if it might earlier. I'd really prefer to walk to the hotel if we can."

"I walked here from my flat. It's cool and overcast, but dry."

"You live nearby?"

"I have a flat in the building where Doncan has his offices," she replied, making a face. "He bought the building years ago and turned the upper floors into flats. He gave me a good price for mine and I'm really grateful, but sometimes I do think that living that close to the office wasn't my smartest decision ever."

"Do you find yourself stopping in the office to do extra work after hours?" she asked.

"It's worse than that," Breesha laughed. "I find myself sitting in my flat thinking that I should go down and do a few things, but never actually doing them."

Fenella laughed. "That sounds like something I would do."

After locking up the apartment, Fenella and Breesha made their way down to the promenade.

"I don't actually know where the Portsmouth Hotel is," Fenella said.

"It's only a few doors down from the other hotel. It's similar in quality and will be just as empty this time of year."

There was a short flight of stairs to the building's entrance. Fenella and Breesha walked up and Breesha pushed the door open. The lobby was only dimly lit and there wasn't anyone behind the reception desk. There was a bell on top of it, but Breesha ignored it and led Fenella through the room and down a short corridor. At the end of the corridor was a small lounge with a few couches, chairs, and tables.

Fenella blinked in the poorly lit space, trying to spot Autumn. As her eyes adjusted to the lack of light, she realized the woman wasn't there.

"Let's get a table," Breesha suggested. They selected one in the back corner of the room. Two young men were sitting together at the next table. Fenella recognized at least one of them as a police constable. While Fenella watched for Autumn, Breesha went to the bar to get a round of drinks. Autumn arrived at the same time as Breesha returned to the table.

"Thank you for coming," Autumn said in a low voice after Fenella had introduced her to "Brenda."

"I'm sorry for your loss," Fenella told her. "I still miss my mother every day."

Autumn nodded. "It doesn't feel quite real. I can't really get my head around it. I keep expecting her to ring me or knock on my door. I don't know if I'll ever get used to her not being here."

"Let me get you a drink," Breesha suggested.

"A glass of wine might be nice," Autumn replied. "Any sort. It all tastes the same to me."

Breesha nodded and then headed back to the bar.

"Randy doesn't understand," Autumn told Fenella. "His mother died when he was seventeen, but it's different for boys, I'm certain."

"I'm sure you're right. I have four brothers and none of them really understood how I felt when our mother passed away."

"I feel as if it's all my fault."

"You mustn't feel that way."

"We wouldn't have even been on the island if I hadn't started digging through our family history. I saw one of the programs on the telly where a famous person finds that he's distantly related to the Queen or to a mass murderer or some such thing. Anyway, I got to wondering who I might find if I went back a few generations in our family. I never expected Mum to get murdered when we tried to find out more about her father, though."

"Of course you didn't."

"Here we are," Breesha said, handing Autumn a glass of wine.

Autumn took a sip and then set the glass on the table.

"We all thought it was a nice hotel. None of us thought Mum would be in any danger if we left her alone for the day."

"It is a nice hotel," Breesha replied.

"People don't get murdered in nice hotels," Autumn countered. "I just keep thinking that it must have been something random. No one had any reason to kill my mother."

Fenella and Breesha exchanged glances. Autumn took another sip of her drink and then nodded.

"Oh, someone suggested to me that you might have wanted her dead, but I don't believe that. I know she was going to sue you, but you're American. I'm sure you've been sued dozens of times before. I've seen it on telly. Everyone is always suing someone in the US because their coffee was too hot or because of a minor accident. You wouldn't have been worried about a lawsuit."

"Even if I had been worried, I never would have done anything to harm your mother."

"Of course not, but then neither would anyone else. I really don't understand what happened. The police won't tell us anything about how she died. Maybe it was just an accident somehow."

"I don't know any more than you do," Fenella told her.

Autumn frowned. "That's disappointing. I thought you were there when the body was found. I was hoping you could tell me what had happened."

"I was there, but I didn't see anything."

"We will be able to find out what happened eventually, won't we?" Autumn asked.

"The coroner's report will be part of the inquiry into her death," Breesha supplied.

"I wish I'd never asked her about her father," Autumn sighed.

"I'm surprised she'd never read the letters before you asked," Fenella said.

"She wasn't ready to read them until later. I asked her about her father maybe six months ago. It may have been a little longer, actually. She told me that she didn't know anything and that she didn't want to discuss it. I thought that would be the end of it, really."

She stopped talking to drink more wine. Fenella followed suit.

"Who brought the subject up again?" Breesha asked after a minute.

"Oh, Mum did. She rang me one day and asked me if I was still interested in learning more about her father. Apparently, when I'd asked, she'd started thinking more about him and the things her mother had told her. After a while, she remembered the locked box of letters. Mum had put all of her mum's things into storage years ago, so it had taken her some time to find the box and then even longer to work up the courage to open it and read the letters inside."

"And then she called you to tell you what she'd found?" Fenella asked.

"Yeah. She was really excited because she'd never known anything about her father. I think she thought that she'd been the result of a brief affair or maybe a one-night stand. She was really happy when she learned that her father had been in love with her mother, even though he couldn't marry her."

"Because of Mona," Fenella sighed.

"I never read the letters," Autumn said, "but that's what Mum told me, anyway. She was pretty bitter about Mona, actually, and I don't blame her. From what Mum said, Mona kept my mother's parents from being together, and she prevented Maxwell Martin from providing properly for my mother."

"But you've never actually seen the letters?" Fenella checked.

"Only the one that Mum had that copy of at the meeting. She showed me that one before we came to the island. She wanted me to understand why she was so upset."

"If the letter is genuine, it was quite upsetting." Fenella said.

"What do you mean, if it's genuine? Are you suggesting that my mother made up the whole story?"

"Not at all," Fenella replied quickly. "It's possible, though, that someone else forged the letters to try to extort money from me or from Max's sister."

Autumn looked surprised and then shook her head. "That doesn't make sense. The letters were in a locked box in storage for years. How could someone have faked them and put them there?"

Fenella looked at Breesha and then shrugged. "Let's hope the police can work it all out," she said.

"Were you going to give my mother some money?" Autumn asked after she swallowed the last of her wine.

"No, and I'm not giving any to Joe Malone, either," Fenella replied.

"Joe? Where does he come in?" Autumn sounded confused.

"He visited Doncan this morning and suggested that we should settle with him on behalf of the family," Fenella explained.

"That's interesting. He never bothered to discuss that with the rest of the family, of course." She pulled out her phone and quickly sent a text message. "I'll just see what my sister has to say about that," she said angrily.

"He would have had to get everyone to agree before there could have been any legal settlement," Fenella told her. "Perhaps he was just trying to get a quick settlement and assumed you would all agree."

"He shouldn't have assumed any such thing," Autumn snapped. "Ah, let's see what my sister says." She glanced at her phone and then frowned.

"Is everything okay?" Breesha asked as Autumn seemed to go pale.

"Apparently, we have bigger problems," Autumn replied. "According to April, our father has just arrived on the island."

"Your father?" Fenella echoed.

Autumn shrugged. "Well, the man that my mother always insisted was my father. It's something of a running family joke that I have a different father to my brother and sister. Mum always denied it, but even she had to admit that I don't look much like my siblings."

"Any idea why he's here?" Breesha asked.

"None at all. As far as I know, he hasn't had any contact with anyone in the family in over thirty years. He and Mum split up when I was two or three, another thing that gives some weight to the idea that I wasn't his child, I suppose. We visited him from time to time right after the split, but within a year or so, he simply disappeared."

"And now he's on the island," Fenella said thoughtfully.

"I suppose my mother's death may have been covered in some of the UK papers," Autumn said. "Maybe he read about it and decided to come over and see if there was anything in it for him."

Fenella must have looked surprised, because Autumn laughed and then shrugged. "From everything my mother has told me over the years, my father was always looking to make a few pounds out of every opportunity. She didn't have very many nice things to say about him, really, which is hardly surprising under the circumstances."

"You don't remember him at all?" Fenella asked.

"Not even a little bit. My mother gave me a photograph of him when I started doing that family research we were talking about, but she'd only kept one, from their wedding. When I asked, she told me that she'd burned every other photo of him. She'd only kept that one because she knew one of us kids would want to see it one day."

"I wonder if your brother or sister remembers him any better," Breesha mused.

"April used to talk about him when we were kids, but I don't think she truly remembered him. It was more made-up talk about how he was really handsome and rich and how one day he was going to come back and take us all to live in a mansion somewhere. Matthew used to get really cross about it, but I loved her stories. I even believed them for many years."

Autumn's phone buzzed loudly. She picked it up and read the message. "I'm afraid I have to go," she said, getting to her feet. "We're having an emergency meeting in April's room to work out what we're going to do about Peter Ballard and his unexpected arrival."

"Good luck," Fenella told her.

"Thanks. I think we might need it," Autumn replied.

Fenella watched as Autumn walked out of the room.

"That was odd," Breesha said.

"Her father turning up like that?"

"The whole thing," Breesha countered. "What did she want?"

"I got the feeling she was leading up to asking me for money before I mentioned that Joe had already beaten her to it."

"You could be right," Breesha agreed.

"I'm surprised she thinks the killing was random, although maybe she just told me that because she didn't want to accuse me of murder before she asked me for a payout."

Breesha laughed. "That wouldn't have been polite," she agreed.

One of the young men at the next table turned and smiled at Fenella. "Ms. Woods, Inspector Robinson told us that this would be an interesting assignment. He wasn't wrong."

"You'll have to let him know about Peter Ballard's arrival," Fenella told him.

"We've already done that," he assured her. "He may ring you later for a full statement on tonight's meeting."

"I'll be home," Fenella sighed.

The constable nodded and then he and his companion got up and walked out together.

"We could have another round," Breesha suggested.

Fenella looked around the room and then shook her head. "I'm happy to have another drink, but I'd rather have it at the Tale and Tail."

"That's a good idea. I love it there."

"You go to the Tale and Tail?" Fenella asked, surprised that she'd never seen the other woman at her favorite pub.

"Not as often as I should, really," Breesha replied. "I think I've been there twice in the past year. I work too much and don't go out often."

The pair walked to the pub, got drinks, and found a table in a quiet corner. While they sipped their wine, Breesha told Fenella her life story and then Fenella shared hers.

"This has been fun," Fenella said as they made their way back out of the building. "We should do this again soon."

"I'm nearly always available," Breesha laughed. "Ring me anytime."

"You can ring me, too," Fenella told her. "I tend to end up at the pub several nights each week."

They parted on the sidewalk in front of the building as they headed in opposite directions toward home. When Fenella got off the elevator on her floor, she was surprised to see Daniel standing in the corridor.

"You told Constable Brown that you'd be home," he said tiredly as she walked toward him.

"Breesha and I went for a drink at the Tale and Tail after we left the hotel," she replied guiltily. "I didn't know you'd want to talk to me so quickly."

"The constable gave me his version of events, but I wanted to hear them from you."

Fenella nodded and then unlocked her door. Katie began to shout at them as soon as the lights went on.

"Is she okay?" Daniel asked.

"I hope so. She shouldn't be hungry. I fed her before I went out."

Fenella found the kitten in the spare bedroom, tangled up in the blanket that had been neatly folded across the bottom of the bed when Fenella had gone out. "What have you been doing?" she asked the animal as she helped her find her way out from between the folded layers.

"Merrwoow," Katie said sharply before she stalked out of the room with her tail in the air.

Fenella shook out the blanket and then refolded it, ignoring a few small snags that must have been created by tiny kitten claws. When she walked back into the living room, she found Daniel on the couch with Katie on his lap.

"Would you like some coffee or something?" she offered.

"I don't want you to go to any trouble, but a cold drink would be nice."

Fenella thought about making coffee anyway as she walked into the kitchen, but then decided that cold drinks were enough work for tonight. She dumped a few cookies onto a plate and then carried that and the drinks into the living room. Daniel took a cookie and ate it before he spoke.

"I shouldn't really be here," he sighed. "We're doing everything strictly by the book this time."

"So why are you here?"

"Because I don't want to conduct another formal interview with you, not tonight, and not about your meeting with Autumn. What I want is for you to tell me about the meeting in your own words, but more importantly, I want your thoughts and impressions. You've helped me solve cases in the past. You have good instincts for this sort of thing. I can't get that from a formal interview at the station."

Fenella nodded. "Autumn arrived a few minutes after Breesha and I got there," she began. It didn't take her long to repeat what she could remember of the conversation she'd had with Rosemary's youngest child.

"What did she want?" Daniel asked when she was done.

"I wish I knew. As I said to Breesha, I felt as if she was getting ready to ask for money when I mentioned Joe. Maybe if I hadn't said anything about him, she would have told me what she wanted."

"Maybe, but then she was interrupted by the news that her father was on the island. I wonder why he's here."

"Can't you ask him that? Surely you have every right to interview the man."

"I do, and I will be trying to interview him as soon as I can. I just have to find him first."

"If he's anything like what Autumn suggested, he may well turn up at Doncan's office tomorrow."

"Or on your doorstep."

Fenella sighed. "I hope not. I feel safe and secure up here. I hope no one actually manages to get to my door."

"The security here isn't bad, but it could be better. If anyone from Ms. Ballard's family does show up here, maybe you should consider moving back out to Poppy Drive for a short while."

"It's been rented out."

"Oh, I didn't realize."

"The new people probably haven't moved in yet, but Doncan said it was snatched up really quickly when it went back on the market. Apparently it's a very desirable location."

Daniel shrugged. "I like living there, but I'm starting to look for something else, actually."

"You are?"

"I don't know what I was thinking when I bought that house, really. I don't need four bedrooms or two bathrooms. I live alone, after all. It was the sort of house that I'd always imagined living in one day, but in my dreams I always had a wife and some adorable children, too. I think it's time to give up on those dreams and focus on reality."

Fenella swallowed a dozen different replies. "Are you planning to stay in Douglas?"

"I think so. It's convenient for work, although I'd consider Onchan as well, as it's much the same thing."

"Maybe you should look at some apartments."

"That was my thought. It would be nice not to have to worry about a garden all summer long. Last year I was always worried that the neighbors were going to complain because I never had time to cut my grass properly. I don't know that I can afford anything in this building, but if I can get something on the promenade, I think I'd really enjoy the views."

"The views are spectacular," Fenella agreed, glancing out the floor-to-ceiling windows that showcased the sea just beyond the promenade. She felt spoiled as she watched the waves washing up on the shore. People all over the world longed for the view that she knew she sometimes took for granted.

"I've been offered another job," he told her, his eyes on the water.

"With another police department elsewhere?" she asked.

"No, with a private company here on the island. They want to have their own department to handle internal investigations. They aren't trying to get around involving the police in criminal matters, they just want their own expert to deal with the police and conduct separate investigations as needed."

"I didn't realize private companies hired people like that."

"It's becoming more common as police resources are increasingly stretched. The thing is, it pays well and the hours would be steady, at least most of the time."

"But?"

Daniel chuckled. "What makes you think there's a but?"

"If there wasn't, you'd be telling me about your new job."

He nodded. "That's why I like talking about cases with you. You understand people. The thing is, I love what I do and I don't know that I'd love doing what they're proposing. Investigating murders is horrible in a way, but it's also fascinating and challenging. I'm not sure that watching shop assistants to make sure they aren't slipping money out of the tills will generate the same level of job satisfaction."

"Have you made a list of pros and cons?"

He shook his head. "Right now I'm focused on Rosemary Ballad's murder. There's a part of me that's hoping that by the time I get that solved, the company will have offered the job to someone else."

"If that's what you're thinking, then you have your answer."

"I know, but I keep thinking about the money."

"Do you need more money?"

"Need? Probably not. I make enough to pay my bills, and some months I have a little bit left over. I have a fairly new car and I'm making my mortgage payments every month. This isn't about need as much as greed," he said with a rueful laugh. "I just keep thinking of all of the wonderful holidays I could have if I were making twice as much money. I could spend my time off work in the Bahamas or seeing America. It's tempting."

"You get what, seven weeks of vacation a year?" she asked.

"That's standard, but they've offered me ten," he told her.

"That leaves forty-two weeks of the year where you'll be doing a job you don't think you'll like. Even with time off for Christmas and whatever, that's a lot of time where you might be miserable."

He nodded. "I think I need to give the whole thing a lot more thought. I didn't come here tonight to talk about that, though. I wanted to hear about your meeting with Autumn. Tell me your impression of her for a start."

"She doesn't seem to think that Peter Ballard is really her father," Fenella said thoughtfully. "In spite of what she said about researching her family history, she didn't say anything about trying to find her real father, though."

"That's interesting. It may not have anything to do with Rosemary's murder, but it's interesting."

"Maybe Autumn's real father lives on the island," Mona suggested as she appeared in a chair. "Maybe Rosemary rang him when they arrived on the island and suggested a meeting. Maybe he killed her so that he doesn't have to take responsibility for Autumn."

Maybe you have an overactive imagination, Fenella thought.

"Just tell Daniel what I said," Mona told her. "It's another possibility."

Fenella took a sip of her drink before she tried to put Mona's idea into words that sounded like less of a leap away from reality. "Is it possible that Autumn's father is on the island?" she asked. "I mean, the man who is really her father, not Peter Ballard. Maybe, while she was here, Rosemary rang him up and suggested a meeting."

Daniel glanced over at her and then shrugged. "Anything is possible. I'm going to have to have another chat with Autumn. Her birth certificate has Peter Ballard's name on it, but that proves nothing, of course."

"I wonder if she'd be willing to take a DNA test," Fenella said. "When we spoke, she seemed quite matter-of-fact about her questionable parentage, but she also didn't seem interested in proving things either way."

"Unless we can find some evidence to suggest that the identity of her father has something to do with Rosemary's murder, I can't see requesting a DNA test from her."

"I'd want to know, especially considering that Peter Ballard left them all those years ago. I can't imagine she'd be heartbroken to learn that he isn't really any relation of hers."

"Maybe one day she'll decide to find out. At the moment, I can't see how it ties into Rosemary's murder, though."

"Unless Autumn's father killed Rosemary," Mona said loudly. "He needs to find Autumn's father and make sure he isn't involved."

"I don't know how you'd go about finding the man, if he even exists," Fenella said thoughtfully. "Maybe Rosemary left the information for her daughter to find after her death."

"We're still trying to track down the safe deposit box that everyone seems to think she had somewhere. There wasn't a key for one on the key ring that was in her pocket when she died."

"She may have lied about the box. She wanted me to think that the letters were locked away somewhere where I couldn't get to them."

"But she may have just had them with her in her hotel room."

"She couldn't have been that stupid. If she was right about the contents, those letters were potentially worth millions of doll, er, pounds. Surely she'd have left them at home, even if she didn't lock them away anywhere."

"The police in London have searched her flat thoroughly. They didn't find any letters or any keys."

"Somewhere in her flat there must be a hidden compartment in a desk, or a safe behind a picture or something," Fenella said. "The police just haven't found it yet."

Daniel shrugged. "I may have them search again. Obviously, we're going through her hotel room very carefully. I'm hoping one of her children might have some other suggestions for places to look."

"Unless one of them killed her and took the letters," Fenella suggested.

"They were all together that morning." Daniel shook his head and got to his feet. "I can't talk about the case with you," he said, sounding frustrated. "Whether I like it or not, you're a suspect this time, and at the moment, one of very few suspects. I shouldn't have come here, but it was a very long day and I really wanted to see you."

Fenella stood up and walked over to him. "I'm glad you came," she said softly. "I understand why you can't talk about the case, but we can talk about other things."

He looked at her for a minute and then pulled her into an embrace. The kiss was short, but it reminded Fenella that there was powerful chemistry between her and Daniel. When he let her go, he stepped away and headed for the door.

"I'll ring you soon," he said as she followed behind him. "Once the case is solved, I'd like to buy you dinner so we can talk. I'd really like your thoughts on my job offer and some other things, but I can't think about them until Rosemary Ballard's killer is behind bars."

Fenella nodded. "I'll call you if I hear anything else relating to the case. With my luck, I'll be hearing a lot."

Daniel chuckled. "You do seem to have a knack for finding yourself at the center of things. In this case, you truly are central to everything." He opened the door and stepped through it. "Be careful," he told her from the doorway. "I worry about you."

"I'll be fine," Fenella assured him before she shut her door. She made sure it was locked and then sat back down next to Katie. "I'll sleep better when Rosemary's killer is behind bars," she told the animal.

Katie jumped into her lap and began to purr as Fenella petted her.

"You shouldn't worry about the killer coming after you," Mona said. "He or she won't want anything to happen to you until you've given the family some of my money."

"Maybe the killer will decide that it would be easier to deal with my heirs," Fenella suggested.

Mona frowned. "What a horrible idea. Who's going to get my flat when you die?"

"That's for my brothers to decide. I've left everything to them in equal portions, but they'll have to decide amongst themselves how they'll divide what they'll inherit."

"They're all older than you, though. What happens if they all die before you?"

"Then the next generation will inherit. Who knows, maybe one of Joseph's daughters will decide to come and live on the island one day. I suppose that could happen."

Whatever Mona was going to say next was interrupted by the telephone.

"Fenella, I'm sorry to be ringing so late, but I didn't want to have to wake you in the morning," Doncan said when she answered. "We need to meet again tomorrow, at eight, if you can manage it."

"Eight?" she repeated, glancing at the clock. "I suppose I can do that."

"I've just been speaking to a London solicitor," Doncan explained. "He's going to be at my office at nine with Peter Ballard. From what the solicitor said, Mr. Ballard is on the island to protect the interests of his children."

"That's lovely, especially as he hasn't been interested in them for the last thirty-five years or more."

"Yes, well, that's between the children and their father. My job is to protect your interests. I still don't think we have anything to worry about, but I get the impression that Mr. Ballard is considering suing just about everyone."

"It might be interesting if he sues Max's sister," Fenella replied. "I suspect she'll quickly reverse her 'welcome to the family' position."

Doncan chuckled. "I have to admit that I'm rather looking forward to watching what happens there. Max's sister's advocate and I have never had a very productive relationship. I won't mind seeing him suffer a little bit over all of this."

"I'll see you at eight, then," Fenella said before she put the phone down.

"Interesting," Mona said. "I wonder if Mr. Ballard's children are aware that he's representing their interests now."

"Autumn wasn't at all happy to learn that he was here. I can't see her agreeing to letting him act on her behalf."

"From what you've told me of Mr. Malone, I can't see him agreeing, either, but then, he didn't ask the others before he started claiming to be acting for them, so he shouldn't really complain."

"If things keep up like this, they're all going to end up suing me individually and I'll have to defend myself in six or seven different court cases."

"It won't come to that," Mona said confidently. "Once Max's sister gets word that someone might be suing her, she'll put an end to her little charade. Maybe she didn't have Rosemary killed. The murder does seem to be spoiling her scheme. It must have been one of Rosemary's children or their spouses, then, but which one?"

"You sit up and try to work it out. I'm going to bed."

Fenella put Katie on the floor and headed for her room. The small animal dashed around her and was already curled up in the center of the bed before Fenella had finished switching off lights and shutting doors on her way to the bedroom.

With her face washed and her teeth brushed, she crawled into bed next to the kitten and fell into a restless sleep. The alarm at six-thirty the next morning startled both of them.

"Merrooww," Katie complained, burying her head under her paws.

"I know, but I need to look as good as possible today. Mr. Ballard is bringing in a London solicitor."

"Maybe you should wear some of your own clothes," Mona suggested a short time later as Fenella began flipping through Mona's wardrobe. "That way you'd look poor, practically homeless," she added.

Fenella made a face at her and then went back to her search. "I don't want to look as if I've made an effort," she sighed as she pulled out and rejected three different outfits in a row. "I just want to look effortlessly fabulous."

Mona chuckled. "It isn't that difficult. Try the burgundy dress in the back."

At first glance, the dress looked too dark and almost matronly for Fenella's taste. "I can't believe you ever wore this," she said to Mona as she held the dress up in front of herself. "It's modest, demure, almost boring."

"Try it on," Mona suggested. "It looks much better on than it does on a hanger."

Fenella slipped into the dress and then blinked at herself in the mirror. Mona was right: Fenella's curves made the dress much more interesting.

"It's almost sexy," she said softly.

"But it isn't quite," Mona laughed. "That's what makes it so perfect. It's glamorous, but it shouldn't be. It covers everything demurely but still manages to be sexy, or nearly sexy. I used to wear it to business meetings and I always got my way."

Fenella twirled slowly in front of the mirror. "I can see why," she said. "I love this dress."

She twisted her hair into a large clip and then applied her makeup under direction from her aunt. "I look wonderful," she sighed when they were done. "It's all going to be wasted on solicitors and men who want my money."

"It won't be wasted. You'll have Peter Ballard and his solicitor hanging on your every word."

"Unless his solicitor is a woman."

"It won't be. He won't be the type to think that women can handle difficult negotiations."

Fenella didn't bother to argue with Mona. Instead, she put what she thought she might need in the handbag that matched the dress and headed for the door.

"Wish me luck," she muttered.

"You don't need luck. You have Doncan on your side."

Fenella nodded. She was worried, but she had complete confidence in Doncan. If anyone could get her out of this mess with her fortune still intact, it was Doncan. Her heels click-clacked along the sidewalk as she headed for his office. The noise made her smile in spite of her nerves.

"Ms. Woods, going to see your advocate, are you?" a loud voice called when she was only a few hundred yards away from Doncan's office. "I reckon you're going to need him and someone who specializes in criminal cases, aren't you?"

Fenella bit her tongue and kept walking. There was no way Dan Ross from the *Isle of Man Times* was going to get her to say something he could use to sell newspapers.

"Do you feel guilty having money that was paid out due to blackmail?" he shouted.

She felt her cheeks flame, but didn't reply.

"I'm sure Mona would have been devastated if she'd known about Maxwell's daughter. She always thought she was the only woman in his life," Dan said.

When Fenella didn't reply, he continued. "If I were you, I'd have done just about anything to get rid of the woman. I suppose you were just lucky someone else wanted her out of the way, too."

The doors to the office building were locked. Fenella pulled on one and then another, trying to get inside. It wasn't easy, but she forced herself to do it as casually as she could, trying to avoid letting Dan know how much he was upsetting her.

"It's odd, though, really, how many murder investigations you've been mixed up in since you moved to the island. Maybe I should ring back to Buffalo, New York, and see what the police there have to say about you. I'm not suggesting that you've actually killed anyone, of course, but you do seem to find more than your fair share of dead bodies," Dan added.

"Go away," Breesha said from behind Fenella. "Stop harassing our client or we'll file a formal complaint with the paper."

"I'm just asking her a few questions. She's spent enough time with the police. She ought to be good at answering questions," Dan replied.

"They have a right to ask her things. You do not," Breesha said sternly. "Now go away. I'm sure there must be a kitten in a tree somewhere about which you can write a story."

Dan opened his mouth and then snapped it shut again. He glared at Breesha for a moment and then turned on his heel and stomped away.

"What a horrible man," Breesha said softly before she turned to Fenella. "I'm terribly sorry I wasn't here when you arrived. I popped to the shops for a few things. I thought I'd be back in plenty of time."

"It's fine," Fenella replied. "I'm just glad you arrived when you did. I don't know that I could have kept my mouth shut for much longer."

Breesha unlocked the door and then ushered Fenella into the building. "Doncan will be with you in a minute," she said as she led Fenella into the small reception area. "I'm going to put the kettle on. Would you prefer tea or coffee?"

"Coffee," Fenella replied. "I think I'm going to need a lot of it today."

Breesha nodded. "I'll get some biscuits, too. Today, I think we need the chocolate ones."

Fenella nodded and then sank down into the nearest chair. It had already been a long day and it wasn't quite eight o'clock yet.

❧ 10 ❧

"I wasn't naïve enough to think that Rosemary's family would just go away quietly after her death," Fenella sighed. She took a sip of her coffee and sat back in the chair in Doncan's office. "I wasn't expecting to get sued by everyone separately, though."

Doncan shrugged. "So far, you aren't actually being sued by anyone. At the moment, everyone is just making a lot of noise. When they don't get the quick out-of-court settlement they're hoping for, they'll have to decide whether they actually want to pursue a lawsuit or not."

"I'm not giving anyone any money," Fenella said firmly.

"Understood. I'm going to push for copies of the letters and a DNA test. As far as I'm concerned, there really isn't anything to discuss until we have both of those things."

"What if Max's sister truly is behind all of this? Could she fake the results of the DNA test to make it appear that Rosemary was Max's daughter, even if she wasn't?"

"I'm afraid I don't know enough about how the tests work, but I imagine it might be possible. If she is behind all of this, though, she might be feeling less cooperative now that Peter Ballard and Joe Malone are both talking about suing her, too."

"I'd feel better about the whole thing if the police would arrest someone for Rosemary's murder," Fenella said. "It must have been one of her children or their spouses that killed her, mustn't it?"

"That's for Inspector Robinson and Inspector Hammersmith to work out. I understand they were all together that morning, but I don't know the details of their alibis."

"They were the only people on the island who actually knew Rosemary, though. I'm sure I look like the most likely suspect, but I know I didn't kill her. It must have been one of them. I'll pick Joe Malone, as he seems the most eager to get his hands on some money now that Rosemary is dead."

"I suggested to Inspector Robinson that it might be useful to work out where Peter Ballard was the day of the murder," Doncan said. "He seems to have turned up here very quickly after his former wife's death. That suggests that he knew something about her whereabouts, although I could be wrong about that. It will be interesting to see what he has to say about that this morning."

The pair chatted a bit more about nothing much. Doncan politely refused to be drawn into a discussion about who might have killed Rosemary. Instead, he steered the conversation around to some of Fenella's investments, inviting her to consider whether she might like to move any of her money around or if she preferred to leave it all where it was currently invested.

"You know I have total faith in you," Fenella said after reviewing the long list of companies in which she held shares. "If you think it's time to move some money around, you go for it. Let me know if I start to run out of funds."

Doncan laughed. "I'd have to criminally mismanage your accounts in order to run you out of money. I just want to maximize your earnings whenever I possibly can."

"As far as I'm concerned, you're doing a brilliant job. I was thinking I might want to start looking at the various properties I own, though. It might be time to sell a few. I don't feel the need to own farms and houses and whatever else I have."

"We can go through your property whenever it's convenient for you. If you'd like, I'll clear a day on my calendar and we can go and visit every single one. Actually, thinking about it, we might need to do it over two days. There are quite a lot of them."

"Let's get through today and whatever comes out of today first," Fenella sighed. "Once everything is settled with Ms. Ballard's family, I'd love to go around the island and see everything that's mine."

Doncan made a few notes on a pad on his desk. "I'll make certain..."

He was interrupted by a knock on the door. Breesha stuck her head around it a moment later.

"Mr. Ballard and his solicitor are in the conference room," she said.

"Very good. Thank you," Doncan replied. He got to his feet and offered Fenella his arm. "Let's go and see what they have to say, shall we?"

Fenella made a face and then stood up and took the arm. When they walked into the conference room a moment later, the two men at the table were whispering together. They stopped and both got to their feet as the door shut behind Doncan and Fenella.

"Ms. Woods? I'm James Diedrich. I'm acting on behalf of Mr. Peter Ballard, in the interests of his children," the taller of the two men said. He held out a hand.

Fenella shook it while mentally pricing the man's suit. Having helped her former boyfriend, Jack, buy suits for many years, she recognized good quality and expert tailoring when she saw it. In contrast, Peter Ballard was wearing a suit that had clearly been bought off the rack and never altered. The sleeves of the jacket were too short and the trousers were too long. The fabric was poor quality, and as Fenella shook Peter's hand, she could see where a seam was coming undone on the jacket.

"It's nice to meet you, Mr. Diedrich, Mr. Ballard," Fenella said.

"Let's not be formal," the solicitor said. "We're hoping for a friendly resolution to everything, after all."

Doncan held a chair for Fenella and she slid into it. The other two men both declined coffee, but Doncan poured cups for himself and Fenella from the pot in the corner before he sat down next to her.

By the time she'd taken her first sip, Fenella had decided that James was far too slick for her taste and that Peter was very nervous.

"Obviously, this is a distressing time for my client," the solicitor began.

"As I understand it, he and Ms. Ballard were divorced over thirty-five years ago," Doncan said.

"Yes, of course, but that doesn't mean he isn't concerned about how the death is affecting his children," James replied.

"Children whom he hadn't seen in over thirty-five years," Doncan added.

Peter flushed. "It was difficult. Rosemary and I had a complicated relationship and, well, I ended up leaving her and the children, something that I regret very much now."

Especially since the children might be in line for some money now, Fenella thought.

"Let's hope this tragedy can bring you all back together again, then," Doncan said.

"It's already doing just that," Peter told him. "I've offered to act in their interests with you and I'm paying for the solicitor out of my own pocket, simply for their benefit."

Doncan nodded. "And they've all agreed, in writing, that whatever agreement you reach with us will be legally binding?"

Peter glanced at James and then shrugged. "Not exactly, that is, not yet. We're still working out the terms, but we'll get there. I'm certain of that."

Doncan sat back in his seat. "Why don't you come and see us again once you've obtained some sort of legal agreement with all three of your children," he suggested.

"We have a number of other things to discuss," James said. "We want some sort of guarantee from you that your client won't attempt to leave the country with money that should belong to my client's children."

Doncan chuckled. "My client is free to live her life as she pleases. If she decides to leave the island, that's her business and no one else's. You've done nothing to this point to suggest that she's in possession of funds that should belong to your client's children."

"Funds obtained through illegal methods are subject to confiscation by the government," James said tightly.

"Fenella inherited her money. There's nothing illegal about that," Doncan replied.

"But the money that she inherited was obtained through blackmail," James snapped. "If I were her, I'd be ashamed to spend it."

Doncan sighed. "I assume you have proof to back up that claim, but you've still no right to pass judgment on my client in that manner."

"We're working on obtaining proof," the solicitor said. "We know that my client's former wife, Rosemary Ballard, had letters in her possession that provide irrefutable evidence of blackmail on the part of Mona Kelly. My associates are working towards locating those letters as we speak."

"Rosemary Ballard made a great many claims," Doncan told him. "I suggest you take care when using phrases like 'irrefutable evidence' until you've actually seen the letters yourself. I would suggest, if Maxwell Martin was cheating on Mona Kelly, that he might have been less than totally truthful with his mistress about the nature of his relationship with Ms. Kelly."

"Is that how you're going to defend this?" James demanded. "By suggesting that Maxwell Martin was simply lying in all of his letters?"

"At the moment, I have nothing to defend," Doncan replied. "If and when you actually produce letters of some sort, then I'll have something with which to work. The first job would be determining if they were actually written by Maxwell Martin or are forgeries. I'd want to do that before I'd worry about anything else."

James nodded. "We'll have copies of the letters by the end of the week," he said confidently. "His daughter knows where they were being kept."

"I'm looking forward to seeing them," Doncan said.

"Once you've seen them, I believe you'll be eager to make some sort of settlement offer," James said. "In the interest in saving my client both time and money, I'm going to give you the opportunity to make that offer today. Obviously, it would be contingent on all three of Ms. Ballard's children agreeing to the terms."

"You can't seriously be expecting us to make a settlement based solely on the threat of letters that may or may not exist," Doncan replied. "There's also the matter of proving Ms. Ballard's parentage. If

Ms. Ballard was not actually Maxwell Martin's child, we have nothing further to discuss."

"We have been in touch with Mrs. Martin-Hardcastle. She is not interested in taking a DNA test at this time," James told him.

Doncan looked at Fenella. "Max's sister," he explained.

"If she refuses, I believe the courts will rule in favor of my client," James continued. "Her refusal will be seen as admitting that Rosemary was indeed her brother's child."

"Surely you would be better off suing her," Fenella said. "If she's admitted that Rosemary was Maxwell's child, Rosemary should be entitled to a share of the man's estate."

"I can assure you that we are looking into that," James said. "That is a separate matter, though, to what we're trying to do here."

"Look," Peter blurted out. "All I want is some money for my kids, that's all. I wasn't there for them growing up, and that's my own fault. I was stupid and let my feelings for Rosemary get in the way of what I knew was right. Whatever, I can't erase the past, but I want to do what I can in the future to help them. Getting them a fair settlement from you would go a long way towards accomplishing that. James told me that you inherited many millions of pounds from your aunt. Surely you can afford to give my kids a million each. That seems a fair settlement, doesn't it?"

He looked plaintively at Fenella, who sighed.

"Mr. Ballard," she began.

"Please, call me Peter," he interrupted.

"Peter, then, if everything you're saying about Maxwell Martin and Mona Kelly is true, then you may be right. Your children probably should be entitled to some money from Maxwell's fortune, either from his estate directly or from Mona's. The problem at the moment is that you haven't provided any proof of anything that has been claimed. Rosemary Ballard could have read about Maxwell and Mona some-where and dreamt up the whole scheme to try to defraud me out of a great deal of money."

Peter nodded. "I'm sure you have to deal with this sort of thing all the time, but this is different. Rosemary always talked about wanting to know more about her father, but when we were together, it was all dreams, you know? Her mum wouldn't ever tell her anything. She wouldn't answer any questions at all. It used to make Rosemary crazy, and then, well, we got married and had our kids and Rosemary seemed to forget about her father for a while. Her mum died and I thought that was the end of it, really. I hadn't seen Rosemary in years, but I can just imagine how excited and happy she must have been when she finally discovered the truth about her father."

"If it actually is the truth," Fenella said gently.

Peter shrugged. "She'd never have gone to all this trouble otherwise."

"There's a great deal of money potentially at stake," Fenella reminded him. "She asked me for five million pounds."

Peter gasped and looked at James, who shook his head.

"Of course, she wasn't planning on going after Max's sister. She told us that she was happy just being welcomed into the family by Mrs. Martin-Hardcastle," Fenella added.

Doncan's phone buzzed. He glanced at it and then rose to his feet. "I'm sure you'll understand that Ms. Woods and I both have other things to attend to this morning. Please ring for another appointment once you have written agreement from all three of Ms. Ballard's children for your acting on their behalf, copies of the letters that Ms. Ballard claimed to have, and absolute proof that Ms. Ballard was indeed Maxwell Martin's daughter. I believe we'll be able to have a much more productive discussion when those things are in place."

James stood up and held out a hand to Doncan and then to Fenella. "We'll get them, and soon," he said in a tone that sounded slightly threatening to Fenella. "You'd have been much better off making a settlement today. I'm going to do some more checking into exactly how much Ms. Woods inherited so that we can better determine our demands going forward."

"You do that," Doncan told him. "Good luck."

James blinked and then looked over at Peter. "Come on, then," he snapped.

"Ms. Woods, let's work this out," Peter said. "I don't want to have to sue you."

"We're still a long way from a lawsuit," Doncan replied before

Fenella could speak. "As I said, we'll be open to discussing a settlement once you have those three things in order."

Peter looked as if he wanted to argue further, but his solicitor grabbed his arm and pulled him toward the door.

"Ring my assistant when you're ready," Doncan reminded them cheerfully as James opened the door and rushed Peter through it.

James glanced back and nodded before the door swung shut behind them.

"That was fascinating," Doncan said as he sat back in his chair. "I'm going to have to find out more about James Diedrich. I'm surprised any solicitor, especially one who looked so successful, would come in here expecting a quick settlement based on nothing."

"I didn't like him," Fenella said.

"No, he wasn't very likable. He wasn't very good at his job, either. I wonder where Peter found him and how he's paying him."

"Maybe James has taken the case on a contingency basis."

"If he has, he's a bigger fool than I thought. He may know something we don't, of course, but I can't imagine what that something might be."

"Maybe he's seen the letters."

"He didn't seem all that confident that the letters will be found, though. It's all very curious." Doncan's phone buzzed again. He checked it and then sighed. "And it gets even more curious. Joe Malone and Matthew Ballard are here, demanding to see me."

"Can you refuse?"

"Of course I can, but what fun would that be?" Doncan asked, laughing. "Do you want to stay or should I sneak you out the back door before I have Breesha bring them in."

"I'll stay. I can't imagine what they want."

"I can imagine a dozen things, but I could be wrong on all counts," Doncan replied. A moment later, there was a knock on the door.

"Mr. Malone and Mr. Ballard," Breesha announced before stepping back to let the two men into the room.

"Coffee, gentlemen?" Doncan asked.

The men exchanged glances and then they both shook their heads.

"Have a seat," Doncan suggested. "Ms. Woods and I were having a meeting, but she agreed to take a break for your visit. I assume you're here in relation to matters that pertain to her as well, but if not, she can wait elsewhere while we talk."

Matthew dropped into a chair and looked at Joe.

"It concerns her," Joe said as he sat down next to his brother-in-law. "We want to know what sort of agreement you reached with Peter Ballard."

"What makes you think we've reached any agreement with Peter Ballard?" Doncan countered.

"He was here this morning," Matthew snapped. "He told us he was coming at nine and that we were to stay well away. He said he'd get us a better settlement than what we could get on our own because he'd brought in some fancy solicitor from London."

"Perhaps you should ask him what was agreed, then," Doncan suggested.

"We're asking you," Joe said angrily. "The settlement concerns all of us, after all. He had no right to negotiate without our agreement."

"That's one of the things I told him, actually," Doncan replied. "I told him that if he wanted to negotiate on behalf of his children, then he needed a signed agreement from all three of them."

"Or both of them," Matthew muttered.

"Both?" Doncan repeated.

"We said before that we don't know who Autumn's father is, but we're pretty sure it isn't Peter Ballard," Matthew said.

"I can't see how that matters in terms of any settlements," Joe said. "What matters for that is who her mother was, not her father."

"So you didn't reach any agreement with Peter about the money?" Joe demanded.

Doncan sighed. "As I said, I told him that I won't negotiate with him on behalf of his children without signed consent from all of them confirming their agreement. Would I be correct in assuming that you aren't interested in having Mr. Diedrich negotiate on your behalf, Mr. Ballard?"

"You can say that again," Matthew barked. "He may biologically be my father, but he wasn't in my life from the time I was five until yesterday. He's just after some share of the money, that's all."

"Does April feel the same way?" Doncan asked Joe.

"April wants me doing the negotiating on her behalf. As her husband, I don't think I need written agreement of that, do I?" he asked with a smirk.

"Actually, I'd prefer to deal directly with the three children, rather than anyone else," Doncan said. "I'll repeat what I told Mr. Ballard and his solicitor. We aren't talking about a settlement in any way until we have copies of the letters and proof that Ms. Ballard truly was Mr. Martin's biological daughter. Once I've been provided with both of those things, we'll be in a position to discuss a settlement or to defend a lawsuit, whichever seems most expedient."

"Surely it would easier to just settle now," Matthew suggested.

Doncan chuckled. "That suggestion is getting old. There's no way we're doing anything without the proof I've detailed. If that's all for today, Ms. Woods and I have other things to discuss."

The two men exchanged glances and then slowly got to their feet. "You won't talk to my father again?" Matthew asked as they walked toward the door.

"I've told him what he needs to arrange before I'll meet with him again," Doncan replied. "If he comes back with those things, I'll meet with him. Otherwise, I don't believe we have anything to discuss."

"If he brings you anything with my signature on it, it's been forged," Matthew snapped. "I wouldn't sign a birthday card for that man."

He walked out of the room, with Joe on his heels. Doncan sat back in his chair.

"Fascinating," he said. "I wonder where Autumn and her husband are in all of this."

"Perhaps she'll call me again," Fenella said. "We were interrupted the other night, after all."

"If she does, I don't want you to meet with her," Doncan said seriously. "There's too much infighting going on right now. I don't want you caught up at the center of it all. Let the siblings fight it out with their father and his solicitor. We'll sit back and wait to see what happens next."

"They don't seem organized enough to sue anyone," Fenella suggested.

"Which is in our favor, assuming it stays that way," Doncan said. "The longer they go on fighting one another, the better, as far as I'm concerned."

"Let's hope they start fighting with Max's sister, too."

"After all of our shared history, it's difficult for me to imagine being on the same side of an issue as Max's sister's solicitors, but in this instance it may come to that."

"Was there anything else?" Fenella asked.

Doncan shook his head. "I want you to stay away from all of them, if you can. I know it's a small island, and you may well bump into any one of them in a shop or pub or something, but please do your best to keep out of their way for the moment. If you do find yourself speaking with any of them, please be very careful what you say and ring me if you possibly can."

"Maybe I should go away for a few days," Fenella sighed. "I could spend half my fortune on an exotic vacation somewhere."

"I don't believe the police want you to leave the island at the moment."

"Oh, yeah, I forgot about that. I'm a bit stuck, really."

"I'm sure Inspector Robinson is doing everything in his power to solve Ms. Ballard's murder. That may make a big difference in everything."

Doncan escorted Fenella to the building's front door. She paused for a minute, looking up and down the street for Dan Ross. When she didn't see him anywhere, she walked out and impulsively turned away from home. A nice brisk walk was just what she needed to clear her head, she thought as she crossed the road and began to stroll along the wide promenade. A moment later she heard her name being called.

"Fenella? My goodness, I've been waving and shouting your name since you walked out of Mr. Quayle's office," Shelly said when she reached Fenella's side. "You looked right through me at least twice."

"I was looking for Dan Ross," Fenella explained. "He chased me down the street this morning, trying to get me to say something stupid for his front page."

Shelly made a face. "He's a horrid man," she said. "If there were any other way to get all the local news, I'd stop buying the local paper because of him."

Fenella laughed. "I never thought about it, but you're right. We could all refuse to buy the paper until they fired Dan Ross, but then we'd have no idea what was going on around here."

Shelly fell into step with Fenella. "How are the party plans coming?" she asked.

"I haven't really been giving the party much thought, not with the murder and all of these lawsuits hanging over my head."

"I thought maybe, with Rosemary dead, the lawsuit idea would just go away."

"I wish. Sadly, it seems that Rosemary's children are still planning to sue me, and her ex-husband is on the island now, sticking his nose in as well."

"My goodness, you do have a complicated life, don't you?"

Fenella chuckled. "My life was perfectly boring and completely ordinary until I moved to the island. I believe it's Mona who had the complicated life. I'm just dealing with the aftermath."

"You can't blame all of the murder investigations you've been involved with on Mona," Shelly protested.

"No, but I can blame the current mess on her. She was the one who was involved with Max for all those years. Who knows, maybe he really did cheat on her. Maybe there are dozens of children out there who are going to start turning up on my doorstep every month or something."

"I can't imagine that. As I said, I never knew Mona when Max was alive, but I knew their story. There was plenty of gossip about the pair of them, let me tell you, and I never once heard anyone suggest that Max was unfaithful. I know Rosemary claims that Max and her mother had their affair in London, but it just doesn't ring true for me."

"I hope you're right."

"If he did have an affair, I think he would have told Mona, anyway," Shelly added, "and no matter what's in the letters that Rosemary has, there's no way I'll believe that she only got things from him through blackmail. Mona was a complicated woman, but she would never have done something like that."

"Again, I hope you're right."

They turned around at the end of the promenade and walked slowly back toward their building. "How's Tim?" Fenella asked.

Shelly blushed. "He's good," she said. "We've been spending a lot of time together. I'm almost afraid to say that things are going really well, because I'm afraid that will spoil it all, but things are going really well."

"Have you spoken to Gordon lately?"

Some months earlier, Shelly had been spending time with Gordon Davison, a man she'd known for many years, who had been friends with both Shelly and her husband, John. They'd gone out frequently, but Shelly had never been certain whether Gordon was interested in taking things beyond friendship or not. Gordon had been traveling frequently for work when Shelly had met Tim, and as far as Fenella knew, Shelly hadn't really spoken to him since he'd been back on the island.

"I bumped into him in ShopFast, actually," Shelly said. "Tim and I were together and we were holding hands when I spotted Gordon. I'm afraid I blushed and stammered and couldn't even properly introduce the two, but Gordon didn't seem at all bothered."

"So maybe he truly did just want to be friends all along."

"I suppose so, which worked out well in the end, even if it is something of a blow to my ego," Shelly chuckled.

"You're happier with Tim, right?"

"I'm much happier with Tim, actually. He makes me feel like a teenager falling in love for the first time again."

"I'm so happy for you."

"How are things between you and Daniel?" Shelly asked.

"He's barely speaking to me because I'm the number-one suspect in Rosemary Ballard's murder," Fenella said bitterly.

"I don't believe that."

"Arguably, I had the best motive. Anyway, he has to be careful not to be seen to be friendly with murder suspects. I understand, but it's, well, it's difficult."

"What about Donald?"

Fenella laughed. "He's bringing a date to Mona's party. She's one of his daughter's nurses, apparently, and he told me he's only bringing her to thank her for her hard work, but the way he talked about her makes me think there's a good deal more to it than that."

"Are you okay?" Shelly asked.

"I'm fine. Donald and I were only ever having fun together. He wasn't the sort of man I could get serious about, really."

Shelly nodded. "I think you and Daniel are much better together."

"Yeah, well, tell Daniel that," Fenella muttered.

"I just might, the next time I see him."

"Oh, goodness, don't do that."

Shelly laughed. "He needs to realize that he can't keep playing with you like this. He told you he cared about you, and then he went away and barely kept in touch. When he came back, he brought that woman back with him, which was stupid. Once she was gone, he dragged you into another cold case, and then dropped you again once you'd solved it for him. What does the man want?"

"I wish I knew. I don't think it's me, though," Fenella said, trying to forget about his visit the previous evening. That visit had suggested that he had feelings for her, anyway. "How's the writing going?" she changed the subject.

"I'm very nearly finished with a very rough first draft," Shelly told her. "I'm excited, but when I think about it, I feel slightly sick, too."

"You're going to let me read it, right?"

"I don't know. Maybe. I need to finish it, and then I need to start over at the beginning and rewrite a lot of it. It's probably going to be months before it will be ready for anyone else to see it."

"Well, you know where I am when you're ready."

The pair had reached Promenade View Apartments. They crossed the lobby and rode the elevator to the sixth floor.

"I know it's not even time for lunch yet, but let's go to the pub tonight," Shelly suggested. "I'm going to work on the book for a few hours and run some errands, but I'll be done with all of that by five or six."

"Want to have dinner together first, then?" Fenella asked.

"Oh, yes, let's," Shelly agreed.

"Let's go to that ridiculously expensive place on the promenade," Fenella suggested. "I'll treat, because I can afford it. If I'm going to get sued and lose my fortune, I want to enjoy my money while I can."

Shelly looked concerned. "Are you sure?"

"I'm very sure. I'm also not worried about the lawsuits, well, not very worried. I have full confidence in Doncan."

"He's very good," Shelly agreed. "Do you want to go out around six?"

"Sure, meet me in the corridor at six," Fenella agreed. "We'll drink too much wine and talk about anything other than Rosemary Ballard and her family."

"That sounds like a plan."

✿ 11 ✿

"Did you make a booking?" Shelly asked as Fenella joined her in the corridor at exactly six o'clock.

"I did," Fenella told her. "Although when I called they told me that they'd always have a table for me, no matter what."

"Is that because you're rich or because of your friendship with Donald?"

"I'm not sure. If it's because of Donald, it may change now that he's found someone else. If it's because of my money, well, that may change if Rosemary Ballard's family get their way."

"They can't get all of Mona's money, can they?"

"I certainly hope not. I'm sure Doncan will fight as hard as he can. They keep suggesting that the courts could confiscate everything, though, if they can prove that all of the money came from criminal activity."

"They'll never prove that because it isn't true," Shelly said firmly. "Let's enjoy dinner and talk about pleasant things."

The line of people waiting for tables stretched out in front of the building. Fenella and Shelly joined the end of the line. The man at the door was as wide as he was tall. He had a Bluetooth headset on and was staring straight ahead through his mirrored sunglasses.

"Do you think we should tell him that we're here?" Shelly whispered to Fenella after a moment. "No one has said a word to him since we arrived. Maybe they've all given him their names already."

Fenella shrugged. "I've no idea how this is supposed to work," she admitted. "I don't usually eat at fancy restaurants. Last time the guy at the door recognized me."

The restaurant door swung open and a tall man in a tuxedo walked out. "That's Ms. Woods," he snapped to the doorman, gesturing toward Fenella and Shelly. "You were told to watch for her."

The doorman glanced at Fenella and then shrugged. "She doesn't look the same as the picture you showed me."

The tuxedoed man frowned and then took a deep breath. He turned to Fenella with a welcoming smile. "My dear Ms. Woods, please come in. I apologize for Jake. He's new and hasn't learned to recognize some of our customers yet."

"It's no problem," Fenella said quickly, not wanting the young man to get into trouble. "I should have told him I was here. We just joined the back of the queue."

The man nodded and then led Fenella and Shelly into the building's cool and dimly lit interior. "I thought you'd like a quiet table in the back. You didn't say if this was a romantic evening or just a friendly dinner."

"It's just friendly," Fenella laughed.

He led them to a small table with an excellent view of the sea. "Did you want to see a wine list or would you prefer some recommendations based on your food selections?"

"Recommendations," the women said together.

A few minutes later the friends had ordered three courses of delicious-sounding food and a bottle of wine they were assured would go with everything. As the waiter walked away, Fenella sat back.

"I think I'm getting too used to being spoiled like this," she sighed. "What if the Ballards do manage to get their hands on all of my money?"

"Then you'll go back to working for a living, like most people," Shelly said. "There are plenty of jobs on the island. Maybe you could teach at the college or work for Manx National Heritage."

"I might like working at the various historical sites," Fenella mused. "They're wonderful to visit and I'd love to learn more about all of them."

"There you are then, the beginnings of a plan. You can't really be worried, though, not with Doncan fighting in your corner. He'll make sure you're okay."

"I know you're right, but sometimes the idea of losing everything terrifies me."

"So let's talk about other things."

Over the next two hours, the pair ate their way through three courses and finished the bottle of wine. They talked about everything from the weather to Tim to a few television programs that they both enjoyed. Fenella was very conscious that she was avoiding any mention of Daniel and the case.

"Everything was delicious," she told the waiter as he cleared away the scraped-clean plates that had held flourless chocolate cake with homemade vanilla bean ice cream.

"I'm glad to hear that," he smiled.

"Just the check, please," Fenella added.

He nodded and then disappeared into the kitchen. A few minutes later the tuxedoed man who'd shown them to their table reappeared.

"Ms. Woods, you know you are always our guest when you are here," he told her. "Mr. Donaldson insists on it."

"I'm going to have a long talk with Donald," she sighed. "He can't keep buying me dinner."

"Well, until I'm told otherwise, we're just going to keep adding your meals to his account," the man said.

Fenella looked at Shelly, who grinned. "I wish I had friends like yours," she said in a low voice.

"Oh, but Mrs. Quirk, you're on a guest list, too," he said. "I believe it was Mr. Hughes who added you to his list. Ms. Woods is on his list, as well, but Mr. Donaldson added her first, so her meals go on his account."

Shelly looked surprised. "Mr. Hughes has a list of people he buys meals for here?"

"Yes, that's right. As I said, you and Ms. Woods are both on his list."

Todd Hughes was a world-famous musician who sometimes played with The Islanders. He and Fenella had gone out a few times, but he traveled a great deal and Fenella was happier staying on the island, at least for the time being. The pair had parted friends, and Fenella wasn't surprised to hear that she was on his list, really.

Shelly looked at Fenella. "Did you know about that?"

Fenella shook her head. "Not at all. You should bring Tim here for dinner sometime."

"I should, at that."

"If Tim is Mr. Blake, then he's also on the list," Shelly was told. "He was here last week with a lovely young woman on Mr. Hughes's tab."

Shelly stared at him for a minute and then nodded slowly. "He must know all about it, then," she said in a low voice.

Fenella grabbed her friend's hand. "Are you okay?" she asked.

"Sure, I'm fine," she replied. "Are we done here?"

"Yes, I think so," Fenella replied. She got to her feet and then helped Shelly stand up. The other woman was a bit unsteady, and Fenella could see tears in her friend's eyes as they headed for the door.

"We're nearly outside," she whispered. "You can have a good cry once we've cleared the line of people waiting for a table."

"I'm not going to cry," Shelly said stoutly. "That would be giving Tim far too much importance in my life."

"But he is important in your life," Fenella argued.

"Are you trying to make me cry?" Shelly challenged.

Fenella chuckled. "Not at all. Cry, don't cry, it's up to you, but know that I'm here for you no matter what you do."

Shelly took a deep breath and then nodded. "I'm not going to cry. Tim and I have never discussed having an exclusive relationship. He's perfectly entitled to take other women out for meals now and then if he chooses."

"And you are entitled to date other men, too," Fenella suggested. "Maybe you should call Gordon."

Shelly shook her head. "I like Gordon as a friend, but that's all. I thought Tim and I were, well, I don't know. I thought we had something special, but clearly I was wrong. I should have realized when he told me he had to work late one night last week, that he wasn't actually working."

"Doesn't he work late sometimes?"

"Maybe, sometimes. I don't know. We don't spend every night together, even when he isn't working." Shelly sighed. "Let's just not talk about it, please."

"Okay, sure, fine," Fenella agreed. "Do you still want to go to the pub?"

"Oh, definitely," Shelly said darkly.

There were a handful of people sitting at the bar at the Tale and Tail, but it was reasonably quiet.

"There's a big group upstairs," the bartender warned them as they got their glasses of wine. "They won't have taken all the tables and chairs, but they might be noisy."

Fenella and Shelly exchanged glances. "Noisy is fine with me," Shelly said with artificial cheer as she headed for the spiral staircase.

Following her, Fenella knew that Shelly was hoping it would be too noisy for them to discuss Tim and what he may or may not have been doing with another woman. As they reached the top of the stairs, Fenella swallowed a gasp of surprise. The entire Ballard family were sitting together in a large irregular circle on one side of the room.

"What's wrong?" Shelly asked as she settled into the first table they reached.

"That's the Ballard family," Fenella whispered.

"Rosemary's kids?" Shelly gasped. "Which one is which?"

Fenella opened her mouth to reply and then realized that April was staring at her. She gave the woman a small wave. April responded by waving back and then gesturing and shouting.

"Come and join us," she called. "There's no reason why we can't all be friends, is there?"

"Millions of reasons," Fenella muttered as she got back to her feet. "I'm supposed to call Doncan if I see any of them," she added to Shelly.

"I'll go downstairs and ring him," Shelly offered. "Then I'll come back up and meet everyone."

Fenella crossed the room and then slid into an empty chair between Autumn and Matthew. "Good evening," she said.

"Your friend didn't want to join us?" April asked.

"She had to make a quick phone call. She'll be right back."

"She had to make a phone call?" Matthew asked. "Is she ringing your solicitor for you?"

Fenella laughed. "Yes, she is," she said, deciding that honesty was the best policy.

Matthew stared at her for a minute and then began to laugh heartily. After a minute the others joined in, all except for Joe.

"If he's coming to join us, I'm leaving," Joe said when the laughter died down. "This was supposed to be a chance to forget all about solicitors and advocates and murder and lawsuits. We were just going to have a few drinks and relax, remember."

"I'm more than happy to forget about solicitors and advocates for a few hours," Fenella told him.

He nodded. "Someone told me you've been involved in murder investigations before. Is that true?"

"Sadly, yes. I've had the misfortune to stumble across a few dead bodies since I've been on the island."

"How long will it take the police to find the killer?" Randy demanded.

"That depends on a hundred different things," Fenella replied.

Shelly rejoined them before anyone else could speak. Fenella quickly introduced her to the others. "This is my next-door neighbor, Shelly Quirk."

Shelly smiled and then nodded at each person in turn as Fenella told her each name.

"What did Doncan say?" Fenella asked when the introductions were done.

Shelly looked surprised. "He's going to be here as soon as he can," she replied.

"He isn't welcome," Joe shouted. "We aren't talking about the lawsuit, anyway. We're going to talk about other things."

"You were telling us how the police solve murder cases," Randy told Fenella.

She shook her head. "I wish I could, but what they do is something of a mystery to me. I'm only ever on the outside looking in."

"They have to consider means, motive, and opportunity," Shelly interjected. "Those are the three keys, at least according to the detective fiction I've read."

"Yeah, I've read some of that stuff, too," April said. "I prefer romance, though. It's more fun than reading about dead people."

Shelly nodded. "I think you're right about that."

"If motive matters, then you must be the number-one suspect," Randy said to Fenella. "If anyone wanted Rosemary dead, it was you."

"Except her death hasn't done me any good at all," Fenella replied. "If anything, it's made things worse because now I'm being threatened by lawsuits from several different people."

"But you didn't know that was going to happen when you killed Rosemary," Joe charged.

Fenella got to her feet. "I'm not going to sit here and be accused of murder," she said calmly. "Have a nice evening."

"Don't go," Autumn said pleadingly. "Ignore Joe. He certainly doesn't speak for all of us. I don't think you had anything to do with Mum's death."

"So who do you think killed her?" April challenged.

"I think she must have disturbed a burglar or something," Autumn shrugged. "Someone probably saw the rest of us leaving and assumed that everyone in our party had gone out. Whoever it was probably intended to go through all of our rooms, taking anything of value, but then they found Mum in her room."

"And killed her?" Viola asked. "You know I love you like a sister, Autumn, but that's a crazy idea. Common burglars don't kill people."

Autumn shook her head. "I just know Fenella didn't do it, no matter what Joe thinks."

Doncan appeared at the top of the stairs and nodded at Fenella as he crossed the room. "Good evening," he said, including everyone at the table in a smile.

"Yeah, you aren't welcome here," Joe snarled. "We're just having a friendly chat about motives and murder."

Doncan glanced around and then pulled an empty chair up to the table. "Don't let me interrupt," he said. "I'll just sit here quietly."

The man glared at Doncan and then shifted his angry look to Fenella. "If you don't want to look guilty, maybe you should stop hiding behind your advocate every chance you get."

"I'm not hiding behind anyone," she replied. "Now, what shall we talk about? How about opportunity? Where were you all that morning?"

"At the Manx Museum," April said, "being bored out of our minds by some woman who wouldn't shut up about rocks and stones and Vikings. It was interminable."

"At least you stuck it out until the end, unlike some people," Autumn said, glancing at Joe.

"I just went outside for a cigarette," Joe replied. "I was only gone for ten minutes."

Autumn shrugged. "You and Randy both need to quit smoking, or at least cut back. You should have been able to get through a few hours without multiple cigarette breaks."

"It was boring," Randy told her. "I would have stayed if there was anything interesting happening."

"Joe didn't even watch the movie," Viola said. "That was the best part of the whole thing."

"Randy fell asleep," Autumn laughed.

"That's why it was the best part for me, too," Randy told her.

Fenella glanced at Doncan. Was it possible that they'd just called the group alibi into question? She was trying to work out the best way to phrase her next question when April began shouting.

"You aren't welcome here either," she said angrily. "Take your fancy solicitor and go back to London where you belong."

Fenella turned and watched as James Diedrich and Peter Ballard crossed the room toward them. She whispered their names to Shelly, who raised her eyebrows.

"April, I understand why you're angry, but please, let's talk," Peter said.

"We'll talk in another thirty-five years," April shot back. "I reckon I'll be ready to speak to you by then.

Peter frowned. "You're having drinks with Ms. Woods and her advocate? That doesn't seem wise."

"If you think we're going to take advice from you, you're crazy," Matthew snapped.

"I understand your anger, but she's on the opposite side of a potential lawsuit. She could use anything you say tonight against you," he replied.

"We aren't going to say anything stupid," Joe told him. "We're just having a nice friendly conversation. We aren't angry at her, anyway, we're angry at her aunt and at Maxwell Martin. She's just a bystander, as it were."

"She's the bystander who got all of the money, though," James said tightly. "You shouldn't be speaking with her without your own advocate or solicitor present."

"You're here," Randy shouted. "You can make sure we keep the conversation light. The weather has been good for February, hasn't it?"

Peter and James exchanged glances. "You've all been drinking," Peter said.

"Newsflash, Daddy," April drawled. "We're all over eighteen now. We're allowed to have a drink in a pub without our father's permission. We don't need Mum's either, which is just as well, all things considered." She swallowed hard and then began to cry quietly.

"Don't cry, April," Autumn said. "You'll make me cry, too."

"Maybe we should go," Viola said to Matthew.

He shrugged. "I'm not leaving my sisters with that man," he said, nodding toward Peter.

"I'm your father," Peter said, sounding hurt. "I know I haven't been the best father ever, but I'm here now and I want to make amends."

"Funny how you turned up right when it began to look as if Mum might have been entitled to some money," Joe snarled.

"I didn't know anything about the money when I came over," Peter replied. "I came because someone showed me the article about Rosemary's murder. In the article, it mentioned that she'd been on the island with all three of her children and their families. I couldn't stay away after I'd read that."

"To see if you were maybe mentioned in Mum's will," April suggested.

"If I am in line to inherit anything from your mother, I'm telling you now, in front of my solicitor, that whatever I get will be divided three ways between my three children."

"Are you including Autumn or do you have another child elsewhere?" Matthew asked.

Peter flushed. "Of course I'm including Autumn. She's my baby girl."

Autumn flushed. "I may have been once, but that was a long time ago."

"While we're busy getting DNA tests for Mum and Maxwell Martin, maybe you and Autumn should take them, too," Matthew suggested to Peter. "At least one of us might have the satisfaction of knowing that they aren't related to you."

Peter looked crushed. "I've never had any reason to suspect that Autumn isn't my child."

"Except she doesn't look anything like you or anyone else in the family," Matthew suggested. "She has a different blood type, too. We found that out years ago."

"What type is she?" Peter asked.

"Mum was O and so are both April and me," Matthew told him. "Autumn is type A."

"What type are you?" James asked Peter.

"I'm A," he replied.

"Does that mean that April and I aren't really your children?" Matthew demanded.

"Not at all," James told him "If the father is A and the mother is O, then the children can be either A or O."

"You seem to know a lot about this," Doncan remarked.

James flushed. "I've dealt with my fair share of custody battles and paternity suits," he said. "With DNA testing, we don't pay much attention to blood types anymore, but years ago they were one way we could begin to work out paternity where it was questioned."

"I remember learning something about it in school many years ago," Doncan told him. "I don't remember anything specific, though."

"As I said, it isn't used much these days, but I can assure you all that as far as blood types go, it is perfectly possible that Peter fathered all three of you."

"That's disappointing," Matthew said. "I was hoping for good news for my baby sister."

Autumn shrugged. "I don't think it much matters anyway. Mum never knew her father and she did okay."

"But maybe your father was a multimillionaire, too," April suggested. "Maybe you can still find him and claim your share of his fortune before he dies."

"She's my daughter," Peter said sharply. "There was never any question of that."

"Maybe not while you were around, but after you left, we all began to wonder," Matthew told him. "April and I thought that was probably why you left."

Peter looked stunned. "That wasn't why I left," he said after a long minute.

"So why did you leave, Daddy dearest?" April demanded.

Peter rubbed a hand across his face. "Things were difficult with your mother," he said. "I, that is, we'd been having trouble before Autumn arrived. I didn't deal well with the responsibilities of marriage and fatherhood. Rosemary thought I should be at home every night and I, well, I still wanted to have some fun sometimes."

"You had an affair," April said accusingly.

Blushing, Peter, waved a hand. "It wasn't quite like that, but, well, I wasn't the husband that your mother deserved, really. She asked me to leave, in the end."

"You cheated on her," Matthew said in a disgusted tone, "and now you think you can come here and be welcomed with open arms?"

"We were having problems long before I ever, well, before I realized that I cared about another woman. I never stopped loving your mother, I just, well, fell in love with someone else, too," Peter said.

"No one here is dumb enough to believe that," Joe said.

"You don't have to believe me, but it's true," Peter replied. "In the end, when I told Rosemary about Sally, she threw me out and told me that she never wanted to see me again. She told me to forget all about her and our children and that she'd never let me see you again, either."

"You could have fought her for partial custody," April suggested. "That would have meant paying some child support, though, wouldn't it? You never paid her a penny after you left, did you?"

"I sent money when I could," he told her. "It wasn't much, but I did what I could. Sally had five children of her own and she wasn't getting any help from any of the fathers. I found myself helping her more and more."

"You helped her raise five children that weren't yours, while ignoring your own children?" Autumn asked with tears in her eyes.

"Your mother told me to stay away from you," Peter argued. "What was I meant to do?"

"Fight for us?" Matthew said. "I mean, that's what I do would do for my kids."

"That's what I have done for mine," Randy said. "I made Autumn move to Liverpool so that I can be close to my kids and I fight with their mothers all the time to make sure I get to see them regularly."

"Times were different then," Peter told him.

"Mum's version of events was very different," April said.

"Mum told you something?" Autumn demanded. "She would never discuss anything with me."

"We talked about it once or twice," April replied. "She said that she thought everything was great until one day when you just didn't come home from work," she told Peter. "She said she never did find out why you'd left but that you never contacted her again."

"She should have filed a missing person report," Fenella said dryly.

"When I pushed her, she admitted that she assumed he'd found another woman, but that she wasn't sure about that. She said she thought for the first few years that he'd come back one day, but he never did. After a while, she stopped waiting, but she never found anyone else."

"She had affairs," Peter said bitterly. "Oh, I still think Autumn is my child, but after Autumn, when things were getting more and more difficult between us, she started seeing other men behind my back. If she'd had another child after Autumn, well, I wouldn't be so sure that one would have been mine."

"Mum didn't cheat on you," Autumn said through tears.

"Your brother and sister don't seem to agree," Peter replied. "They were both questioning your paternity a minute ago, remember?"

Autumn looked from Matthew to April and back again. "Mum didn't cheat," she said firmly.

"Wouldn't you rather have a different father?" Matthew asked her.

Autumn swallowed hard and then looked at Peter. "Yeah, sure, but so would you and April. None of us are going to get what we want, though, are we?"

"I'm sure he'll take a DNA test if you want," Matthew said.

"I will," Peter agreed. "If you think that would give you peace of mind."

"I'm not sure what it would give me," Autumn sighed. "I'll think about it."

"I'm sure all of this has been very entertaining for Ms. Woods and her friends," James said. "I'll just remind you again that we're on opposite sides of a lawsuit. Meeting socially is inappropriate."

"It wasn't intentional," Joe said. "As I already said, anyway, we aren't upset with her, but with her aunt and Rosemary's father. That's one of the reasons why I'd like to reach a quick and easy settlement with her. We don't want to destroy her or take every penny from her. We just want a fair settlement for what Rosemary had to endure as an abandoned child."

"She had a good childhood," Peter countered. "Her mother loved her dearly and spoiled her as much as she could."

"But her childhood could have been significantly better with Maxwell Martin's millions at her disposal," Joe replied. "You can't argue with that."

"I think that's quite enough," James said. "I'm going to suggest that we leave immediately," he told Peter. "You've already said more than you should have and, as your solicitor, I'm going to advise you to stop speaking and come with me now. As a courtesy to your children and their significant others, I'm going to make the same suggestion to them. You all need to stop talking and go back to your hotel. If you truly must drink, do so in your rooms or in the lounge there, where Ms. Woods and her advocate won't join you."

A few people exchanged glances. After a moment, Joe stood up. "Even though I hate to admit it, he's right," he said. "We should go."

April stood up and then fell back into her chair. She giggled and then let Joe help her back out of the seat. "I may have had too much to drink," she told the others in a loud whisper.

"That makes two of us," Autumn sighed as Randy pulled her to her feet. "Now I just want to sleep."

"It's a good thing we can walk back to the hotel from here," Matthew said. "Let's go."

Fenella stayed in her seat and watched as the three siblings and their partners made their way across the room. When the elevator doors shut behind the group, Peter sighed deeply.

"I truly never intended for thirty-odd years to go by before I saw them again," he said plaintively. "I loved them all, I just wasn't ready to be a father to them. After I left, I kept telling myself that I had time to make things up to them. I was always going to send cards for birthdays or Christmas. I know, I know, best intentions and all that." He sighed and then looked at James. "We should go, shouldn't we?"

"Yes, indeed," the solicitor said firmly.

The pair walked away, leaving Fenella and Shelly with Doncan.

"That was interesting," Doncan said. "I didn't get the impression that the siblings are ready to have Peter look after their interests."

"No, it certainly didn't seem like it," Fenella agreed. "They didn't seem to be getting along all that well among themselves, either."

"Can I buy you ladies a drink?" Doncan asked.

Shelly touched Fenella's arm. "I think I want to go home, but you stay and have a drink if you want."

"No, I'm ready for home and bed," Fenella told her. "It's been a very long and incredibly odd day."

Shelly nodded sadly. "It has."

Doncan insisted on walking them back to their building.

"How are the plans for the party coming?" Fenella remembered to ask as they walked.

"From what I've been told, nearly everyone has replied in the affirmative. It should be a good evening."

"What happens to the party if I'm being sued?"

"You aren't paying for the party. The party comes out of a different pool of money, to which you have no access. I suppose the Ballards could sue for that money, too, but this year's party is already mostly planned and nearly everything had been prepaid. The party will go ahead no matter what."

Fenella nodded. "I'm not sure if that's good or bad, but at least I know."

Doncan laughed. "It's going to be a wonderful occasion," he assured her. "Inspector Robinson has a week and a half to find Rosemary's killer before the party. It will all be fine."

Fenella didn't share his confidence, but she didn't argue. She and Shelly walked away, taking the elevator to their floor. "Come in," she told Shelly. "You don't want to be alone right now."

Shelly hesitated and then shook her head. "I'm okay. I'm sad, but I'm also tired. I think a good night's sleep will help a lot."

"Are you sure?"

"I have Smokey for company. I'll be fine for tonight."

Shelly had adopted Smokey, an older and very dignified female cat, a short while after Katie had made herself at home in Fenella's apartment.

"Call me if you need me, even if it's the middle of the night," Fenella told her.

"I will," Shelly promised. "Speaking of that, do you think you should ring Daniel and tell him about tonight?"

Fenella shrugged. "I don't know. Yes, probably, but maybe I'll wait for morning."

The question was very much on her mind as she washed her face and changed into her pajamas.

"Tell me about your evening," Mona insisted as Fenella paced around the living room. "Something must have happened or you'd have gone to bed already."

Fenella sighed. If she had to repeat everything that had happened that night to Mona, she might as well just call Daniel and tell him the story at the same time she thought, as she headed for the phone.

❧ 1 2 ❧

"**I**'m sorry to bother you so late," Fenella began when Daniel answered his phone.

"It isn't that late," he replied.

Fenella glanced at the clock and was surprised to see that it was only nine-thirty. It felt much later. "It's been a long day," she told him.

He chuckled. "That's very true."

"Shelly and I had dinner together and then we went to the pub," she said, switching the phone to speaker mode. Mona dropped into the chair next to her, looking eager to hear what had happened at the pub.

"Don't tell me you bumped into someone from the Ballard family there," Daniel sighed.

"We bumped into the whole family. All three siblings, their spouses, and even their father showed up for a short while."

"Tell me everything."

Fenella sighed. "I actually met some of the family earlier in the day, as well. Doncan and I had a meeting with Peter and his solicitor and then Joe and Matthew came to see Doncan while I was still there."

She repeated what she could remember from her day. When she was done, she sat back and sighed again. "I didn't go looking for any of them."

"No, I understand that, but you also didn't have to join them for a drink at the pub."

"I didn't want to be rude."

Daniel laughed. "And you didn't want to miss a chance to ask them all a few questions."

"Maybe. From what I heard, none of them has an ironclad alibi for the murder, anyway."

"Hmm."

"What does that mean?"

"It means I'm not going to discuss the case with you."

"I don't know anything about the murder weapon. I suppose it's too much to hope for that whatever killed her was rare and exotic and only one person had access to it?"

"That would definitely be too much to hope for," he agreed. "It's going to be in the papers tomorrow, so I can tell you that the murder weapon was an ordinary kitchen knife. You may well have some of the exact same knives in your kitchen right now, although I suspect yours are better quality. The hotel kitchen uses them, and they aren't even certain if they're missing any, they're so ubiquitous there."

"Are they sold anywhere on the island?"

"They're sold at several shops on the island, as well as at hundreds of retail shops across the UK."

"Did the Ballards fly over or come on the ferry?"

"They came on the ferry," Daniel told her. "So, yes, it is entirely possible someone brought a knife with them. They brought two cars, and vehicles aren't searched."

"They brought two cars? Where were the cars parked while the children were at the museum?"

"At the car park for the hotel. One was Ms. Ballard's car and the other belongs to her son, Matthew. Matthew left the car keys in his hotel room, so there's no chance anyone used it to sneak from the museum to the hotel and back again."

Fenella sighed. "It isn't that far, if someone wanted to walk," she suggested.

"We're looking at all possibilities."

"None of this makes sense. I can't understand why anyone in the family would have wanted to kill her."

"That's one of the challenges we're facing. From what I can see, Rosemary was potentially about to come into a great deal of money. Killing her before she'd received any settlement seems like a bad idea."

"The family are still fighting for a settlement, though, and I've been told they're pursuing Max's sister, as well. Rosemary didn't want to sue her, for some reason or other."

"I much prefer it when things are simple," Daniel sighed. "Last week someone in a pub in Ramsey stabbed the friend he was drinking with. We were able to make an arrest before he'd even managed to get home."

"Is the other man okay?"

"He'll be fine. It was just a flesh wound. Hopefully, he's learned a lesson from the experience, but last I heard he was trying to raise the money to bail his assailant out of prison."

"It's a weird world."

Daniel laughed. "I can't argue with that. I see that every day."

"Have you given any more thought to the other job?"

"I've turned it down. Money isn't everything. I love what I do, most of the time, anyway, and I'd always wanted to be a police inspector. Maybe when I get a bit closer to retirement age, I'll think again about changing jobs, but for now I feel as if I'm right where I belong."

"That's one worry off your mind, anyway."

"Yes, and a big one at that. I didn't realize how stressed I was about the whole thing before I rang and told them no. I may even sleep tonight."

"I hope you do, and I hope you find Rosemary's killer tomorrow."

"That would be nice."

They talked for a few more minutes, but Fenella was too uncomfortably aware of Mona's presence to do more than chat about generalities. When she put the phone down, Mona was frowning.

"What's wrong?" she asked her aunt.

"There's something about blood type," Mona replied, "but I don't know what it is."

"Do you think Autumn isn't really Peter's daughter?"

"I don't know about Autumn and Peter. I was thinking of Max and Rosemary. I'm going to have to go and talk to Max, I think."

"Does he know his blood type?"

"I'm sure he does. The question is, does his blood type rule him out as Rosemary's father? That might be too much to hope for, but, well, we'll see."

Mona faded away before Fenella could ask her any further questions. Since she knew next to nothing about blood types, not even her own, she pushed the thought out of her head and went to bed. There would be plenty of time to look things up on the Internet later if she needed more information.

"It's the blood, you see," Rosemary Ballard told her.

"Oh, no," Fenella replied. "It's bad enough I have to live with Mona. I'm not having any other ghosts in this apartment."

"You could make the effort and refer to it as a flat, you know," Rosemary said. "You've been on the island long enough to stop using American words for everything."

"Why are you here? What do you want?" Fenella demanded.

"The blood is going to be the key. Remember that."

Fenella stared at her as she faded away. "I don't want any more ghosts in here," she said loudly.

"Not even me?" a voice asked.

"Who are you?" Fenella asked, feeling confused as she looked at the man in his fifties who was wearing an ugly suit.

"I'm Alan Collins. You found my body months ago. I can't believe you've forgotten all about me."

"Of course I remember you. What are you doing here?"

"Just visiting. I thought it might be fun to have a wander around the place, but it isn't really. Everyone is asleep, except for the couple in 409. They're having a screaming row about whose turn it was to do the washing-up. People are incredibly dull."

"Maybe you should go back to the spirit world or wherever you came from," Fenella suggested.

"It's not much better there. Everyone sits around all the time complaining about being dead. I think I need a holiday."

"Great idea, off you go."

Alan sighed. "You aren't very nice. If this is how you treat Mona, no wonder she complains about you so much." He faded away before Fenella could reply.

"She complains about me?" Fenella shouted pointlessly.

"Everyone complains about you," Tiffany Perkins told her. She smiled brightly and then began jogging around the room. "No one likes you, especially not Daniel."

"You're not a ghost," Fenella snapped. "You aren't supposed to be in this dream."

Tiffany shrugged. "You'd probably rather dream about Daniel, wouldn't you? You're never going to get him, not if I can stop you."

"You've gone back to the UK where you belong. You need to stay there and stay out of my dreams."

"Are you sure this is a dream?" Tiffany asked. "Why don't you pinch yourself? That would be fun."

Fenella frowned at her and then slowly squeezed her own arm. "Ouch," she exclaimed as her eyes opened. She sat up in bed and looked at Katie, who was glaring at her. "Sorry about that," she muttered as she lay back down.

Katie shrugged and then curled up again and went back to sleep. "What was that all about?" Fenella asked herself in a whisper. As she didn't know how to reply, she rolled over and tried to fall back to sleep. It couldn't have been much before seven when she finally drifted off. Katie woke her, of course, at exactly seven to demand breakfast.

"I had a bad night," she reminded the kitten. "Could you wait an extra hour?"

Katie sighed and then jumped off the bed and disappeared around the corner. Fenella squeezed her eyes shut and tried to get back to sleep. Guilt had her dragging herself out of bed a few minutes later.

"I'm going to be grumpy and exhausted all day," she told Katie as she filled up her bowls, "but at least I'm not a bad kitten mother."

Katie looked smug as she began to eat. Fenella was considering going back to bed when the phone rang.

"Ah, Maggie, darling, you're home," a familiar voice said.

"Jack, it's seven in the morning. Where else would I be?"

Fenella's former boyfriend sighed. "I didn't think about the time difference. I am sorry. It's the middle of the night here, but I couldn't sleep, so I thought I'd call you and see how you are. We haven't spoken recently."

Jack and Fenella had been a couple for over ten years, working together at the same university and spending nearly all of their spare time together as well. Fenella had been unwilling to live with Jack, even after all those years together, which should have told her everything she needed to know about the relationship. Jack was kind and intelligent, but also slightly helpless and frequently annoying. When he'd visited the island recently, he'd discussed making some big changes in his life. The last few times he'd called, Fenella had been out and Jack had done nothing more than leave a message to say that he'd call back another time.

"I'm fine. How are you?" Fenella replied.

"I'm, well, unsettled. I want to make some changes in my life, but I'm not certain exactly what I want to do."

"The last time we spoke, you were going to Las Vegas. How was your trip?"

"Strange. I stayed in a hotel right on the Strip. That's what they call the main road that's full of hotels and casinos."

"I have heard of it," Fenella said dryly.

"Oh? Well, that was where I stayed. I had a short interview one day and then a full day of interviews the second day, but otherwise, I was free to explore the city."

"And what did you think of Vegas?"

"I didn't really care for it."

Fenella wasn't surprised. "What about the university?"

"It felt very different to here. It was hot and sunny and everywhere had air conditioning. I didn't like anything about it, really."

"So if they offer you the job, you'll turn it down," Fenella concluded.

"They already offered me the job, and yes, I turned it down. It just wasn't the right place for me. Now I'm trying to work out where the right place might be."

"Didn't you tell me that you applied for several jobs when you were here?"

"Yes, the one in Las Vegas and three others. The only other one that I was interviewed for was in Miami."

"You've been to Miami since we last spoke?"

"Yes, I have. I have called several times, but you're never home."

"So how was Miami?" she asked.

"Also hot and sunny. It isn't for me, either."

"Maybe you need to look for positions closer to home."

"You could be right about that. Or maybe I should look for something quite a bit further away. I didn't get to see much of England, just airports, really, but maybe I'd like to live there."

"In England?"

"Yes, I really liked the Isle of Man. England is similar, isn't it?"

"I suppose so, but it would be a huge culture shock for you."

"You've managed."

"Yes, but," Fenella stopped and took a deep breath. "Have you actually applied for any jobs in England? I'm not sure how you'd get a visa to work there. You'll have to find out about all of that."

"Yes, of course, it was just a thought. I'm really simply feeling out of sorts and in need of an adventure."

"An adventure?" she echoed. In their ten years together the man had never once suggested an adventure. What had Mona done to him?

"Yes, although not like the sort of adventures you seem to find yourself having. It seems as if every time we talk you've fallen over another dead body. Please tell me you haven't found any this week."

Fenella sighed. "I don't want to talk about it."

"Seriously? I was kidding, or I thought I was. You found another dead body?"

"Not exactly, but I'm caught up in another murder investigation, anyway."

"Who died this time? Someone you knew?"

"Not exactly. I really don't want to talk about it."

"That's okay. I'll just look it all up online. I'm sure there will be tons of media coverage of the murder."

"No doubt. I'll let you go, then, so you can start reading all about the island's latest murder."

"Wait, wait, what about my life? Have you any suggestions for how

I can change my life? Maybe you'd like to come and visit and help me in person. How caught up in this case are you? Are the police refusing to let you leave the island?"

"I have no interest in leaving the island, whatever the police think."

"That's a yes, then, isn't it? My goodness, you do seem to find yourself in the middle of a mess over and over again, don't you? These things never happened when you lived in Buffalo."

"Yes, I'm well aware of that. I also have to go. Have a nice day."

"Wait, if you're stuck there, maybe I should visit you again."

"Jack, you need to get on with your life and forget about me."

"I want us to stay friends. We have a lot of shared history.

"We do," Fenella agreed. "And I'd like us to stay friends, too," she admitted.

"Good, and now I'm going to go and see what I can find out about your murder. I'll keep track of the story online and once the murder is solved, I'll call again. Maybe, once you don't have the murder to worry about, you'll have some ideas about what I should do with my life."

"Not likely," Fenella muttered as she put the phone down. She still cared deeply for Jack, but he irritated her more than anyone else in the world. Between the murder and his phone call, she was feeling really grumpy.

She took a shower and made herself toast with honey, which improved her mood slightly. A long walk on the promenade seemed like the best way to work out some of the annoyance she was still feeling. From her apartment window, she stared out at the light rain. That's why I have a raincoat, she told herself. A few minutes later she was marching purposefully down the promenade, determined to put Jack and the murder out of her head.

When she reached the end, she turned around and began a slightly slower walk back toward home. There was no point in rushing, as she was pretty wet already. A bit more rain wouldn't make any difference. Her apartment building was in sight when she recognized the woman walking toward her.

"Good morning," she called to Autumn Tate.

Autumn jumped and then gave her a tentative smile. "Sorry, I was a million miles away," she said. "Good morning."

"It's not a very good one, of course," Fenella replied, holding out a hand and watching the rain splash against it.

"I like the rain," Autumn told her. "I've always liked the rain. Matthew and April think that's further proof that I have a different father, because they hate rain."

"Everyone is different. I hardly think having a different opinion about one thing is proof of anything at all."

"Thank you. It's, well, it's odd. The three of us used to talk about it when we were younger, imagining that my father was a prince or a millionaire or something else wonderful and exciting. Of course, in our fantasies, when he finally came to claim me, he always took April and Matthew back to his mansion with me. They were just games, really. I never took any of it seriously."

"I remember pretending that my parents weren't really my parents. They were older than my friends' parents. I'd been a late surprise. I used to pretend that my oldest brother was really my father and that it was all a big family secret. I never told anyone else, though, I just pretended to myself."

Autumn nodded. "We never talked about it with Mum. Even when we were small, I think we knew that there was something inappropriate about mentioning it to her. Oh, it came up later, of course, but not until we were much older. I've been dreaming of my real father since I was tiny, though, and now, well, things are just all wrong."

"Do you think Peter Ballard is your father?"

"I don't know. His solicitor was right about blood types. I checked online last night and just going by blood type it is possible that he's my father. I don't know what to think."

"You never asked your mother?"

"She used to get upset whenever the topic was mentioned, understandably, of course. When she started finding out things about her own father, I tried asking her again, but she just told me that Peter Ballard was my father, the same as April and Matthew, and that I should stop questioning her."

"Maybe she was telling the truth."

Autumn shrugged. "She may have been, but there's always going to be some level of doubt, unless I have a DNA test. I always resisted before, telling myself that it didn't really matter, but the older I get, the more I want to know the truth."

"How will you feel if Peter Ballard is your father?"

"Disappointed, really, although that's crazy, because at least he was around for a few years after I was born and he's here now. If he isn't my father, who is? My mother is gone now. It isn't as if I'll be able to force her to tell me anything now."

"Maybe you're better off not knowing."

"That's what I keep coming back to, even though it's disappointing. I think what I really want now is to just go home and put everything that's happened on the island out of my head. Back in Liverpool, I can even forget about Mum, really. We didn't speak on the phone every day or anything like that. I can just sort of ignore the fact that she's gone, at least part of the time."

"You need to do whatever works for you as you deal with your grief."

"I miss my son, too, although he's on his own and doesn't need his mother bothering him all the time."

"I hope Randy is being supportive."

"He's trying, but he doesn't truly understand. We were talking last night, just him and me, about who might have killed my mother. He agrees with me that it was probably just random misfortune. We tried to come up with a way to convince the police of that, but we couldn't."

"They don't like the idea of random murders."

"No, I can understand that, but no one had any reason to kill my mother. Motive is important, and there simply isn't one."

"When money is involved, motives are sometimes almost too obvious."

"But Mum didn't have any money. Okay, she might have been getting some from you, but if it goes to court, it could be years before anyone gets anything, and then it will be mostly the solicitors and advocates who win, won't it?"

"Probably. That's usually how it works, anyway."

"I don't understand why you won't just make a settlement, then," Autumn said quietly. "It doesn't have to be a lot, you know. I think my brother and sister would agree to a fairly small amount, maybe a million for each of us."

"I hardly think three million pounds is a small amount."

"Dad's solicitor says you're worth a good deal more than that. You'll probably pay your advocate that much fighting against us. Wouldn't you rather see myself and my siblings benefit than your advocate?"

"I might, if I believed that your mother was actually Maxwell's daughter," Fenella told her. "Until that's proven, though, there's no point in discussing a settlement."

"If the DNA results come back and prove that Mum really was Max's daughter, you'll give us each a million pounds, though?"

"I'm not agreeing to anything at this point," Fenella said firmly. "There are still far too many unanswered questions about the whole thing."

"Meanwhile, my father is paying a huge sum to his solicitor every day," Autumn sighed.

"That's his choice and nothing to do with me."

"I just want everything resolved."

"As do I."

Autumn stared at her for a minute and then shrugged. "I suppose we've nothing further to discuss, then."

"You know how to reach me once you have the DNA results."

"We're waiting for Mrs. Martin-Hardcastle to agree, but Dad's solicitor doesn't think that's going to be a problem."

The rain had begun falling more heavily while the pair had been talking. Fenella felt soaked through as she walked away from the other woman. Making another call to Daniel didn't appeal to her, but she knew she had to tell him about her conversation with Autumn.

"I'm sorry, Inspector Robinson isn't available right now," the voice on the other end of the line told her when she called the Douglas police station.

"If you could tell him that Fenella Woods called, I'd appreciate it," she replied. She put the phone down and then went into her bedroom and looked in the mirror. Mascara was running down her cheeks and her hair was hanging in a limp mess of tangles.

"Umbrellas are useful," Mona said as Fenella reached for a brush.

"I was wearing a raincoat with a hood."

"Were you wearing the hood?"

"I tried, but it kept blowing off."

"They do make waterproof mascara, too."

"I thought this was waterproof mascara."

Mona chuckled and then settled on the bed. "Who was the woman on the promenade? I assume she's something to do with Rosemary Ballard's murder."

"That was Autumn Tate, her youngest daughter."

"Really? I wish I could have seen her more clearly. I wonder if I can get binoculars from somewhere. I don't imagine you'd like to invite the whole family to a meeting here? I'd like to meet them all. I could probably pick out the killer once I'd met them all."

"I'm not having them in this apartment. Once they saw it, they'd start demanding even more money."

"Yes, there is that, of course. What did Autumn want?"

"We just happened to bump into one another. We talked about her uncertainty over who her father might be and she suggested that I should give each of Rosemary's children a million pounds to make them go away."

Mona sighed. "I do wish they'd all stop trying to get money from you."

"Yes, I quite agree with you on that."

She'd just finished reapplying her makeup when someone knocked on the door.

"I hope it's Autumn, no, I hope it's Joe Malone. I think he's the most likely candidate for Rosemary's murder. Maybe it will be Matthew. I can't see him killing his own mother, though."

Fenella shook her head at Mona's babbling and pulled open the door. When she saw Daniel on the doorstep, she glanced at Mona, who looked disappointed.

"We got the message that you'd rung," Daniel said.

"We?"

"Hi," Mark Hammersmith said, waving from where he was standing behind Daniel.

"I assume you rang because you've more information to share.

Mark and I are starting another round of interviews, and we thought we'd start with you."

"Come in," Fenella offered. "Do you want coffee or cold drinks or anything?"

"Coffee would be wonderful," Mark said. "It's cold and wet out there."

"Yeah, I know. I took a walk on the promenade this morning and got soaked. I only just finished drying my hair and fixing my makeup," Fenella replied. She led the men into the kitchen and then waved them into chairs at the island. It only took her a minute to fill the coffee maker.

"Was I right? Do you have more to share?" Daniel asked.

"I ran into Autumn while I was out walking," Fenella told him. While they waited for the coffee to brew, she told the two men about the conversation she'd had with Autumn. When she'd filled three mugs, they took their drinks into the living room so that everyone could enjoy the view while they talked.

"I love it, even when it's raining," Mark sighed. "I could sit here all day, watching the rain and the cars and the people."

"It's very tempting to do just that," Fenella replied.

The pair asked her a few questions, having her go back through what she'd done the day Rosemary had died. After a while, Daniel sighed. "We're going to go back and talk to all of the family members, including Peter Ballard. Do you think we would do best to focus on anyone in particular?"

"Tell them Joe," Mona urged her. "He's the most likely, unless it was Matthew or Randy. April doesn't sound very nice, either, of course."

Fenella gave Mona an incredulous look and then shook her head at Daniel. "I wish I could tell you that I suspected someone, but I still can't work out any clear motive for any of them."

"It was about money," Mark told her. "Maybe someone thought she already had lots or maybe one of them thought they'd get a faster or bigger settlement if Rosemary was out of the way."

"That's a thought, actually," Fenella said. "Rosemary wasn't demanding anything from Max's sister, but I understand the family is now considering suing her as well. They may have better luck getting a quick settlement from her, anyway. If she truly had accepted Rosemary as her niece, maybe she'll be happy to give each of Rosemary's children a lump sum."

"That woman wouldn't give a blind, starving beggar a penny even if her purse was full to bursting," Mona scoffed. "She's not going to meekly hand over anything to Rosemary's children. They'll have to take her to court and be prepared to fight long and hard if they think they're ever going to see anything from her. I guarantee she'd rather spend every penny she has fighting against them than agree to a settlement."

"We've spoken to Mrs. Martin-Hardcastle once and plan to speak to her again," Mark told Fenella. "When we spoke, she talked about Rosemary as her dear niece. I wonder if she'll change her tune if she gets sued by her dear niece's children."

"I think we need to put her on the list for later today," Daniel said.

"After we've spoken to the three children and their spouses," Mark replied. "Maybe we'll be able to find out for certain if they are going to sue Mrs. Martin-Hardcastle or not."

"Is there any way she could be behind everything that's happened?" Fenella asked.

"Are you suggesting that she pretended to accept Rosemary as family and then sent someone to the island to kill her? I spoke to her doctor, there's no way Mrs. Martin-Hardcastle came over here and killed Rosemary herself," Mark said.

"Could she have found someone to kill Rosemary? I mean, I don't have the first clue how to hire a contract killer. It doesn't seem the sort of thing that Max's sister would know about, either."

Daniel shrugged. "She may not have found a contract killer, but she might also have enough connections to have someone hire one on her behalf. If you have enough money, I understand you can always find someone to take care of whatever you need."

Fenella shuddered. "What a horrible thought."

"What do you think of Rosemary's children?" Mark asked.

"April seems angry at the world. Matthew didn't strike me as the brightest of men, but I can't see him as a killer, either. Autumn seems sweet and slightly confused. I think she's also devastated by the loss of her mother. She certainly seems the most upset about her death."

"And the spouses?" was Mark's next question.

"Joe is thoroughly unpleasant. He was nasty to Matthew and he tried to get me to agree to a deal without his sisters knowing about it. I don't like him at all. Viola is too quiet for me to have any opinion on her, really, and I'd almost say the same about Randy. He seemed nice enough, but I've barely spoken to him and he doesn't say much when he's surrounded by the others."

"What about Peter Ballard?"

"I don't know what to think of him. I find it odd that he just happened to turn up on the island within days of his ex-wife's death. His children are hostile toward him, and understandably so, but when I talk with him, I almost find myself feeling sorry for him. He acts as if he genuinely wants to reconcile with his kids, but he hasn't any idea where to even start."

"Do you think he's Autumn's father?"

"I think only a DNA test will answer that for sure. I wouldn't blame Autumn if she decided not to take one, though. As she said, if it isn't Peter, who is her father?"

"If it isn't Peter, maybe he could make some suggestions as to where she might find a likely candidate," Mark suggested. "He must know who else his wife was sleeping with back then."

"Maybe, but Autumn may be happier not knowing."

Mark nodded and then looked at Daniel. "Was there anything else?" he asked.

"I don't think so. Thank you for your time," Daniel said formally.

Fenella walked the two men to the door and then watched as they walked away together.

"Max was asleep when I went to see him last night and he isn't up yet," Mona told her with a sigh as Fenella shut the door. "I don't want to anger him, but I really want to wake him up and ask him about blood types."

"I'm sure he'll be up soon. It's nearly noon."

A knock on the door startled both women.

"Daniel? Did you forget something?"

"I think I dropped a pen," he told her. "I thought I put it back in my pocket as we were leaving, but I don't seem to have it."

It only took Fenella a moment to spot the pen. Katie was batting it back and forth across the kitchen floor.

"Sorry about that," she said as she handed it to Daniel.

He laughed. "No harm done."

She walked him to the door and then reached for the knob. He caught her hand and then muttered something under his breath before he pulled her close. The kiss was short but full of pent-up frustration and passion. When he let her go, Fenella felt dizzy.

"I needed that," he told her. "I miss you. Once this case is solved, we're going to sit down and have a long talk."

He opened the door and disappeared back down the corridor before she could reply.

"I didn't even notice him dropping that pen on purpose," Mona told her. "He did it very cleverly."

Fenella nodded, still feeling weak from the kiss.

❦ 13 ❦

Fenella made herself some lunch from the rather slim pickings in her refrigerator and pantry. "I need a trip to the grocery store," she told Katie, who gave her a concerned look.

"Meerow??"

"No worries. I have plenty of cat food," Fenella laughed.

Katie nodded and then curled up in a quiet corner for a nap while Fenella made a shopping list. She considered taking Mona's fun, fabulous car, but as the rain was still falling, it seemed impractical to take the convertible, especially since it had such a tiny trunk.

The grocery store felt oddly empty as Fenella worked her way through her list. Whenever she went shopping, she told herself that she was going to cook healthy meals every night for a week, and now she found herself putting heads of broccoli and bags of apples into her shopping cart. She carefully selected chicken breasts and beef for stew, vowing to use them all. Most often, Fenella found herself calling out for pizza or getting Chinese food from the nearest restaurant. While she wanted to believe that she was going to do better starting today, she was realistic enough to throw freezer bags into her cart as well.

Back at home, she unloaded all of the shopping and then quickly started a big pot of beef stew. It would be ready far too early for tonight's dinner, but she could freeze some and keep the rest in the refrigerator for later. Feeling as if she'd accomplished quite a lot that morning, she settled in with a book while the stew bubbled on the stove.

When someone knocked some time later, Fenella blinked and then dragged herself away from the Florida Keys.

"I hope I'm not interrupting anything," Shelly said apologetically when Fenella opened the door.

"Not at all. I was reading a book, but not enjoying it. It's set in Florida, and on a cold and rainy day I got quite grumpy reading about the heat and sunshine."

Shelly laughed. "My book is set on the island, so it's full of rain and cold. I hope you'll enjoy that more."

"Romance is supposed to be about fantasy. Weren't you tempted to set it somewhere more glamorous?"

"I was tempted, but as I've never been anywhere glamorous, I wasn't sure where to start."

"Never mind, I'm sure the island will seem exotic to people who've never been here."

"We can only hope, not that it will be a problem if you're the only person who ever reads it."

"We can argue about that later, once it's written," Fenella told her. "What can I do for you?"

"I just didn't want to be on my own anymore," Shelly admitted. "This thing with Tim is really bothering me, even though it shouldn't be."

"Of course it should be. You thought you and Tim were a couple. Obviously you don't want him going out with other women."

"But we've never discussed it. He has every right to go out with other women."

"Maybe now would be a good time to discuss it, then," Fenella suggested.

"I just don't know how to bring it up, and it's scary, too, because it means taking the relationship to a different place. If we agree not to see other people, well, that means we're serious about one another, doesn't it?"

"You're probably asking the wrong person. Jack and I never had a discussion like that. I suppose, in theory, either of us could have dated someone else during our years together, but neither of us ever did. I'd like to say it was because we had an unspoken agreement, but I'd have probably gone out with anyone who'd asked, but no one did."

"I can't imagine why. You're beautiful and smart, and you've had no shortage of admirers here."

Fenella shrugged. "A male friend once told me that I gave off an 'I'm taken' vibe. He said he would have asked me out otherwise, but I seemed unavailable."

"You should have told him to ask you out anyway."

"I might have if we hadn't been having the conversation in front of Jack," Fenella sighed. "I never wanted to hurt Jack's feelings, even though I knew I wasn't madly in love with him."

"So what do I do about Tim?"

"What do you want to do?"

"I want to go back to last night and not have the waiter tell me that Tim had another woman there."

Fenella gave her friend a hug. "You need to ask him about it. Mention that we went there and see what he says. If he doesn't say anything, just ask him flat out about what we were told. I think we're all too old to play games."

"I know I'm too old to play games. I'm just worried that I'm too old for romance, too."

"You are never too old for romance," Fenella said firmly.

"Would you like to come to dinner with me and Tim tonight? Then you can be there when I ask him and it won't be so awkward."

"How will it be less awkward if I'm tagging along?"

Shelly sighed. "I don't know. I'm not good at confrontation. John never cheated on me. I honestly don't think he ever so much as looked at another woman after we met. I never once worried about what he was doing if he rang to say he had to work late. It was naïve of me to give Tim that same level of trust before I really got to know him, I suppose."

"You said yourself that he wasn't doing anything wrong, even if he was with another woman."

"Yes, I know. I'm just confused and upset and a dozen other emotions that I can't even classify. Just ignore me."

"I won't ignore you. I even understand how you feel. Is Tim picking you up at home tonight?"

"Yes, he's going to be here around six. We're supposed to go and see a movie and then get fish and chips."

Fenella frowned. "That sounds good, but I made beef stew for dinner."

"You can always freeze it."

"Except I made enough to freeze a ton anyway. I'm not going to be tempted away from my lovely stew by your greasy fish and chips."

"Thanks," Shelly said, making a face.

"I didn't mean to insult your dinner plans. I'm just trying to talk myself out of going along and getting some myself."

"I did ask you to come to dinner with us," Shelly pointed out.

"And I can't do that. I'm not crashing your date just because Tim may have been out with another woman last week. What I will do, though, is hang out at your place until he gets here. Maybe I can sneak something into the conversation that you can use later when you talk to him."

"That's a great idea," Shelly said, clearly relieved. "Or maybe you can just tell him what we were told last night and see how he responds. I can hide in my bedroom while you do that."

"I'm not sure that's the best plan, but we'll see how it goes," Fenella laughed. "What time do you want me to come over?"

"Why not come over now and bring Katie? She hasn't had a play date with Smokey for ages. I'm sure they miss one another."

Fenella checked on her stew and then switched it off. "I'll have to pop back in a little while to put it away," she told Shelly. "Remind me."

Portions of stew were safely stowed in both the refrigerator and freezer by the time Tim arrived at Shelly's door.

"Come in," Fenella invited him. "Shelly's just changing."

"I hope not. I'm rather fond of her exactly as she is," Tim replied.

Fenella smiled. The man seemed so incredibly nice that she found it hard to believe that he was involved with another woman. Fenella knew he sometimes worked a lot of extra hours for ShopFast. That was what Shelly had been told, anyway.

"How are you?" Tim asked.

"I'm very well. I won't stay long. We just wanted to give the cats some playtime together."

"Hello, Smokey," Tim said, getting down on his knees to pet the cat for a moment. Katie immediately demanded a share of his attention. Tim laughed and then sat down on the floor and let both cats climb into his lap.

"How have you been?" Fenella asked as she watched the cats lapping up the man's attention.

"I'm okay. I've been working too much and neglecting Shelly, but hopefully the next big project is more or less done, from my perspective at least, and I'll have more time for her going forward."

"And I'll get to see less of her," Fenella laughed. "I was enjoying having her around a bit more. We even went to that fancy place on the promenade for dinner the other night."

Tim named the restaurant. "It sure is nice, but I didn't enjoy it the last time I was there," he said.

"Why not?"

"It was just last week, too," he told her. "We're working on a top-secret project in Liverpool. I'm not even supposed to mention that much, but whatever. Anyway, a woman from an architecture firm in London came over to meet with me to discuss certain things. We spent far too many hours arguing over trivial details and then she demanded that I take her to the island's most prestigious restaurant. I really wanted to take her for fast food, but she'd already heard of the place on the promenade. I thought I could put her off because it's almost impossible to get a table there, but when we showed up, we were treated like VIPs because of Todd."

"Yes, we were treated very well, too," Fenella said, feeling incredibly happy for Shelly. She just had to hope that the other woman was listening to the conversation.

"You're treated well because of who you are, though," Tim laughed.

"It was a new experience for me. Anyway, my colleague from London enjoyed it very much, but she just kept talking and talking, and after the starters I simply stopped listening and thought about how much I'd rather have been there with Shelly. I actually called the stupid woman Shelly three times because she was on my mind so much. Luckily for me, my work colleague was too busy talking about herself to notice."

Fenella laughed. "I hope you won't have to see her again?"

"If she comes back, I'm making the vice president take her to dinner next time. I'll only go along if I can take Shelly with me."

Shelly walked into the room with tears in her eyes. "I'm sorry," she said softly.

Tim got to his feet with a confused look on his face. "You're sorry?" he echoed.

"Someone at the restaurant told us that you'd been there with another woman and I thought you were seeing someone behind my back," she told him.

Tim stared at her for a minute and then pulled her close. "I've had my fair share of women in my life," he said. "The only one I ever truly cared about, well, she ran away with another guy from the band. After she broke my heart, I said I was never going to let myself fall in love again. You've made me rethink that and a lot of other things, too. We've never talked about it, but I haven't done as much as smile at another woman since the night we met, and I truly hope you aren't seeing other men, because I'm falling in love with you and I don't want to share you with anyone."

Shelly and Fenella both had tears streaming down their faces as Tim pulled Shelly into a kiss that Fenella was embarrassed to witness. She scooped up Katie and headed for the door. "Bye," she shouted as she let herself out.

It only took her a few minutes to reheat her stew for dinner. "And it's every bit as good as fish and chips," she told Katie.

Katie nibbled her way through her own dinner happily. As far as Fenella knew, the kitten liked everything she was given. Perhaps that was the key to the kitten's happiness.

After dinner, she settled in front of the television to watch an old movie. She was just getting up to make herself some popcorn when Mona glided into the room. She smiled at Fenella, looking very much like a woman who knew an extremely juicy secret.

"What?" Fenella demanded.

"Whatever do you mean?" Mona asked, giving her a wide-eyed, innocent smile.

"You look as if you've worked out who killed Rosemary," Fenella replied.

"I wish I had, but that isn't what I'm excited about."

"So what are you excited about?"

"I know for certain that Rosemary wasn't Max's daughter."

"You've talked to Max?"

"Not about Rosemary, of course. It would never do for him to think that I'd ever doubted him, not that I did. I talked to him about blood types."

"What about blood types?"

"When you mentioned the discussion from the other night about Rosemary's children having different blood types, I remembered something about Max. He had a rare blood type. We found out all about it when he fell ill near the end of his life."

"And?"

"And he was type AB, which means he couldn't have had a child who was type O," Mona said triumphantly.

Fenella sat down and took a deep breath. "You're sure about that?" she asked. "About all of it?"

"I'm very sure. Max remembered his blood type, and so did I. I'm sure you can have his doctor look at his records. It will be there."

"And you're sure he couldn't have a child who was O?"

"I went and spoke to an expert myself," Mona told her. "The man did some groundbreaking work in genetics back in the nineteen-forties. I could give you all of the details, but they don't really matter. What matters is that Rosemary wasn't who she claimed to be."

Fenella stared out at the sea for a moment. "What do I do now?" she asked.

"You tell Doncan, and he tells Dan Ross, and Dan writes an article about how Rosemary came here to try to exploit money from you. I'm not certain how we can prove that Max's sister was behind it all, but maybe Dan can dig something up if the police can't."

"The police are more concerned with finding Rosemary's killer than anything else. What would you suggest that I tell Doncan, though? If I tell him that my dead aunt told me that her former lover had type AB blood and therefore can't be Rosemary's father, he'll think I'm crazy."

Mona sighed. "Do I have to do everything for you?" she asked. "Just tell him that after the talk about blood types, you started wondering about whether they could help with the current situation. Suggest to him that he ring Max's doctor and find out his blood type. Doncan is smart. He'll work things out from there."

"And if you're right and Max wasn't Rosemary's father, we just need to get everyone together and tell them that. They should leave me alone after that."

"I should think so. Whatever letters they may have, if Rosemary wasn't Max's daughter, they aren't entitled to anything."

"The letters are still a worry, though, in terms of your reputation if nothing else."

"I've decided not to care," Mona told her. "People can believe what they want. I know Max was faithful to me, and I know exactly why he gave me gifts and treated me so well."

"You did know his secrets."

"Yes, I did, but he knew I'd never tell, not even if he'd cut me off without a penny. We both played our parts, though, for many, many years. He gave me what he could afford to give me because he was generous and kind. I gave him everything I had in return."

Fenella frowned at her. "What was Max's secret?" she asked.

Mona smiled enigmatically. "I'm not sure I'm ready to talk about that yet. There are many reasons why I've never told it to anyone."

"You will tell me one day?"

"One day, maybe, when it seems to be the right time."

"I'm going to call Doncan and see if he can start things rolling.

Maybe if the lawsuit issue gets taken off the table it will be easier for the police to solve Rosemary's murder."

"If she was killed because of her possible claim on my fortune or Max's, learning it was all for nothing might flush the killer out," Mona suggested.

Fenella called Doncan at home and asked him to see what he could find out about Max's blood type. "Her children said that Rosemary was type O," she added. "That might be significant."

"I'll ring Max's advocate in the morning," he promised. "I'm sure he'll be happy to clear things with Max's general practitioner to release that information to me."

"Let me know what comes of it."

After she put the phone down, Fenella found herself pacing back and forth across the living room. "What if the family all believed that Rosemary was telling the truth?" she asked Mona. "One of them might have killed Rosemary in an attempt to get his or her hands on more of the money whenever any settlement is reached."

"I think that's the most likely scenario," Mona agreed. "From what you said, Rosemary told them all that she was getting the money for herself, not for them. Maybe one of them didn't like that idea."

"I don't think any of them liked the idea. They all seemed to feel as if Rosemary should share her newfound wealth, assuming she ever actually got anything, of course."

"If she were going to confide in any of her children, tell them what she was planning and how she thought she could get away with it, which one would it have been?"

Fenella thought for a minute. "I would pick Autumn, except that Autumn lives in Liverpool now and I can't see Rosemary telling her the whole story over the phone, so maybe April."

"If anyone knows the truth, then, it's April. Would she have confided in her husband?"

"I've no idea. If I were married to Joe Malone, I wouldn't tell him anything, but she must love him, mustn't she?"

Mona shrugged. "For her sake I hope not too much, just in case he is the killer."

They talked in circles for another hour about the siblings and their partners, but couldn't reach any final conclusions.

"I think Joe did it," Mona said eventually. "I'd put Randy second and Matthew third, but that may just be because I can't imagine a daughter killing her mother."

"There's always Viola," Fenella suggested. "She's barely said two words every time I've seen her. Maybe she has hidden depths."

"Maybe, but are they murderous depths?" Mona asked.

"I think I'm going to go to bed," Fenella sighed. "There's nothing else we can do tonight. We're just wasting our time and energy going over everything again and again."

Mona nodded and then followed her into the bedroom. Fenella washed her face and brushed her hair while Mona sat on the bed.

"My heart might have broken if she'd really been his daughter," Mona said after a minute.

"I thought you had total faith in him."

"I did, I do, but even so, it made me pause. It worried me. I knew Max would never have had an affair with anyone, but that didn't stop me from having a moment or two of doubt."

"I'm glad it's all worked out, then."

"Max only had one secret, really," Mona continued, "but I wasn't the only one who knew it. That's one of the reasons why I knew the letter was fake."

"Oh, really?"

"It was a fairly simple secret, too, one that maybe wouldn't even matter now."

So tell me, Fenella thought, biting her tongue.

Mona laughed lightly. "Anyone could read your thoughts when they're that obvious."

Fenella shrugged. "Obviously, I'd love to know Max's secret, but I'm also tired, and depending on what Doncan finds out, tomorrow could be a long and stressful day. Do you want to talk about it or leave it for another night?"

"Max fell madly and passionately in love only once in his life," Mona told her, with tears in her eyes. "He was sixteen and that was it for him. He never loved anyone else. That was his secret."

"I thought Max was older than you when you met and that you were eighteen."

"That's right."

"So you weren't Max's true love?" Fenella asked, feeling confused. She turned around and saw tears streaming down Mona's face.

"He loved me, I truly believe that, but not in the way that he loved Bryan."

"Bryan? Wait, his business partner?"

Mona smiled. "I don't think I ever identified him as Max's business partner, only as his partner. They were partners in every sense of the word. They started their business together, made their fortune together, and loved each other with a devotion that was truly incredible to see."

"But Bryan was married."

"In those days, on this island, you could be birched for being gay," Mona told her. "Both Max and Bryan did what they could to protect themselves. Samantha knew what she was getting into when she walked down the aisle. She'd worked for Bryan for years and he offered her everything she'd ever wanted. Once they were married, she traveled whenever she felt like traveling, she had almost unlimited financial resources for whatever she wanted to buy, and she was able to help out her mother, who had serious health issues. Believe me, Samantha was more than happy with what she got out of that marriage."

"And what did you get out of your relationship with Max?"

Mona waved a hand. "All of this and more. I'm sure Doncan has given you an idea of exactly how much my estate was worth when I died. Max was incredibly generous to me, not to buy my silence, but out of gratitude for my continued willingness to play my part. We pretended to have a passionate and volatile relationship and no one ever suspected the truth."

"Why did you do it?"

"As I said, Max showered me with gifts. I was eighteen when we met. I never had to work a day in my life. You still haven't visited my safe-deposit boxes. Wait until you see the jewelry he gave me. It was all part of the fantasy, of course: the jewels, the clothes, the cars, the houses. And everyone on the island believed it."

"From everything I've heard, you were very convincing. What about Max's sister?"

"She would have had a fit if she'd known Max's secret. His parents were the same. They would have cut Max out of their lives if they'd as much as suspected that he might be gay. He moved to the island to get away from them. Luckily, Bryan was willing to move here as well."

"So his sister never knew?"

"Never, and I'd rather she didn't find out now. It's far too late for her to do anything, of course, but I'd prefer it if Max's secret remained a secret."

"I won't tell anyone," Fenella assured her. "Of course Bryan and Samantha knew. Did anyone else know?"

"I don't think so. As I said, Max fell in love once and that love never wavered. Bryan was the same, fortunately. They were devoted to one another and Bryan was happy to have me in Max's life. I was there when they discussed Samantha, before Bryan proposed. They were in complete agreement about bringing her into our little circle."

"What was she like?"

"She was smart, really very smart. If she were a young woman today, Bryan would have made her managing director of the company rather than marrying her, but women had limited opportunities in those days. Marrying Bryan was a smart move on her part."

"And she never cheated on him?"

"I don't think she was terribly interested in men. Not that I think she was interested in women, I just don't think she was very sexual. Some people aren't, of course. As far as I know, she was faithful, but as I said, she traveled a lot. She could have had very discreet affairs while she was traveling and no one on the island would have ever known. I've no doubt Bryan would have accepted any unexpected children that might have arrived as part of the price of having a wife."

"What about the other men in your life?"

"There weren't any other men," Mona told her. "I flirted outrageously with everyone, and one or two men thought it would be clever to tell others that they'd slept with me. At first I was outraged, but Max persuaded me to let it go. He insisted that the more wild people thought I was, the more easily they'd believe that our relationship was real. He was right in the end, although it took me some time to see that."

"So all the fights I've been told about, they were all faked?"

"Mostly. We used to sit in my rooms, back when this was a hotel, and talk about exactly what we'd fight about at the next big party. After a while, we both realized that no one was really paying any attention to our arguments, so we stopped bothering with having substance to them. Instead, when the time was right, I would just start shouting at Max." Mona laughed. "It became a joke between us, my shouting. As I said, no one really listened or understood, so I used to shout outrageous things. One of my favorites was the night I spun around and yelled 'There aren't meant to be pandas on the buffet,' at him."

"Pandas?"

"We'd been watching a documentary that afternoon about pandas in China," Mona explained with a sad smile. "While everyone on the island was convinced that we were either fighting or having amazing sex, we mostly watched television and talked when we were together. Max knew something about everything. He was sophisticated and worldly. He'd traveled everywhere." She sighed. "Anyway, he apologized for the pandas and I refused to believe that he was sorry, and then I stormed out and demanded that his driver take me home. That left the way clear for Bryan to offer Max a ride back to his flat."

"It sounds like you had an interesting relationship, anyway."

"It was certainly never boring, although many women would have found the real Max, the one with whom I spent hours watching television or just talking, to be quite dull. In public Max was always at the center of every party and every gathering, but he was a very shy person really. His public persona let him keep people at a distance. Everyone thought they knew him, but no one truly did."

"You did."

"I hope I did. I always thought I did, which was why Rosemary Ballard's allegations were such a shock. I didn't believe them, but they raised doubts, doubts I never wanted to feel about Max."

"If he was gay, surely he didn't father a child with anyone."

"Some gay men decide to try other things, maybe just once. I had to concede that it was remotely possible that he'd been in London and been lonely and had had a one-night stand. I never believed for one second that he'd knowingly had a child with another woman and not supported that child, though. He would have married the mother, if he'd known about the child. I'm sure of that."

"And the letters?"

"He never would have written such horrible things about me. Not because he was afraid of me sharing his secret, but, I truly believe, because he loved me, in his own way. We were like brother and sister, I suppose, or maybe even father and daughter. He took me, at eighteen, and showed me the world. He taught me everything I know about everything, really. He knew I'd never have betrayed his secret, no matter what he did."

"I'm still not sure I understand why you did it," Fenella said. "I mean, I understand that you were well compensated, but you gave up a lot, too. You gave up the chance to have a husband and children, for example."

"I'm not ready to tell you my secret," Mona said. "I only had one that mattered, too, but not even Max knew it. Maybe another day."

Mona faded away before Fenella could object.

"What do you think of that?" she asked Katie, who was sitting on the bed staring at the spot where Mona had been sitting.

"Meeroow," Katie replied.

"Yes, exactly," Fenella said. She changed into her pajamas and crawled into bed, her mind racing. She wasn't sure how she felt about everything that Mona had revealed. It all seemed almost sad somehow, but she wasn't sure for whom she was feeling the most sorry.

She turned off the light and then jumped when she realized that Mona had returned. Her aunt gave off a slight glow that revealed more tears on her cheeks.

"I decided if I was going to tell all, that I should answer your question," she said softly. "My secret was very similar to Max's actually. I only fell in love once in my life, too, and I fell madly, crazily in love. I would have done anything for the man I loved, even spend my entire life pretending to be his lover while sleeping alone every single night."

Fenella watched the tears run down Mona's face. "You were in love with Max."

"I'll always be in love with Max. He was the only man for me, and in spite of everything, I'd do it all exactly the same again if I had the chance. I willingly gave up everything for him, marriage, children, because I loved him and I always will."

Mona faded again before Fenella could reply.

❧ 14 ❧

After all of Mona's surprising revelations, Fenella had trouble falling asleep. When Katie woke her the next morning, she was grateful that she couldn't remember any of her dreams from overnight.

"I didn't sleep very well," she told Katie as she poured cat food into a bowl, "but I don't want to go back to bed this morning. I'm afraid I'd just have nightmares. Although, as it's morning, I suppose they should be called daymares, shouldn't they?"

Katie looked at her as if she'd lost her mind, which made Fenella laugh.

"Yes, I'm babbling," she admitted. "My brain is in overdrive, trying to work through all the things I've learned in the last twenty-four hours, that's all. I didn't sleep well and I'm a little bit worried about Mona."

"Worried about me? How very kind of you," Mona said as she came into the room. "You've no reason to be, but it is sweet."

"You were upset last night."

Mona shrugged. "Some things from my past are more difficult to talk about than others. It was a conversation that we needed to have, especially in light of recent events, but it isn't one that needs repeating or rehashing. Nothing has changed. You simply understand me a bit better."

Fenella nodded. She had dozens of questions for the woman, but if Mona wanted to drop the subject, she felt she should honor that desire. "What shall we talk about, then?" Fenella asked.

"Are you ready for my party? It's coming up quickly and you want to be prepared."

"I have my dress and shoes picked out. What else do I need to do?"

"You should go over the guest list to see who has been invited and who is actually coming," Mona told her. "I'm sure Doncan would be happy to share that information with you."

Fenella sighed. "He emailed me the guest list before it went out, but as I don't know who most of the people on it are, I didn't pay much attention."

"Let's go over it together," Mona suggested.

An hour later, Fenella felt as if her head were spinning. Mona had told her anecdotes about dozens of different people, and Fenella had already resigned herself to the fact that she was never going to remember which ones belonged with which people, even if she did remember any of the stories.

"Ah, Herman," Mona sighed, pointing to the next name on the list. "He chased after me for many years, but he was just, well, incredibly dull. His family has oodles of money and he used to give me a diamond every time he saw me. I had them all put together into a bracelet. It's in one of my safe-deposit boxes. You'll love it."

"How old is he?"

"Now? He must be eighty-five, I suppose. He's younger than I was, but not by much. His father did some business with Max, and Herman decided when he was about fifteen that he loved me. As I said, it took me years to discourage him."

"Did he ever find anyone else?"

"Oh, goodness, yes. He's had three wives so far and knowing him, he's looking for a fourth. His first wife was the true love of his life. They met when he was nearly forty and they were married for twenty-five years. When sadly, she passed away, he married one of his old friends who had recently been widowed herself. She died only a few years later. Herman found his third wife when he was on holiday. She was quite a bit younger, but she seemed nice enough. I believe they were happy together until she lost control of her car on a rainy evening. He's been alone for a few years since then, but I'm sure he's looking for someone. He doesn't like to be alone."

"I should be taking notes," Fenella sighed. "I'm never going to remember all of this."

"That's probably for the best. You'd struggle to explain how you know so much about everyone without telling anyone about me."

"I should have Doncan sit down and go through the list, then, shouldn't I? Just in case I slip up and mention something I'm not supposed to know."

"Doncan won't tell you the same things I'm telling you. He'd stick to the facts and to what's public knowledge. You should see if Breesha is free for a chat. She knows everything about everyone, but she never repeats anything. Maybe she'd make an exception for you, though."

The phone provided a welcome interruption to the review of the guest list.

"I've heard back from both Max's doctor and the coroner. There's no way Rosemary Ballard was Maxwell Martin's daughter," Doncan told her.

"That's a huge relief."

"I'm going to invite Rosemary's children and their spouses to a meeting to discuss the matter," he continued. "The sooner we can finish this thing, the better, so I've cleared my afternoon for them if they are all available."

"Are you going to invite Peter Ballard and his solicitor?"

"That might be best."

"Maybe you should add Daniel or Mark Hammersmith to the guest list," Fenella suggested. "If Rosemary was actively attempting to defraud me and any of her children knew about it, it's a police matter."

"That's a good idea. I'll do that. Breesha is trying to contact the Ballard family now. Once they've agreed to a time, she'll let you know. Hopefully, I'll see you later today."

Fenella put the phone down and smiled at Mona. "Max wasn't Rosemary's father," she said.

"Yes, we've already established that," Mona retorted. "Now we just have to work out who killed her, although as she was clearly not a nice person, I imagine anyone might have wanted to kill her."

"I still think it was one of the family."

"I still think it was Joe Malone. Maybe, when he finds out that there isn't going to be any settlement from my estate, he'll confess."

"That would be good, but I can't see it happening," Fenella sighed.

Breesha rang a few hours later, while the pair were still talking about the party guest list. Fenella had given up on trying to remember people's names and which stories went with them and was simply sitting back and enjoying learning more about Mona's past and the people she'd known.

"We're all set for two o'clock," Breesha told her. "The three children will be here with their partners, along with Mr. Peter Ballard, Mr. James Diedrich, and Inspector Daniel Robinson."

"It almost sounds like a party," Fenella replied.

"I don't think anyone on the guest list is going to feel like celebrating once they hear what we have to tell them."

"No, I'm sure you're right about that."

Mona kept Fenella entertained with more stories about the men and women who were coming to the party through lunch and right up until time for Fenella to leave for Doncan's office.

"I'm starting to look forward to your party now," she told Mona as she changed into a plain black dress. "I know I won't remember any of the stories, but I'm still excited to meet all of the people we've been discussing."

"I'm looking forward to it as well," Mona said. "I'm fairly certain that I'll be able to attend, at least for a short while. It may drain a lot of my energy, but it will be worth it."

"You should bring Max."

Mona smiled. "He doesn't realize he's dead yet. He isn't up to the journey."

Fenella glanced at the clock. She didn't have time to ask Mona all of the questions that the woman's comments raised. "I have to go," she said.

"Good luck. I hope this solves the case as well as getting rid of the threatened lawsuit."

Fenella nodded and then grabbed her bag and headed for the door. She gave Katie a quick pat on her way out, rushing to catch the elevator that was just closing as she'd shut her door behind herself.

"We're going to be meeting in the conference room again," Doncan told Fenella when Breesha escorted her into his office a short while later. "We'll just wait for everyone else to arrive before we head up."

A minute later, Breesha stuck her head into the room. "Inspector Robinson is here," she said.

"Bring him in here. He can wait with us," Doncan replied.

The trio were exchanging pleasantries when Breesha reappeared. "They're all here. I started a pot of coffee brewing. It should be ready when you get there."

"Thank you," Doncan said. He got to his feet. "Ready?" he asked Fenella.

She shook her head, but stood up anyway. Daniel took her hand and gave it a squeeze. "It's going to be okay," he whispered as they followed Doncan out of the room.

"You do enjoy keeping people waiting, don't you?" Joe snapped as they walked into the conference room a moment later.

"I hope you weren't waiting long," Doncan replied. "Did anyone want coffee?"

"We want to know why we're here," Joe said. "We all have better things to do today."

Doncan sat down. Fenella took the seat next to him and Daniel slid into the seat on her other side.

"You've brought the police? That doesn't seem appropriate," James said nervously.

"Yeah, why are the police here?" Joe demanded.

"As attempted fraud is a criminal activity, it seemed best to have a police inspector in attendance," Doncan replied.

"Be very careful about making any accusations," James warned.

Doncan nodded. "Let's start with a few basic facts, then. My client was present during a conversation among yourselves about blood types. The issue under discussion was whether or not siblings could have different blood types. I believe the result of the conversation was an agreement that it was possible, and that Autumn's blood type didn't rule out Mr. Peter Ballard being her biological father."

"Yeah, so?" Randy snapped. He reached for Autumn's hand and gave it a squeeze.

"During the course of the discussion, someone mentioned that Rosemary Ballard had blood type O," Doncan continued. "Is that correct?"

"I think so," April said. "I could be wrong, though. That was just what I remembered. We were just talking amongst ourselves. I didn't realize that everything we said was going to be reported back to the police." She gave Fenella a dirty look.

"You remembered correctly," Doncan told her. "I checked with the coroner and Ms. Ballard was definitely type O."

"Great. Was that all you wanted?" Joe asked.

"I also checked with Maxwell Martin's general practitioner. Mr. Martin was type AB."

Several people shrugged before James spoke.

"Are you certain?" he asked tightly.

"Positive. I have a sworn affidavit that confirms it," Doncan replied.

"May I see it?" James asked.

Doncan passed him a sheet of paper. James read it and then sighed. "That's the end of that, then."

"What's the end of what?" Joe shouted over everyone else's similar questions.

"A man who is type AB can't father a child who is type O," James explained. "Mr. Martin wasn't Rosemary Ballard's father."

"This is a trick," Autumn said angrily. "Mum wouldn't lie about such a thing. We'll wait for the DNA results, I think."

"There is no need for DNA testing at this point," Doncan told her. "Mr. Martin is conclusively ruled out as her father."

"I don't believe it. What about the letters?" Autumn demanded.

"What about the letters?" Doncan replied. "If any letters between Charlotte Sharp and Maxwell Martin do exist, and to my mind that's still unproven, their content is irrelevant, as Mr. Martin was not the father of Ms. Sharp's child."

"You're suggesting that Charlotte lied to Max Martin," Matthew said slowly.

"As I said, the existence of the letters is yet unproven, but that might be one possible explanation for them if they do exist," Doncan replied.

"I don't believe any of this," Autumn said. Randy pulled her into a hug and she began to sob loudly on his shoulder.

Joe turned to April. "Did you know about this?" he asked her. "You and your mum were really close this last year. Did she really think she was Maxwell Martin's daughter?"

"Of course she did," April said stoutly. "We wouldn't be here if she hadn't believed what she'd read in those letters."

"So perhaps Ms. Sharp simply made a mistake when she attributed her daughter's parentage to Mr. Martin," James suggested.

Doncan shrugged. "I'm not sure that I care who was lying to whom at this point. As long as you all understand that any threat of lawsuits against my client are out of the question now, you can decide amongst yourselves where the blame for the confusion lies."

"My mother never lied to me," Autumn said fiercely. She lifted her head and glared at Doncan. "We were close, closer than she was to April or Matthew. She never lied to me, not ever. When she told me about the letters, she was so excited. She'd finally found out something about her father. That was what she was most excited about, really. This wasn't about money, not primarily. She just wanted her fair share, what she was entitled to as the daughter of a millionaire."

"Except she wasn't the daughter of a millionaire," Peter said quietly. "When we first met, she introduced me to her father. I suppose I should say she introduced me to the man that her mother had always told her was her father. He'd been married when he'd had his affair with Charlotte, but his wife had died a year or so before I met Rosemary. That was when he decided to find Charlotte and try to make amends."

"So you knew that Rosemary's claims against my client were fraudulent?" Doncan asked.

Peter shook his head. "I just assumed she'd found out about Mr. Martin later. The man I'd met, the one she'd thought was her father, passed away just a year or so after Rosemary and I got married. I never gave the matter any more thought, but it's possible that she did find the letters she told you about after her mother died."

"She told us that she grew up never knowing anything about her father," Fenella said.

"She must have meant her real father," Peter said, waving a hand. "I'm sure it was a shock to her, learning that someone else might be her father."

"I don't think we need to debate this any longer," Doncan said. "It will up to the police to decide if they want to try to prosecute anyone for taking part in the attempt to defraud my client."

"No one ever actually filed any lawsuits," Joe said quickly.

"No, but several people pressed her for a financial settlement," Doncan replied.

"We were only acting on what Mum told us," Autumn interjected. "I should say we were only acting on what Mum believed to be true."

April laughed. "You really think you and Mum were that close, do you?"

"What do you mean?" Autumn asked.

April shook her head. "I'm not saying anything that might incriminate me, but Mum didn't tell you everything, I'll tell you that much."

Doncan glanced at Daniel and then cleared his throat. "It's possible that the attempted fraud was perpetrated by someone else altogether. I find it difficult to believe that Ms. Ballard was capable of creating the letter that she showed me without outside assistance, most likely from someone who knew Mr. Martin well. I believe the police would be interested in hearing anything anyone might know about exactly where that letter came from, even to the extent of agreeing not to press charges against minor players in the charade."

April frowned. "Are you talking to me?"

James laughed. "He's suggesting you should tell the police what you know if it will help them catch the person behind the fraud, assuming it wasn't your mother, that is."

"As we believe that the fraud attempt was tied to Ms. Ballard's murder, we need every bit of information we can get," Daniel said.

April glanced at Joe and then shrugged. "I didn't really know much, just that most of what Mum said wasn't entirely true."

"I don't believe it," Autumn shouted. "Mum told me everything."

"Not everything," April sneered. "Did she tell you about the advert that she answered?"

"Advert?" Autumn repeated.

"Yeah, it was in the back of some newspaper or magazine. Some company was looking for women who had been born between certain years and who didn't have a father listed on their birth certificates. According to the ad, the company was doing some sort of survey and would compensate anyone who replied," April said.

"I can believe that Mum would have replied to something like that," Matthew said. "I'm sure she thought it was interesting, and she wouldn't have wanted to miss out on any compensation."

"Exactly. After she replied to the advert, she got sent a train ticket to meet someone at a café in Milton Keynes. There, she was met by a woman in her forties who took her picture and asked her loads of questions and then gave her a thousand pounds," April continued

"A thousand pounds for a few questions?" Randy exclaimed. "She should have known right then that there was something wrong."

"A few days later, someone rang her and arranged a meeting in London at a café. The same woman, she told Mum she was called Norah, turned up and told Mum what she wanted her to do," April told them.

Daniel was taking notes as April spoke. Now he looked up. "Maybe we should have this conversation at the station."

"We don't need to go to the station. You said you wouldn't press charges if I told you the truth," April replied. "I want my baby sister, Mum's favorite child, to understand what really happened, anyway. She always thought Mum told her everything and that they told each other all of their secrets, but this time Mum went to me with her secret."

"I'm glad I didn't know," Autumn snapped. "Mum didn't tell me because she knew I wouldn't agree to go along with anything criminal."

April laughed. "You'd have gone along. The plan was foolproof.

Mum didn't tell you because she knew you'd fall apart if the police questioned you."

"You're the one telling them everything," Autumn replied.

"Because Mum was murdered and the woman in London must have been behind it," April retorted. "She gave Mum that letter and promised that there would be a lot more of them to come. She also promised Mum that if she took a DNA test, the results would match."

"How was she going to manage that?" Daniel asked.

April shrugged. "I've no idea. Mum wasn't worried about the details, anyway. Norah told her that once she showed Ms. Woods the letters, Ms. Woods would settle without a DNA test."

"But she never gave your mother more than the one letter?" Doncan asked.

April shook her head. "We weren't meant to come over to the island until later, but Mum decided she didn't want to wait. Maybe Norah needed more time to get the letters together."

"You mean to fabricate the letters," Fenella interjected.

"Norah told my mother that the letters were real and that Maxwell Martin really did have an illegitimate child, but that the child had died when he was six. Mum felt as if she was fighting for the rights of that poor little boy."

"Who never existed," Fenella muttered.

"Whatever, Mum rang Norah last week and told her that we were going to come over now and see what happened. Norah was upset at first, but in the end, she agreed," April said. "That's why I think she killed Mum. She thought Mum was trying to cheat her out of her share of what she was going to get from Ms. Woods."

"What was her share meant to be?" Daniel asked.

"They were going to split everything fifty-fifty," April replied. "Mum was going to try to talk her into making that sixty-forty once the settlement was paid, but she never got a chance."

"Tell me more about this woman," Daniel requested.

"Mum just said she was in her forties, with brown hair that was already going grey. Mum assumed that she was working for someone else, but she never pressed Norah for more information."

"So your mother agreed to go along with this woman's attempt to defraud me," Fenella said. "Norah told her what to do, but wanted her to wait until she had more letters ready, but your mother went ahead anyway?"

"Mum was tired of British winters. She wanted to take her millions and go and soak up the sun somewhere," April explained.

"Wasn't she worried about what Norah might do?" Fenella asked.

"Nope. She reckoned she had enough material to get money out of you without Norah's help," April replied. "If she'd only been able to get a few million, she would have taken it and disappeared to somewhere where Norah wouldn't have been able to find her."

"None of this sounds like the mother I knew and loved," Autumn said sadly.

"You'd understand better if you'd been around more lately," April told her. "Mum was tired of living in London. She wanted to retire somewhere warm where she didn't have to work two jobs just to pay her bills. This woman offered to help her fulfill her dreams. Ms. Woods is worth tens of millions of pounds. She wouldn't have even missed a few of them."

"Do you have any proof of any of the things you've been telling me?" Daniel asked April.

"I have the original advert that Mum cut out of the paper," she told him. "She told Mum not to keep any of her emails, but Mum did anyway. They're all printed out and in a safe place in my flat."

"You should have told me," Joe said in a low voice.

"The fewer people who knew, the less likely the secret was to come out," April replied. "Mum only told me in case something happened to her. She didn't really trust Norah, you see."

"And yet she was murdered several days ago and you didn't say a word," Daniel said.

"I thought Ms. Woods killed her," April told him.

Fenella gasped. Doncan held up a hand to stop her from replying.

"You still should have told us everything," Daniel said. "Norah has had plenty of time to cover her tracks now."

April shrugged. "If I would have told you, it would have ended our chances of getting any money from Ms. Woods."

"And that was more important to you than finding Mum's killer?" Autumn asked.

April grinned. "Well, yeah, of course it was. With Mum gone, we wouldn't have had to share anything we got with Norah. That's why Joe and I were going to go after Mrs. Martin-Hardcastle, too. Norah was insistent that Mum not bother her, but if we didn't know anything about Norah, we could sue everyone."

"You never told me about Norah," Joe said plaintively.

"Don't worry," April laughed. "I'll go on record that you knew nothing about any of this." She looked over at Daniel. "Honestly, I never told Joe anything about Norah. He genuinely believed that my mother had found the letters just the way she said she had. I was the only one who knew the whole story."

"You should have told me," Joe said, his face pale.

"Mr. Malone, perhaps we should go down to the station and have a chat," Daniel said, rising to his feet.

"Why?" Joe asked. "What do you want to talk about?"

"You seem upset about everything your wife is saying," Daniel replied.

"I am upset. I truly believed Rosemary's story. I thought she was telling the truth."

"We all did," Autumn said bitterly.

"I didn't," Matthew interjected. "I had a long talk with Mum after the first meeting we had with Ms. Woods. Things didn't quite add up in my mind, so I confronted her."

"What did she tell you?" Daniel asked.

"Parts of the story, anyway," Matthew sighed. "She didn't tell me everything, but what she did tell me matches what April has been saying."

"So you knew that Ms. Ballard was trying to commit fraud," Doncan asked.

Matthew shrugged. "I stayed out of it after that. I told her it was all between her and Ms. Woods. I even told Viola that if Mum got a lot of money, we wouldn't take any, well, not much." He flushed and looked down at the table.

"He told me that we'd take just enough to fund one attempt at

IVF," Viola said quietly. There were tears rolling down her cheeks as she glanced up and then looked back down at the table. "We can't afford it any other way. I didn't want to agree, but I truly am that desperate to have a baby."

"I'm going to need to get statements from everyone in light of this new evidence," Daniel said. "We should really move this down to the station."

"It's really nothing to do with me," Joe said quickly. "April told you that I didn't know anything about any of this."

"I'll just need to get that into a formal statement," Daniel told him.

Joe shook his head. "I don't want to answer any more questions."

"I suggest you get yourself an advocate," James said. "I get the feeling you have things you want to hide."

"I don't," Joe shouted too quickly. "Maybe an advocate would be a good idea, though. Can you recommend one?"

"I'm available, but I'm expensive," James replied.

"Dad is paying you," April said.

"I was paying him," Peter corrected her. "I was paying him to look after your interests in what I thought was a legitimate attempt to recover money that should have rightly been Rosemary's. I'm not paying him to defend anyone against a murder charge."

"What murder charge?" April demanded. "No one has suggested that Joe had anything to do with Mum's murder." She turned and looked at her husband. "Tell him he's crazy," she said sharply.

"You're crazy," Joe said in a shaky voice.

April stared at him for a minute and then began to shake her head. "You didn't have anything to do with Mum's death," she said loudly. "You were with me at the museum that morning."

"He skipped the movie and the first half of the tour," Viola said. "We laughed about at the time, remember?"

"He was having a cigarette, that's all," April insisted. "He didn't have any reason to kill Mum."

"Maybe he wanted to get his hands on the settlement he thought was coming her way," Peter suggested. "Knowing your mother, she had plans for spending every penny on herself."

"She was going to move somewhere sunny and leave us all behind,"

Joe said bitterly. "She made us all come with her so that we could see her moment of triumph, but she wasn't going to share anything with anyone else."

"She had to give half of everything to Norah," April said.

"But I didn't know there was a Norah," Joe said tightly. "I thought your mother's claim was legitimate. You told me that it was."

"It wasn't safe for anyone to know the truth," April argued.

"But if I'd known..." Joe trailed off and then looked down at his hands. "If I'd known..." he repeated softly to himself.

"You killed Mum," Autumn said. "You killed her so that you could get a share of the lawsuit money."

"I think it's time to take this to the station," Daniel interrupted. He'd taken his phone out of his pocket a few minutes earlier and Fenella had watched him sending text messages. Now Breesha pushed the conference room door open.

"There are several uniformed constables here," she said uncertainly.

"They're with me," Daniel told her.

Fenella sat in silence as Daniel had each person escorted out of the room in turn. April was crying silently as she was led away. Joe still looked confused as he went. Autumn was openly sobbing as she and Randy left together, with Daniel's approval. Matthew and Viola were also allowed to remain together. They both looked pale, and Fenella found herself worrying about Viola, who looked as if her dreams had been shattered as well.

Peter insisted on keeping his solicitor with him as he went. When the door shut behind them, Daniel sat back down next to Fenella.

"I'm going to send someone here to take a statement from you and from Doncan," he told Fenella. "I may see you later, but I may be tied up with this mess for a long time."

She nodded, but didn't get a chance to reply before he was back on his feet and out of the room.

❀ 15 ❀

Fenella was telling Shelly the whole story that night when Daniel knocked on the door. Mona moved away from her seat on the couch next to Shelly, taking a seat a bit further away as Fenella let the man into the apartment.

"You look tired," she said.

He nodded. "It's been a long afternoon. I had a stale sandwich at some point, but nothing else. I don't suppose I could talk you into giving me a few biscuits and a cup of tea?"

"How about an omelet?" Fenella offered.

"Anything would be much appreciated," he replied.

He followed her to the kitchen with Mona on his heels.

"I'm going to head home," Shelly announced. "I told Tim that I would come and watch the band tomorrow night, so I really need an early night tonight. I can let myself out."

Fenella nodded and then gave her a quick hug before she left. Daniel sat at the counter watching as Fenella scrambled eggs and chopped up ham, cheese, and onions. "Okay?" she asked as she began adding things to the frying pan.

"Perfect," he sighed.

As the omelet was cooking, Fenella boiled a kettle of water and made him a cup of tea. He added sugar and then took a sip. "This is helping," he told her.

"Good."

She refilled his cup just before she slid the omelet onto a plate. After a few bites, Daniel began to look a little better.

"Thank you," he said softly.

"You're very welcome."

"I don't usually let cases bother me, but this one did."

"Are you sure that Joe was the one who killed Rosemary, then?"

"He's given us a full confession. I think he was so stunned when he found out that Rosemary had been lying about everything that he didn't know what else to do. He truly believed that Rosemary was the rightful heir to Max's fortune. From what he told me, he was upset that she wouldn't sue Mrs. Martin-Hardcastle and he decided to take things into his own hands."

"Except Mrs. Martin-Hardcastle was behind the whole thing," Fenella said.

"I don't want that name being said in my flat," Mona told her.

"We don't have any evidence to support that theory, at least not yet," Daniel replied. "We're looking into it, obviously, but if she's at all clever she'll have covered her tracks well."

"You need to find Norah, the woman who met with Rosemary in London."

"We're working on that. April is going to share everything she has with me once she gets back to London. That's complicated by the fact that her husband is not leaving the island for the foreseeable future, of course."

"What is she going to do about him?"

"I don't think she knows. She's upset and angry and not thinking clearly at the moment. We have a specialist counselor working with her. She seems to blaming herself for her mother's death because she didn't tell Joe the whole story."

"It's all so convoluted that I don't even know who I feel sorry for," Fenella sighed. "I mean, April and Rosemary were trying to steal my money, but that doesn't mean that Rosemary deserved to die."

Daniel nodded. "Her other two children are both badly shaken, as well. They've been given permission to leave the island tomorrow and I think they'll both be on the first flight out if they can get seats."

"I'm relieved that it's all over, but it certainly isn't a happy ending."

"My sister arrives in a few days, so when I'm not at work, I'm going to be busy trying to get my house cleaned up and ready for the invasion. Deborah won't care about the mess, but my nephews will get into anything and everything they come across. I won't have much spare time between now and their arrival. Maybe, once they're gone, you'd like to have dinner one night?"

"I'd like that," Fenella said.

"Stop being so available," Mona told her.

Fenella made a face at her and then turned back to Daniel. "I hope you have fun with your sister. I'm sure your visit will go better than my visit with my brother did."

Daniel chuckled. "I'm not planning on finding any dead bodies while my sister is here."

She walked him to the door a short time later. "Thank you for dinner. It was wonderful," he said.

"It was just an omelet."

"So maybe it was the company that was wonderful," he replied. He pulled her into a kiss that might have turned into something more if Mona hadn't suddenly started coughing.

Fenella reluctantly pushed Daniel away. "We need to take things slowly," she reminded him.

"I wish you weren't right," he replied. "I'll see you at Mona's party."

She nodded and then watched as he walked down the corridor to the elevators.

The next few days seemed to fly past.

"You look perfect," Mona told Fenella as she twirled slowly in front of the mirror. "Don't change a thing."

Fenella nodded. "I feel like a princess or something."

Mona nodded. "I'll see you at the party," she said before she vanished.

Fenella wasn't sure how that was going to work. She and Shelly had agreed to take a taxi to the venue together. It was close enough to walk, but neither of the women wanted to risk messing up their hair or makeup.

"My goodness, you look incredible," Shelly gasped when she saw Fenella. "That must be one of Mona's dresses."

"Of course it is. That is too, isn't it?" Fenella replied. She'd given Shelly a handful of dresses out of Mona's wardrobe over the past months. This one was a blue-green that Fenella hadn't liked when she'd first seen the dress, but now, on Shelly, it looked stunning.

"Yes, I hope you don't mind."

"Of course not."

A few minutes later their taxi arrived at the back of what looked like a very long queue of limousines and expensive-looking cars.

"Maybe we shouldn't have come in a taxi," Shelly muttered as they inched their way forward.

Fenella shrugged. "We'll know for next year."

Mona had suggested that she hire a limousine, but she'd dismissed the idea for such a short journey. She hadn't really thought about how the other guests would be arriving, though.

When they finally reached the front of the queue, a man in a tuxedo opened the door and helped them each from the car.

"This is incredible," Shelly whispered as they walked into the huge ballroom that Fenella hadn't known was inside the luxury hotel she'd walked past a dozen times.

An hour later, Fenella was feeling slightly overwhelmed by everything. She'd talked to dozens of people and they'd all shared stories with her about Mona. While many of the stories had been funny and most had emphasized Mona's wild side, several of them had also been about times when Mona had been kind and generous. Fenella felt as if she were learning about a very different side to her aunt.

"She saved my life," one woman told her. "When my husband died, I wanted to die, too. Mona told me to go out and find a new man. I thought she was crazy, but then I found my Stanley. We've been married for thirty-seven years now and I have Mona to thank."

"I was in love with her," a man told her. "She could have had any man on the island, you know, but she and Max had something special. I never did understand it. She introduced me to the woman I ended up marrying and I never regretted giving up on my fantasy life with Mona in order to marry the real-life woman who's been by my side for forty years."

Shelly and Tim appeared to be having a wonderful time, Fenella noted as she made a circuit of the room.

"Fenella, you look stunning," Donald said as she literally bumped into him.

"Thank you so much. I'm glad you made it."

He nodded. "This is going to sound terrible, but it's nice to get away from Phoebe for twenty-four hours."

"It doesn't sound terrible. I understand."

"This is Betty," he told her.

Fenella shook hands with the petite blonde. She looked about fifty-five and not at all the sort of woman who could usually be found on Donald's arm.

"It's nice to meet you," Fenella said.

"Oh, likewise. I wasn't sure about coming to this, but Donald insisted that it would be fun. It's a bit overwhelming, though. I'm not used to this sort of thing."

"Neither am I," Fenella told her. "This was all Mona's doing."

The woman laughed. "Donald has told me so many stories about Mona that I almost feel as if I know her."

"We talk a lot," Donald said. "There isn't much else to do in a hospital room all day, every day."

Fenella gave him a hug. "She's lovely," she whispered in his ear. "I'm truly happy for you."

He gave her a rueful smile as she pulled away. "Thank you," he said softly before she continued on her way.

"There you are," Daniel said as she stopped in front of one of the huge tables full of food. "You need to meet Deborah and Michael."

Fenella smiled through the introductions, trying not to be too obvious as she studied Daniel's sister. There was a superficial resemblance, Fenella decided as the foursome chatted about nothing much.

Michael's phone interrupted the conversation. "It's the constable we left in charge of the children," he said with a frown. "I need to take this."

He and Deborah quickly headed for the door. Daniel frowned. "I hope everything is okay."

"So do I. Do you need to go, too?"

"Maybe. Deborah will text me if they need to leave."

"How's the visit going?"

"It's fun having them here, but the boys are hard work. I always thought I'd have kids some day, but now I'm not sure I'm sorry that I haven't."

Fenella swallowed a dozen replies. "Have you been able to show them much of the island?"

"We've visited a few sites and hope to do a few more before they go back. They've been exploring on their own while I've been at work, too. They both like the island a lot, but Michael loves what he does too much to contemplate moving here."

Fenella nodded. Deborah was back before she could reply.

"Nothing's wrong," she announced. "He just wanted to check exactly how much ice cream the boys were allowed to eat after dinner."

Fenella laughed. "I suppose that's better than just letting them eat it all."

Deborah nodded. "Michael actually ran into someone he knows. He'll be talking about work for half an hour, knowing him."

Daniel nodded and then frowned as his phone began to buzz. "And now I need to take this," he sighed as he began to walk away.

"He was badly hurt before," Deborah said as they watched Daniel leaving the room.

"Was he?"

"He hasn't told you about his ex-wife?"

"Not really."

She sighed. "Ask him about her. It really isn't my place to tell you anything."

"I can try. He doesn't seem to like to talk about himself."

"That's very true, but you need to know what you're facing. I know that he cares about you, but your money is a real concern."

"My money?"

"His ex-wife inherited some money; not a fortune, just enough to give her ideas about giving up work and traveling the world. Daniel is too dedicated to what he does to agree to such a thing, of course. In the end, she decided that she'd rather travel on her own than stay with Daniel."

Fenella winced. "How awful for Daniel."

"It was pretty rough. She found someone else, of course, within a few months, actually. They're still traveling the world, at least as far as I know. Daniel told me about you months ago, when he first met you."

"But then he met someone else when he was in Milton Keynes."

"Yes, and that's something else you need to talk about with him."

"We never seem to find the time to talk."

"If you care about him at all, you may have to make the time to talk and force him to do it," Deborah said. "Communicating doesn't come naturally to my darling brother."

By the time Daniel rejoined them, they were chatting about the food and the wine. His face was grim.

"What's wrong?" Fenella asked.

"London police have located the woman who met with Rosemary Ballard to set things up for the lawsuit against you. The one who was calling herself Norah," he replied. "Or rather, they've located her body."

"Her body?"

"It looks as if it was suicide, but they aren't ruling out murder yet. She left a note, but those are easy enough to fake, especially as it was typed and printed on a standard inkjet printer."

"Maybe she was mixed up in more than just the Rosemary Ballard fraud."

"The woman's partner has come forward," Daniel continued. "He gave the police an envelope that she'd given to him in case anything happened to her."

"And?" Fenella asked.

"And the police have arrested Mrs. Martin-Hardcastle for attempted fraud."

Fenella surprised them both by laughing. "I'm sorry," she said, "but after everything I've heard about Max's sister, I'm quite happy to hear that she's been arrested."

A short while later, as Fenella stood on her own on a balcony that overlooked the party, Mona joined her.

"It's a lovely party," Fenella told her. "Happy birthday."

"Max's sister has been arrested," Mona said happily. "That's far and away the best birthday gift I've ever received."

"Really?"

"Well, Max did once give me an entire hotel for my birthday. That was pretty special, too, but I do think this tops it."

"Everyone I've met speaks very highly of you."

"They should. They were my friends, after all."

"I've heard a lot of stories about you tonight. You were much nicer than you seem."

Mona laughed. "I'm not sure how to reply to that," she said. "I did my best to be a good person. My reputation was not entirely deserved, as you know, whatever other people think of me."

"Were you happy?"

Mona shrugged. "I'm not sure how to reply to that either. I don't have any regrets, that's a certainty. Look down there. Those people, all of them, were my friends when I was alive. I was blessed with friends who cared about me. I cared about all of them, as well."

Fenella nodded. "I'm glad you don't have any regrets."

"But why are you hiding up here?" Mona demanded. "You're missing the party. If you never learn anything else from me, you should learn to enjoy every minute of every hour of your life. Dance, laugh, flirt, love, share, enjoy, celebrate."

Mona faded away, leaving Fenella to head for the stairs and rejoin the others. She had a few drinks, danced with several men who were probably nearly twice her age and laughed more than she had in years. The sun was coming up when she finally strolled home with Shelly, Tim, and a few other friends who lived along the promenade.

"That was wonderful," Shelly told her at her door. "I can't wait for next year."

The next day Fenella met with Doncan.

"Are you sure about this?" he asked.

"Quite sure," she assured him.

He had her sign the checks and then gave them to Breesha to mail. "You don't owe them anything, you know that, right?"

"I know, but they were as much victims of Mrs. Martin-Hardcastle as I might have been. It isn't a lot of money, really, but it should be enough to pay for April's divorce, for Autumn's son's education, and for Matthew and Viola to have a few rounds of IVF. I hope it makes a difference for all of them."

Doncan smiled at her. "Mona used to do things like this all the time," he told her. "You're a lot like her in many ways."

Feeling incredibly flattered by the comparison, Fenella walked home to her apartment confident that she was happier than she'd ever been before.

ACKNOWLEDGMENTS

Many thanks to my editor, Denise, who works at least as hard as I do on these books.

Thanks to my beta readers, who have to read books that aren't quite as polished as they could be and who never complain.

Linda at Tell-Tale Book Covers has done another amazing job with this cover. I'm hugely grateful for all of her hard work.

And thanks to you, dear reader, for spending more time with Fenella and Mona. I hope you've enjoyed it as much as I have.

MARSUPIALS AND MURDER

Release date: February 14, 2020

Fenella Woods has been living on the Isle of Man for a year, and it now seems as if every charity there feels it's appropriate to start soliciting her. Most of the letters get turned over to Fenella's advocate to deal with, but one request catches Fenella's eye. Darrell Higgins wants her help monitoring the wild wallaby population in the Curraghs wetlands area of the island.

When she agrees to spend an hour in the wetlands one morning, the man in her life, Daniel Robinson, offers to join her. After a boring hour in the cold and rain, they both can't wait to get indoors, but on the walk back to Daniel's car, they find Darrell under a bush, dead.

There isn't any shortage of suspects, from volunteers with the charity to business colleagues of the dead man, not to mention a quartet of ex-wives and one current girlfriend, but motive is harder to determine. Can Daniel and Fenella work out who killed the island's main marsupial supporter before the killer chooses another victim?

ALSO BY DIANA XARISSA

Aunt Bessie Joins

Aunt Bessie Knows

Aunt Bessie Likes

Aunt Bessie Meets

Aunt Bessie Needs

Aunt Bessie Observes

Aunt Bessie Provides

Aunt Bessie Questions

Aunt Bessie Remembers

Aunt Bessie Questions

Aunt Bessie Solves

Aunt Bessie Tries

Aunt Bessie Understands

Aunt Bessie Volunteers

Aunt Bessie Wonders

The Markham Sisters Cozy Mystery Novellas

The Appleton Case

The Bennett Case

The Chalmers Case

The Donaldson Case

The Ellsworth Case

The Fenton Case

The Green Case

The Hampton Case

The Irwin Case

The Jackson Case

The Kingston Case

The Lawley Case

The Moody Case

ABOUT THE AUTHOR

Diana grew up in Northwestern Pennsylvania and moved to Washington, DC after college. There she met a wonderful Englishman who was visiting the city. After a whirlwind romance, they got married and Diana moved to the Chesterfield area of Derbyshire to begin a new life with her husband. A short time later, they relocated to the Isle of Man.

After over ten years on the island, it was time for a change. With their two children in tow, Diana and her husband moved to suburbs of Buffalo, New York. Diana now spends her days writing about the island she loves.

She also writes mystery/thrillers set in the not-too-distant future as Diana X. Dunn and middle grade and Young Adult books as D.X. Dunn.

Diana is always happy to hear from readers. You can write to her at:

Diana Xarissa Dunn
PO Box 72
Clarence, NY 14031.
Find Diana at: DianaXarissa.com
E-mail: Diana@dianaxarissa.com

Printed in Poland
by Amazon Fulfillment
Poland Sp. z o.o., Wrocław